The Dark Moon Series
Book Two

Under a Dark Star

Anna Faversham

**Copyright
Anna Faversham
©
2016**

All Rights Reserved

No part of this book may be reproduced or stored in any form, by photocopying or by any electronic or mechanical means, including information storage or retrieval systems, or recording, or otherwise, without prior written permission from the author.

This is a work of fiction. The places in this book are either real or imagined. Some events are loosely based on reality. The characters are fictitious. Any resemblance to real persons, living or dead, is purely coincidental.

For my Brothers

Table of Contents

Prologue		1
Chapter One	"The sea ran red"	2
Chapter Two	"Are you calling my officers chickens?"	9
Chapter Three	"The imperious voice of God"	14
Chapter Four	"All that it takes"	19
Chapter Five	"Bailing or vomiting"	22
Chapter Six	"Surly Silence"	28
Chapter Seven	"Akin to the fires of hell"	36
Chapter Eight	"The Dark Star"	41
Chapter Nine	"Weasel! We're not eating weasel"	48
Chapter Ten	"They failed spectacularly"	55
Chapter Eleven	"More than could be explained"	61
Chapter Twelve	"Lord of the Manor"	67
Chapter Thirteen	"A date was set"	75
Chapter Fourteen	"By thunder! What goes on here?"	81
Chapter Fifteen	"You underestimate the devil"	86
Chapter Sixteen	"Get this dog off me"	94
Chapter Seventeen	"There is a third condition"	100
Chapter Eighteen	"An orange glow"	106
Chapter Nineteen	"A curious crowd"	111
Chapter Twenty	"A malevolent, swirling fog"	118
Chapter Twenty-One	"The scent of her"	126
Chapter Twenty-Two	"A real godsend"	133
Chapter Twenty-Three	"A stink of dogs"	137
Chapter Twenty-Four	"There must be more cake"	141
Chapter Twenty-Five	"Dark, shifting shadow"	148
Chapter Twenty-Six	"Someone to come home to"	156
Chapter Twenty-Seven	"Permanently thwarted"	162
Chapter Twenty-Eight	"The sound of hope"	168
Chapter Twenty-Nine	"The plan was simple"	172
Chapter Thirty	"Hound from Hell"	181
Chapter Thirty-One	"As cold as the grave"	187

Chapter Thirty-Two	"Plague of eyes"	190
Chapter Thirty-Three	"The guilt grew"	194
Chapter Thirty-Four	"Through the deep waters"	200
Chapter Thirty-Five	"Weasely servant of hell"	208
Chapter Thirty-Six	"Where, be damned, were you?"	214
Chapter Thirty-Seven	"A wail of sheer misery"	220
Chapter Thirty-Eight	"A graceful form, perfectly balanced"	227
Chapter Thirty-Nine	"Not quite the naval way"	237
Chapter Forty	"Escaped the sawbones"	244
Chapter Forty-One	"A sense of foreboding"	254
Chapter Forty-Two	"He'd enjoy every minute"	264
Chapter Forty-Three	"Overwhelming agony"	269
Chapter Forty-Four	"Tomorrow, sometime, somehow"	278
Chapter Forty-Five	"Let not your past echo...."	284
Twenty Questions for Book Clubs		289

Under a Dark Star

Prologue

Dressed all in black, he was confident he could not be seen on this stormy, moonless night as he lay flat on the grassy cliff top. A rabbit peeped out of its burrow, smelt danger, turned tail and disappeared.

"Don't be concerned, little fellow," he whispered to the fluffy, white tail, "I have bigger prey than you in mind."

He picked up his telescope again and trained it on the shoreline where a gang blatantly ambled down to the beach in groups of ten or more. On the rocks leading out into the sea stood one man. Crashing waves created white spray – the perfect backdrop to expose the figure holding a teapot-shaped spout lamp giving the order to make ready.

The ill-fated sailing ship, making its perilous way around the wild, southern shore of the island, came into view.

Two hours later, stiff with the winter's icy cold, the onlooker had seen all he needed to. Sea spray should never be blood red.

Under a Dark Star

Chapter One
Bethlehem Farm, Wintergate, Kent, England - Daniel
"The sea ran red"

Dark star *(Newtonian mechanics, 18th century), a star that has a gravitational pull strong enough to trap light…*

January 1823
Lieutenant Karl Thorsen arrived, as usual, like a drum roll prior to battle. Dismounting from his black stallion, he flung the reins around the hitching post and strode across to the open door of the early eighteenth century farmhouse.
"I need your help."
"Another impossible task you wish to undertake?" Daniel Tynton dipped his head in greeting to his old foe, now promoted to almost a friend. "What is it this time?"
Karl gave him a wry smile and stamped his feet impatiently after his long, cold ride. "All that it takes for evil to triumph is for good men to do nothing. Would you agree?"
Daniel, a little taller and fairer than Karl, stood aside to allow him to enter. "A notion you have acquired from your Parliamentary friends?"
Karl did not respond but turned so that the new housemaid could assist with removing his cloak and riding hat.
Daniel continued. "I'll grant you it's a worthy thought and one with which Mr Raffles will no doubt agree, would you not?"

Under a Dark Star

Parson Raffles, having only just arrived at his friend's house, took up most of the doorway to the small parlour. "If good men do nothing, evil flourishes." He furrowed his brow then looked delighted. "I shall take this theme for one of my sermons."

Karl and the parson bowed to each other before they all joined Daniel's wife, Lucy, who was enjoying a pot of tea, salty biscuits and cheese from the farm.

Lucy stood, greeted Karl with apprehension, and sat down again. "I've called for Martha who will bring more tea." Her welcome was less than warm, yet she had much to thank him for. Daniel gave her an encouraging smile so she added, "Martha will be overjoyed to see you. Have you ridden all the way from Whitchester Manor this morning?"

"Indeed." Karl's eyes twinkled. "Midnight covers the distance in just over an hour."

Lucy thought it probably took longer.

Daniel watched his wife and Karl tiptoeing around each other's feelings.

Parson Raffles, as always, came to the rescue. "Ah, there's nothing so cheering as a blazing fire on a winter's day and here's Martha, bringing her own special joy: a beaming smile and more biscuits."

A baby's cry caught everyone's attention. Lucy leapt up and promptly sat down again. Daniel laughed and fondly put his arm around his wife's shoulder and explained gently, "Lucy's mothering instincts are in good order."

Martha, having worked for all three of the families represented in the room, could not contain her joy and burst through the doorway. "Lieutenant Thorsen, I'm so… so… fluffled to see you. And you just wait 'til you see young Freddie! Aw he's all pink and plump." Still clutching the tray, she turned to Lucy, "Shall I tell Nurse to bring him down?"

Under a Dark Star

Daniel held up his hand. "Not yet, Martha, thank you. And we'll all be pleased if you put the tray on the side table by Lucy."

Martha, rather small, pink and plump herself, grinned despite her lack of a full set of teeth, and said, "I've got cake too. Look, a whole plate of it. When I heard those thundering hooves, I said to myself, *That'll be the lieutenant; good thing I made some cinnamon cake.* Oh and Midnight has been stabled. He'll be well looked after. And..."

"I think Lieutenant Thorsen has some matters to discuss, Martha, and if he has an inclination to stay..." Daniel glanced across to Karl who raised an eyebrow and nodded, "please have a bedroom prepared for him."

Undeterred, she beamed and continued, "The Lieutenant's saddlebag is in the hall and I'll take it up..."

Daniel looked across at his wife and they exchanged suppressed smiles. "Thank you, Martha, that will be all for now. We'll ring for you when we need you again."

Martha bustled out of the parlour and after a few seconds of silence Lucy chuckled, desperately trying not to be heard. She moved closer to the fire, while Daniel, Karl and the parson rearranged their chairs around the parlour's small table near the window.

Karl took a seat which enabled him to comfortably see Lucy. He turned to Daniel and said, "And how is business?"

"No visitors at the moment, of course. It's a quiet time for Lucy and me, though the building work still goes on for which I have a very capable manager." Daniel, though a good farmer, had overriding business ambitions. To support these ambitions he had taken advantage of the proximity of a thriving holiday trade in a nearby seaside town and built holiday accommodation on his land.

Parson Raffles added, "There's still the animals to be attended to, I'm very glad to say. You know this farm still provides milk

Under a Dark Star

for most of Wintergate? And his mother's farm provides for hamlets nearby." He gave a little chuckle and grasped Daniel by the shoulder. "He is undoubtedly the most important member of our parish."

"I was schooled expertly." Daniel nodded his acknowledgment to the parson, the man who had taught him so well. "And how is life as a Member of Parliament, Karl?" He took the tea cups offered by Lucy and passed them to Karl and Raffles.

"Like the campaign to abolish slavery, all progress is slow." Raffles leaned forward and took a large slice of the cinnamon cake placed before them. "Wasn't there an Act of Parliament to do with abolition, some years ago now?"

"Yes. Only partially effective though. It went a long way to curtailing the slave *trade* in the Empire, but not slavery itself." Karl paused for a moment then slapped the table and hurried on. "A conversation with William Wilberforce, who is the leading campaigner for the abolition of slavery, suggested to me that the prevention of smuggling should not be abandoned. He commended the work we have done in this part of Kent but said complete eradication is a drip by drip process." Karl took a moment to gulp down his tea and seize a piece of cake. "Do excuse my lack of courtesy, I have much to convey."

"Fine Christian, that Wilberforce," Raffles said, nodding his head and stroking his several chins.

"Take all the time you need," Daniel said with a smile. "The day is not half over and I am keen to hear about this help you require."

"I'm coming to that." Karl grinned and appeared to relax a little. "Wilberforce was not being impertinent. His meaning was that slavery and smuggling will be defeated little by ceaseless little."

"A wise man," Raffles said.

Under a Dark Star

Karl nodded in agreement. "He suggested I take a look at the Isle of Wight."

"I believe my dear wife has connections with the island," said Raffles, "a cousin with a farm. She's always suggesting we visit." He looked thoughtful before hurriedly saying, "My apologies, I have drifted from a most important matter."

"No need to apologize, Mr Raffles, such information might be helpful." Karl dipped his head to indicate his gratitude. "I visited the island and what did I find?" He paused, he did not want to alarm Lucy. "On a dark night, I watched from a cliff top, and I saw..." he glanced across to Lucy.

Daniel understood. They'd return to that subject later. So he asked, "What else did you find on the island?"

"I found rotten and pocket boroughs!"

Daniel looked surprised. "Is this technical terminology or your opinion?"

"They're technical terms meaning that votes in such boroughs are mostly bought or representation is handed from father to son – nepotism. Corruption. And that is no way to govern a country."

"Are you saying the island...?"

"No. They exist all over the country. Reform is urgently needed – but that battle must be put aside while I deal with something worse than corruption."

"Wrecking?"

Karl stared at Daniel, his eyes showing not surprise but respect. "Yes. Wrecking. And it's extensive. It seems the whole of the island is either involved in smuggling or its prevention. Then there's the wreckers. No one dares attempt to stop these vile men, and corrupt officials turn a blind eye – like our brave Admiral Nelson they see only what they want to see." Fighting to contain his energy, he shifted in his seat before continuing in a whisper. "Wilberforce has heard of an American ship that was making its way through the Channel with a cargo of cotton and tobacco. The ship was wrecked off what they call 'the back of the Wight'. On board were twenty-four affluent American passengers returning to visit their English families. All were killed. Not just accidentally drowned, but beaten to death so no survivors could bear witness." The business he had come to discuss destroyed conviviality. Shocked silence prevailed. Karl, never one to waste time, seized the opportunity to evaluate their expressions and his impact, masked by taking another mouthful of cake.

Meanwhile, Daniel's thoughts raced over old territory. Karl's father had been left to drown on the treacherous sands a mile out to sea by Daniel's drunken, smuggling father. Karl left his estate, and became the hated head of the Riding Officers in order to track down the man responsible. He didn't stop until he was caught and hanged. Karl and Daniel were sworn enemies – on opposite sides of the law. But since that time, revenge assuaged, he had noticed a slow emergence of a compassionate nature in his old foe. Today, however, that iron resolve seemed to be reappearing. He was once ruthless in pursuing his cause – which he saw as justice for the murder. Yet, a while ago, Lucy had commented on Daniel's influence on Karl and how their growing respect for each other drew forth from him the pursuit of a different kind of justice. It was no longer personal. She was right, as always.

Karl resumed in rapid, clipped tones. "I need all the information you can give me as I intend to return to the island in disguise. I shall mingle with the local inhabitants and take part in some of their appalling activities."

Lucy looked up and exchanged worried glances with Daniel who shook his head.

Raffles was aghast. "You are a gentleman, Karl. Even as a lowly but respectable Riding Officer you looked out of place."

Under a Dark Star

"However," said Daniel clasping his chin, "coming from the mainland, islanders might expect you to be different, but I doubt you could become one of them. You'd be an outsider. And if you are to challenge wreckers rather than smugglers, you are directly threatening men who clearly have no regard for taking lives. *Your life will mean nothing to them.*"

Karl no longer whispered – he had to convince his friend. "A ship lured onto the rocks, smashed, looted. Crew and passengers desperately struggling to the safety of the shore. Throats slit. The sea ran red!"

Lucy shuddered.

Daniel glanced at his wife, her big brown eyes now staring at him. He looked at the parson and read his mind. Why had Karl crudely spilt the lurid details of this atrocity in front of her? Why was he always so dramatic? Then a pinpoint of light, like a star on a dark night, flashed into his blue eyes. Leaning forward he whispered, "You've come for more than information."

Karl grinned. "If you and I put our energies and strengths together, we'd be a formidable force."

Chapter Two
"Are you calling my officers chickens?"

"It's as though they are in league with the devil!" exclaimed the parson, shivering as he walked.

Daniel knew that Raffles had intended his visit to be short. *"Just a little stroll by the sea,"* he'd said, and Daniel's mind couldn't help but add *and pass by the farm for a little tea and some biscuits*. But Karl, like his surname, Thorsen – son of the god of thunder – had changed all that like a thunderbolt from a cloudless sky. How good it was that Raffles had been persuaded to stay and scatter a few wise, considered words and listen to Karl's latest passionate challenge.

Karl momentarily looked thoughtful. "A God-given insight. I feel it in my soul."

Daniel refrained from voicing any thoughts about Karl's soul. Even Josh, Daniel's long-haired black and white dog, gave Karl a dubious look.

The three men, now wrapped up warmly, were ambling around the farm. Daniel showed Karl the work he'd undertaken since he had last visited. "There are now eight cottages completed for letting to visitors. So much better than just a room in a hotel, don't you think? And if it doesn't provide a profit, I can make them available for permanent renting."

"Oh there'll be plenty of profit. You should have been here in the summer, Karl." Raffles took pride in the way Daniel was developing the holiday retreat. "Carriages arriving every week

Under a Dark Star

with families bringing their servants too. And children playing on the beach, and fine ladies and gentlemen strolling along the cliffs. As hoped, they have spent their money around the farm, buying crafts from the villagers, and the whole enterprise is extremely successful."

"Just as it should be," said Karl with a wry smile. "No more skulking around on dark nights with tubs of brandy, killing honest revenue men and never doing a proper day's work."

Daniel ignored Karl's description of the constant struggle the smugglers had endured trying to feed their families. Since Karl had arrested nearly all the local gang and sent eighteen to the gallows, smuggling had ceased and Daniel had taken the opportunity to put his long-held plans into action. Widows whose husbands were hanged or transported now sold handicrafts; returned soldiers who'd lost limbs in battles, either with the French or the revenue men, were using old skills like carpentry to make furniture. Visitors brought wealth, and the dignity of labour had returned. Yes, he could ignore Karl's words. Karl was incorruptible, forthright and permanently campaigning for a cause. And Daniel knew they were good causes. He and Karl were on the same side now.

"I foresee a few problems, Karl."

"That's the primary reason I'm here. I knew you would and I need you to tell me what they are."

Parson Raffles rubbed his hands together and blew on them. "Mighty cold today."

"Forgive me," Daniel said. "I don't want to alarm my wife with our discussions. If we talk quietly, the dining room is a better place. Come, we'll leave the farm's progress for some other time. Follow me!"

Josh, always ahead in the game of life, was already standing with one paw on the door of the farmhouse as Daniel pushed it open and showed his guests into the dining room. Martha was just disappearing through the other door to the kitchen. As ever, she had anticipated their need and lit the fire in the impressive stone hearth. They each pulled a chair close. Josh, sensing important business, lay across the doorway nearest the parlour.

"One of the problems, Karl, is exactly what Mr Raffles has said. Even as a Riding Officer, you stood out like a bull in a chicken house."

"A chicken house! Are you calling my officers chickens?" Karl spluttered almost as much as the sparks from the fire.

"Gentlemen! We are straying from the reason you have come. Yet Daniel has said what we both thought."

"My apologies, Mr Raffles. I thought we made an effective force for good."

"You did," said Daniel. "Of that there is no doubt. But the very thought of you arriving on an island pretending to be a wrecker is akin to signing your own death warrant."

"I realize I sound reckless – so you must impart to me…"

Daniel raised a finger to interrupt Karl. "That is not the only problem."

Raffles joined in. "How can you fulfil your duties as a Member of Parliament and be isolated on an island?"

"That is not a problem at all. As you know, my constituency is a two member seat so I have more time than most. The other M.P. covers for me when I have work on my estate and I do likewise for him." Karl gave a broad smile. "Currently it enables me to make better headway with my campaign to lower taxes on the goods being smuggled. Now I foresee it as being the means to stay on the island long enough to defeat this evil."

"Another problem," said Daniel who was keen to stop Karl thinking it would be easy, "is that you may be recognized as a

Under a Dark Star

Member of Parliament by the authorities on the island who might not be trustworthy."

"I have not made any official visit to the island. Wilberforce agreed that wouldn't be wise. I doubt anyone of any consequence would recognize me."

Daniel scoffed. "Anyone of any consequence! The people of consequence in your operation include those you regard as the scum of the earth – the wreckers! And they're often led by someone of importance but unknown to all. Think, Karl! The real leader of our North Kent Gang wasn't me or my father, it was Lucy's father, Sir William Harper." He omitted to say that Lucy was his illegitimate daughter; she was in all ways a lady and he'd found her father a decent man trying to do the best for everyone, including himself, of course.

Raffles brought order. "It is important we know what the objective of this exercise is, then we can give some thought as to how we can help."

"The objective," said Karl "is to stop the wrecking. That and that alone. Preventing smuggling will be achieved by my Parliamentary work, slowly but surely taxes will be lowered."

"Twenty-four innocent people brutally murdered," mumbled Raffles with a sigh. "What will the Americans think of us?"

"Quite!" exclaimed Karl.

Daniel allowed a moment's thought before saying, "It is clear to me, Karl, that if you value your life and your work in Parliament, you must not attempt to infiltrate the wreckers. I have a relative on the island, a Tynton. I've never met him but my father spoke well of him – which probably means he is a rogue."

"It is as I thought. You are indispensable. Would you pay him a visit; maybe arrange lodgings with him for me? If you stayed for a short while, you could help me integrate."

Under a Dark Star

Daniel knew how Karl's mind worked. He was being drawn inexorably into this ill-thought-out mission. "I suppose you already know more about him than I do?"

Karl adopted an innocent air. "It seems I must be absolutely honest with you." He raised an eyebrow. "Before he died, your father boasted of his extensive network of relatives who would retaliate, including some on the Isle of Wight but he didn't say exactly where." Dismissively he added, "I had no use for the information at that time."

Raffles attended to the fire and pulled his cloak close around him while he squeezed into his chair. "You cannot pretend to be a smuggler, Karl. I cannot give my blessing to such an irresponsible undertaking."

Daniel sat back in his chair and stared at his old opponent. "A *Tynton* arriving, with a history of leading the greater part of the North Kent Gang, could easily blend in and then it is not such a big step to joining the wreckers."

"No, Daniel, do not start thinking in such a way." Raffles looked him straight in the eye. "Think of Lucy; think of your baby not yet six months old. These wreckers are murderous ruffians."

Why had Karl burst back into his life? Why had he mentioned wrecking? Now Raffles' words would hang over their heads like daggers waiting to drop. Despite his thoughts, he felt compelled to ignore the warning.

"You will make a very poor smuggler, Karl, but a very good Riding Officer. You go as the law and I will go as the wrecker."

Under a Dark Star

Chapter Three
"The imperious voice of God"

Sunday 26th January

Lucy and Daniel, as usual on Sundays, prepared to go to the service at Wintergate church. Karl had thundered away on Midnight shortly after breakfast and Daniel was sure Lucy had caught their conspiratorial air as they parted. Was he doing the right thing?

On the short journey to the church, he explained. They argued. Lucy pleaded with him to reconsider. He tried, but much as he loved her and his new-born son, something inside him urged him on. What was it? Did he miss the excitement of the old days? The comradeship? The successful planning? Winning against all the odds? Or was it what Karl had said?

"If you are going – I am going too, and so is baby Freddie!"

Daniel grasped her shoulders gently and kissed her forehead. "I shall be back before the summer and you cannot possibly bring Freddie. We don't know what Emmeline's cousin's farm is like." Though she resisted, he drew her into his arms, hugged her and reassured her.

She struggled free to say, "Emmeline said she'd write and if it sounds suitable, I shall stay there. I shall not become involved with your dirty deeds."

"Don't say that, Lucy." Daniel still carried guilt in his heart for all he'd seen and been involved with. He could defend the smuggling: soldiers who'd returned from the war with France had few chances of making a living wage any other way. It was his father's violent ways he would not defend. He'd been no more than a boy when his father had taken him on the darkest of nights and he'd seen terrible violence towards the revenue men trying to do their duty. Tied up, staked out on the beach in a rising tide, how could his father...?

Lucy noticed his expression and her voice softened. "Daniel, I know the memories are still with you, but you have done much to change the lives of so many people. Surely you can't desert them now?"

They drew up to the lychgate in their modest carriage pulled by the two horses Karl so generously gave them as a wedding gift. Their stable hand was also the coachman and he helped them alight. They walked through the church doors to the front pew. Parson Raffles was such a popular preacher that even on this snowy day the church was full. The times when Lucy had sat at the back and Daniel had stood assessing all that happened were long gone. Now Lucy wore a cape trimmed with fur; then she had worn a patched dress. Every time they came, Daniel knew she remembered the days when she was scorned and he was feared. She had been viewed as a spy by both the revenue men and the smuggling community. Having been brought up as a young lady in her formative years, she had been pulled from her roots by her mother and planted here in Wintergate to earn a living. And that is how he'd met her. She toiled at his father's farm whatever the weather and he fell in love with her. She intoxicated him: innocent, pretty blond curls, and a way of speaking that he'd never heard before. He had won her heart against all the odds. And she was his. Not Karl's. Now she wanted to go to the back of the Wight, the wild and lawless part of an island off the south coast. Yes, this revealed the depth of her love, but how could he justify

Under a Dark Star

allowing her to go? He'd wanted to make a better life for her and their baby, not take her to who knew what.

The organ played, the congregation sang, and his good friend and confidante, Raffles, once more turned into 'Parson Raffles'. Going to the island would be like the misnamed good old days when as a child, his family had scratched a living and respectability was not even considered worthwhile when compared with having food in your belly.

His wandering thoughts came to an end when Parson Raffles started *his* wandering. Literally. He left the pulpit and stood looking down the centre aisle which meant he was standing just a foot or two away from Daniel. There was complete silence except for the sound of the parson's padding footsteps as he shuffled from foot to foot.

"Last Monday morning..." he stamped his feet, "...last Monday morning, I realized I have never told you about a man I once knew." He smiled gently at the congregation. "He is unknown to you." Having established the fact he was not a gossip, he smiled broadly. "He was, shall we say, on the wrong side of the law for most of his life. A petty thief who turned to violent robbery as he grew older."

Daniel felt a little uncomfortable. Many of this congregation knew people like that.

"Shall we call him Tom?" Parson Raffles, relaxed and smiling, continued. "Tom would often ask to speak with me after our Sunday morning service and we would sit at the back of the church; he would not come to the front. He told me how he'd returned from Van Diemen's Land having been sent for a whole record of misdemeanours, and one by one we brought them to our saviour Jesus." The parson walked backwards and forwards across the front of the pews before he threw his arms in the air and roared, "Under the blood!" Then quietly, so those at the back strained to

Under a Dark Star

hear, he added, "When nailed to the cross, with blood trickling down, Jesus cried out, 'My God, My God, why hast thou forsaken me?'" Back and forth he marched, gathering speed all the time. "Forsaken? Forsaken! Yes, Jesus was truly carrying the sins of the world and what does sin do? It separates us from God!" He paused and stood at the front of the aisle and, once more quiet, he said, "So Jesus, with *our* sins – not his – felt forsaken and separated from the Father.

"Now all of this I explained to Tom and Tom, having been punished enough, confessed his sins and repented. He'd worked hard, and become moderately wealthy and married a decent-living wife who kept a comfortable home. He considered ways to make restitution to those he had robbed or harmed. He then received the blessing of forgiveness. His sins were given to Jesus and his heart was clean.

"Now you may think this is the end of my story." Parson Raffles smiled. "Oh no. Oh no, no, no! Tom asked to speak to me again the following week, and each week until three weeks went by, I laboured to explain that he, Tom, had a clean heart and he should begin his new life and sin no more. 'But I haven't sinned all week,' cried Tom. 'Not like I used to.' So I prayed with Tom yet again. And then," the parson grinned, "then something wonderful happened. Into my head popped these words, 'What sins?'" Turning around on his heels to face the altar, he bellowed, "What sins? Yes there we were, week after week confessing the same iniquities, and asking for the blessing of forgiveness, and what? God did not remember what we were talking about!" He chuckled, and the congregation joined him in the merest murmur of the thought of God 'forgetting'.

The parson turned around to face his flock again and with head lowered he said, "I was young but I should have known what the book of Hebrews says, '…and their sins and their iniquities

Under a Dark Star

will I remember no more.' A new covenant – Jesus takes away our sin." Then he spun on his heels again, faced the altar and flung his arms wide. "If we are truly repentant and have confessed and given our sins to Jesus, God doesn't expect to hear us mentioning them yet again."

Daniel suppressed any visible sign of his tangled feelings. His name might not be Tom, but he too carried terrible guilt despite his remorse. It was time to recognize that he was a *pardoned* offender. Time to leave it all behind. But was this God's way of saying he should not go to the island? Or was God saying he should go to the island to help others? Why doesn't He make things clear? And how could he leave the woman he'd loved since the day he first saw her?

"So Tom, clean as fresh fallen snow, asked only that God would protect him from transgressing again. I remember his words: 'My wife will be dismayed but I shall return to live amongst my own kind and I shall work for *their* benefit.' And Tom did, despite the seemingly wise words of his wife who begged him not to return to his old haunts." Parson Raffles stamped his feet as if they were cold – or was it for emphasis? "Returning to an impoverished area enabled him to buy – yes, *buy* a rather dilapidated house." Then he mumbled, "With a little help." He took a deep breath then bellowed, "He and his wife have opened it to orphaned Workhouse children. You see," said the parson raising his eyes to the rafters, "Not even the pleading voice of a woman's love must silence for us the imperious voice of God".

Daniel now knew the answer.

Chapter Four
Lucy
"All that it takes"

The snow had been fluffy and light on the previous Sunday and only yesterday there was still merely a scattering of flakes on the far fields and none around the house. But as Lucy gazed out of her bedroom window early on this bitter Thursday morning, the crescent moon shone on a blanket of snow. The icy cold seeped through and her breath misted the pane. There was no sound, all was peaceful.

She'd been woken by the snuffling noises from the cradle alongside her bed. Freddie now slept through the night but this morning he'd stirred before the servants were up. She pulled the curtains closed again, wrapped a shawl around her shoulders, climbed back into bed, and lifted him to her breast. This would settle him for a little longer and Daniel would be able to sleep uninterrupted.

She loved this first feed of the day. It was a time when she lay in the warmth of her marital bed, treasuring the coos and snuffles of her first born and listening to the sound of Daniel's gentle breathing. Seeping into her heart was the recognition of silence. She turned to place a hand upon his shoulder; usually so comforting to know he was beside her. Fear shot into her heart and Freddie opened his eyes wide – Daniel wasn't there. She looked down into her baby's face and smiled. "Papa is attending to the animals and he'll be back soon." Her soothing voice allayed his

Under a Dark Star

alarm and even calmed her own for a fleeting moment but then her fear grew and she knew Daniel would not be back soon. Once she'd fed Freddie and laid him back in his cradle, she crept along the hallway and peeped out of the window overlooking the front of the house. There were his footprints leading to the stables adjoining the barn where the animals were sheltering, and there were Fiddle's tracks in the snow trailing away from Bethlehem Farm and all that he had worked for.

Disregarding her usual routine, she dressed herself, throwing on the warmest clothes she could easily find in the dark bedroom, and hurried down the stairs to the parlour where she lit one of the lamps. She cleared the grate, and laid and lit a fire. As she stood up, she noticed on the mantelpiece a letter addressed to her. Hesitating, she opened it.

"My dearest Lucy,

I hope you will forgive me. I could not bear to see the pain and reproach in your eyes nor hear the gentle morning coos from Freddie so I have taken Fiddle and Josh and am riding first to Jerusalem Farm."

For a brief moment, she stopped breathing. Fleetingly she wondered if he was only seeing that his mother, aunt and uncle were coping with the snow. She realized this hope was futile. She had thought him so perfect, and no longer cool and reckless. She took a deep breath and read on.

"I remember our first kiss which I stole from you when you worked at the farm. I loved both you and your voice, and I knew I wanted you forever. When, much later, I discovered that Sir William Harper was not only the real magic behind our successful smuggling but was also your father, my life began to make sense, and all the work I had done became worthwhile.

"Now that we have turned from the old ways, life provides a worthwhile challenge. It also provides comfort for you and

Under a Dark Star

Freddie – a priority. But I cannot rid myself of what Karl said. 'All that it takes for evil to triumph is for good men to do nothing.'

"Earlier this week, I arranged for my mother to continue to live at Jerusalem Farm. She is not alone as you know, and I'm sure the farm manager and his wife will be adequate for the needs of the property. My aunt and uncle will temporarily move back here into their old house and he has agreed to manage the farm in the bottom fields. My mother will assist with any visitors who arrive before I return.

"We already have a competent overseer taking charge of the building projects and Benson is delighted to be promoted from just stable hand to also being temporarily responsible for the many attractions we now offer our visitors should any arrive before I return.

"Aside from my uncle and aunt, these people understand they must please you or you will reassess their positions within our household.

"Under the table in the parlour you will find my trunk. I am unable to transport it at the moment but Karl will arrange for it to be sent.

"I take with me, as always, the curl I cut from your hair that day we stood together on the rooftop of Watch House. I also take with me the thought of you and Freddie awaiting my return. I leave you all the love I have in my heart and I go, as Parson Raffles said, surrounded by the strength of God's love."

He'd signed it with a kiss.

Lucy reeled. Karl had come between them yet again. And Parson Raffles hadn't helped either. She could not allow this. She also could not allow her next thought to take root: was Daniel missing the excitement of his old life?

Chapter Five
Isle of Wight - Daniel
"Bailing or vomiting"

Saturday 15th February 1823
"No dogs and donkeys! D' yer 'ear?"
Daniel stared at the block-shaped man and suppressed his retort which he deemed unsuitable for the ears of any ladies waiting to board the small wooden steamer. "I can't leave them behind so how do they get across to the island?" The Solent separated the Isle of Wight from the mainland of Britain and he peered across the heaving sea and saw nothing but low, grey clouds and rain.
"Show us yer silver and we'll tow 'em."
Daniel dug deep in his pocket and pulled out a half crown and offered it to the man who stood barring his way.
"That'll do for the dog. Did yer wanna take the donkey too?"
He patted his other pocket and a few nails and coins jingled. He fingered another half crown and a shilling, drew them out and said, "Take good care of them." He nodded towards Josh and his mother's new donkey, Nancy. "They're all I've got." He'd left his trusted horse with his mother.
"Get in the boat then; we 'aven't got all day and it ain't gonna be easy in this weather."
Daniel unstrapped the saddlebags and slung them over his shoulder. Two young women were making friends with Josh who wasn't at all sure about this whole journey; his tail was between

Under a Dark Star

his legs and his head hung low. He scooped him up and one of the girls leant forward and whispered, "Carry him on board underneath your cape. Pa's not as bad as he sounds. He's as blind as a mole so he probably won't even notice."

He smiled. The journey to this southern port opposite the island had been a battle worthy of a prize kingdom and it looked like the worst was yet to come. A little assistance was very welcome. The girls returned his smile in no uncertain manner. "My thanks to you, ladies." They giggled. "Josh thanks you too." Daniel put his right hand to his left shoulder to show that they were friends and Josh, though awkwardly tucked under his arm, put up a paw.

The girls were entranced and jostled to be the first to shake his paw. "Sit with us, sir. We're used to the crossing and we won't be sick all over you. That lot might."

"And we'll get seats near the boiler too. Pa always sees to that!"

'Pa' plodded across to them and gave his daughters a gentle push towards the open steam boat. "Stop yer smatter and get aboard or I'll leave yer behind."

Daniel followed, sat between the girls next to the warm smoke stack, put the cumbersome saddlebags on the deck by his feet, and pulled his cloak tightly around Josh and himself. Poor Nancy, she was tied to a post on an open boat which wasn't much more than a glorified raft and being towed a few yards behind. She had a man with a bucket, and two horses and a carriage for company but from the sound of her hee-hawing, she was not a happy donkey.

The sea tossed the boat around and the passengers were soaked by both the torrential rain and the huge waves hurling themselves into the vessel. 'Pa' had given his daughters a wink, and a tarpaulin to shelter beneath. To everyone else he gave

Under a Dark Star

buckets and instructions to bail out. All except Daniel and his two young friends were either bailing or vomiting.

"See," said one of the girls lifting the tarpaulin a little, "that's Ryde church and Pa steers towards the steeple."

Not to be outdone, the other called across him saying she could see Ryde Pier and they'd soon be mooring alongside.

He confessed he'd never seen such a long pier and the girls giggled again. They gave each other a conspiratorial look then gave him two half crowns.

"Pa overcharges mainlanders, and we do the counting of the money, so he won't know."

"Ladies, you are too kind and..." He nearly said that ferrying him and his animals across was worth at least one half crown but stopped in time – it would be unwise to offend them or appear too wealthy.

"And what?"

He smiled at their bold attitude. "And perhaps we could visit a coffee house before I complete my journey? That is if your Pa won't mind."

"Nah," said one, "he'll not even know."

"He's just bringing us back home, so he won't wait around for us," said the other.

He'd wondered whether to ask if they were twins, but listening to their banter confirmed they were identical, except one had long hair straggling around her shoulders and the other had hers stuffed under her bonnet.

"We know a café in Ryde, don't we?"

~

The boat smelt of vomit and salty water; the warm, steamy café smelt of coffee, and the starched, white cotton tablecloths with beeswax candles in brass candlesticks gave the place a look of quality. Daniel would have stopped for some refreshment even without the urging of the twins. For twins they were: Jilly and Jessie Joliffe. And he was now having a cup of coffee with them and sharing a large treacle tart.

"She's French," said Jilly, nodding at the woman behind the counter. "There's some that like her too much and then there's some that don't like her at all."

"Tis true, but she's got what Pa calls 'style'," said the other. "See, she's wearing silk."

Daniel could always suppress a smile when he needed to. These twins, probably no more than nineteen or twenty, clearly aspired to silk chemisettes and more. Such a pity they lived on the north side of the island and he had to make his way to the south. He mustn't spend more than a few more minutes with them then he'd have to take his leave.

"The French woman does have style – I can see that, but you girls have it too." He flashed a smile at the twins who collapsed into a fit of shy giggles. "Will you mind if I think of you as the jolly Joliffes?"

"We'll like that!" said Jilly, the one with her long, brown hair hanging around her shoulders.

"And we are at your service, sir," said Jessie. The smile she gave him was innocent, confirmed by her next words. "We're not used to compliments here on the island. The men are all pretty rough, 'specially down south. Tis a pity you're not staying here in the north."

"When you come this way, you must let us know," said Jilly. This could be useful. "And how might I be able to do that?"

Jessie and Jilly conferred, then Jessie leaned forwards and whispered, "Our uncle's a carter and he'll always bring us a message."

Jilly added, "He and Pa are saving to buy a hotel. Pa hates ferrying. He says he's getting too old."

Under a Dark Star

"A worthy ambition. And very fashionable too," responded Daniel.

"Fashionable?" Jessie looked pleased.

"The rich are travelling so much more these days and need good hotels." This was a fortuitous meeting. Here were people who might not be averse to making extra money should he need a reliable local man.

"With regret, I must leave you now." He stood and carefully pulled out the chairs the twins were sitting on, just enough to help them leave: he didn't want them sitting in a public place discussing him. He paid the bill, then walked across to the girls who were now standing by the door. "Kaddakay is a fair journey and I should press on." He opened the door for them and stood on the path outside. Josh, tethered to the same post as Nancy, looked hopefully at his master. "This is not what you like, Josh, but this slice of treacle tart will have to do. I'll stop at the horse trough and you can both have a drink, though it seems to me you've reduced that puddle considerably."

"Our uncle knows the roads, him being a carter. Shall we get him?" Jessie seemed anxious. "You being a gentleman, you'll need a bit of help."

"Gentleman?" Damn, damn, damn. Despite wearing his old working clothes, he'd not successfully concealed what he'd become since he'd known his dearest Lucy. "You flatter me. I'm afraid my prospects and aspirations…" No, he definitely sounded all wrong for the task ahead of him. He changed tack. "I'm a working man with one donkey and a dog and I'm in search of my kinsfolk here. You need not concern yourselves with my well-being, I'm practised in the art of…" Damn, he must change – and fast. "I'm well able to take care of myself. It's only in the presence of you two ladies that I appear to be something better than I deserve."

26

The twins did not giggle. "Tis clear you are a gentleman in what Pa calls 'reduced circumstances'. Nobody round here gives a dog treacle tart," said Jessie firmly.

He was highly amused at what constituted being a gentleman in the eyes of these young women.

"We are honoured to meet you," Jilly said in as fancy an accent as she could muster. She gave him a bob, as a maid to a master, and Jessie followed her lead. "We shall be pleased to see you again."

"Ladies," said Daniel, "I bid you farewell." He mounted Nancy who was still letting it be known that this was not a good day nor week, and he took hold of the rope tied around Josh's neck; Josh wasn't happy either despite the treacle tart. At least it wasn't still raining hard, just drizzling. The day was improving. He marvelled at his own thoughts: drizzling, windy, cold, a grumpy donkey, a disapproving dog, and all of them very wet and he'd just thought the day was improving.

Under a Dark Star

Chapter Six
"Surly Silence"

"Tynton? Nah, nobody round here called that."
"He's my cousin."
The Kaddakay innkeeper cast suspicious eyes over Daniel again. "Where're you from?" The menace in the innkeeper's voice equalled the look in his eyes. He intended to keep his customer waiting.
Daniel took his hat off and shook it dry. The Ship Inn was one of the worst he'd ever been in. Empty barrels were used as tables and two three-legged stools stood either side of the door, the rest were scattered, mostly upturned. "Mainland."
"North Island! That's what us'ns calls that great lump north of us." The innkeeper showed no interest for a few moments, then his curiosity surfaced. "Ain't seen nobody with a big cape like that afore."
Damn! The twins had given him enough warning and he should heed it. "Fits well, eh?" He held out his arms and gave a lopsided grin. Mustn't *smile*. "Rained a lot on the way. Wouldn't have been right to leave it rotting in someone's old barn, would it?" If he wanted to stay alive, these tales would be his only defence and they'd have to be watertight. This one was: the cape had been hanging in his own barn.
"Good leather that." The innkeeper screwed up his eyes to take a clearer look. "You planning on keeping it?"

Under a Dark Star

Daniel rubbed his fist in his palm: his old ways were returning. "Aye, I'll keep it."

The innkeeper slammed a tankard of ale down in front of Daniel and held out his hand. "Shilling."

"And one for Polly." A green feathered parrot screeched from a cage atop the end of the bar.

Any other time he might have been amused – but not today. "Shilling! Most of it's on here." Daniel pointed to the puddles on the bar.

"Shilling." The innkeeper insisted.

"Shilling this time." He flexed his fingers before grasping the handle and staring hard at the short, stout man, he whispered slowly, "Never again."

"Never again," screeched Polly.

He ambled over to a barrel, set the tankard down, picked up a nearby toppled stool and sat down facing the only other three patrons of the inn. He'd been a master for so long now that he must take care to integrate with the working men from the 'back of the Wight'. "Tynton? Anyone know of a Tynton round here?"

No one replied. The scrawny looking men shook their heads, then stared down into their tankards. He mustn't throw his money at them, at least not until he'd established a visible source of income, but he was equally sure he was not going to become a timid toady.

It was nearly dark and Josh and Nancy were tethered outside, resenting every step of the last three days' travelling across the island. Somewhere to sleep in the warm and dry was needed. He downed his ale and strode towards the innkeeper. "Have you got a room for the night?"

The innkeeper's eyes gleamed, then lost their spark. "Might have."

Under a Dark Star

"I'll take it." Daniel took some small coins from his pocket and counted them out. The innkeeper looked unimpressed. "And I'll need stabling and feed for my donkey. The dog stays with me." Hesitation showed on the innkeeper's face. "And if my donkey's still there in the morning, there'll be a further shilling."

"And one for Polly."

Polly was ignored.

"What did you say your name was?"

"Tynton. Daniel Tynton."

One of the men sitting across the room spluttered and knocked his tankard on to the floor as he hurried to the door. Daniel's muscles were taut. He was still staring into the eyes of the innkeeper who now looked down and muttered, "I'll take your bags up and show you the room."

Daniel picked up his saddlebags and waved the innkeeper on. "And your name is?"

"Tollervey. Everybody calls me Tolly."

Jilly, Jessie, Tolly, Polly.

~

So they'd heard of him – or perhaps his father. Good. That would make things easier. Daniel lay on what passed for a bed, turning over his thoughts and the plans he'd made with Karl. He'd had to be firm with him, he was so keen to arrive and clean up the coast. If he appeared too soon, suspicions would be aroused. Josh, laying by the fire, stirred and put his long snout on Daniel's hand. "Given you a hard time, haven't I?" Josh raised his eyes to look forlornly into Daniel's. "But now that you've had a good brushing, we can all see what a fine fellow you are." Josh was not impressed. He was a long-haired black and white dog, and soggy long hair and muddy legs and belly were not appreciated. "Yes, I know what you're thinking, Josh, some food would be welcome. I'm thinking the same." He rubbed Josh's ears. Hard to explain to a dog why he had to leave his comfortable life and trek a hundred miles in snow, hail and torrential rain.

His thoughts turned to Bodger. Dear old deaf mute Bodger. He'd always been such a reliable member of the North Kent Gang. Devoted – not too strong a word to describe how Bodger was always there, always willing to do anything. His death last winter had left a gaping hole in their lives. Lucy was devastated. He could do with Bodger now. Here. Someone who was never noticed as he went about Daniel's business. He'd lost a good friend but he kept the memory. With a loud sigh, he stood up and leaned across to the chair in front of the fire and pulled off his dried breeches, which though old were still too fashionable. He pulled off two of the buttons on one leg, and three from the other leg. This would leave them gaping just below the knee. He put them on, and turned the chair back under the small table in front of the window. Then he tied a rope around his waist and slipped a knife in the strap on his boot. The old days were back. It was dark now with only the glow from the dying fire. He could hear noises coming from downstairs. Tolly – stupid name for a bald, fat man – had said he'd bring up some stew before it got busy. Where was it? He opened the door and nearly tripped over a small pot on a tray on the floor. There was a lamp burning low on the landing and after he'd put the tray on the table, he grabbed it, took it into his room and hung it on a hook. Warm food, warm room, warm glow – things could be worse.

Before leaving Josh to finish the bowl of thin stew, he showed his faithful companion the door latch. "Have a nap by the fire, Josh, but keep one ear cocked." He silently went down the rickety stairs and pushed open the door to the noisy bar. The babble rippled to silence in less than two seconds. The crowd parted and walking towards him was a man, perhaps a couple of years older, with a thatch of light brown hair topping a rugged, scarred face.

Under a Dark Star

Whereas most of those in the inn were short and scrawny, this man was taller and well-built and his gait reminded Daniel of a picture of an ape Raffles had once shown him. An ape in fine clothes. Not fashionable, but a good woollen coat was worn over a velvet waistcoat. Light-coloured breeches, with all their buttons, led his eye to strong leather boots.

"You Tynton?" the man said.

"I am."

"What d'yer want here?

Daniel knew he needed every one of these men to trust him and draw him into their band of wreckers.

"I'm looking for my cousin. Tynton. Know him?"

"Huh!" His sneer implied Daniel might as well be looking for a unicorn. "What's happened to the magician?"

"Oh, so you know my father then?"

The ape took a step closer. "You on the run?"

That was a good line to pick up; it would give him a believable reason for coming to the island. He decided against it. One word would suffice. "No."

"I heard the magic ran out," scoffed the ape.

"My father is…" he'd been going to say "no longer with us" which is what Lucy would have said but it sounded soft so he said unwaveringly, "the old man is dead." There was a murmur from most of the customers of the inn and Daniel caught the gist. They'd heard his father had been hanged and gibbeted. "But I am still here."

"That 'cos you done the dirty on him?"

"Never!" said Daniel with menace. "Who are you?"

The ape stood his ground. "You ain't looking to leach off us, are you?"

Daniel resisted the temptation to say the ape didn't seem to be very good at smuggling. From the looks of the scraggly lot in the bar, the runs were not very successful. Or did the ape keep it all for himself? For now, he'd be conciliatory. Peace-making had been easy in Wintergate – everyone knew the Tyntons were not to be trifled with. If Daniel said there'd be no truck there'd be no truck. No dealing in goods unless he said so. An enforced peace. But in this place it looked like this ape was the master. A smile had to be suppressed – this man had probably never seen a picture of an ape. Better not to mention the word though, not just yet.

"I'm looking for my cousin – that's what I'm looking for. No leaching. Wouldn't mind earning a bit though." Would the ape fall in with this?

No one spoke; all watched with squinty eyes as each opponent said his piece. Then a donkey brayed and kept on braying. Bad timing.

"That'll be Nancy." Josh knew it too and began barking. The ape stood squarely in front of Daniel. "Nancy doesn't take kindly to being 'napped." Daniel moved forward and ducked all in one swift move as the ape's fist smashed into the solid door post and his mouth filled the room with curses, but Daniel was out of the door before anyone else moved and Josh was right behind him.

The clouds had cleared and in the light of a quarter moon Daniel could see two men attempting to drag Nancy away from the inn. Josh, like a bullet, shot across to the men and circled them, all the time nipping at their ankles. Daniel took the rope from around his waist and pulled it tight around one of the men's neck. "Let go of the donkey," whispered Daniel in his ear. He didn't need to explain why. "Enough, Josh." Josh allowed the other man to flee.

"We were paid to," said the roped man. "Don't kill me. Paid to."

"Who by?"

"I beg you, don't ask. He'll kill me."

Under a Dark Star

"So who do you wanna be killed by? Me or him?"

The man had one of his thumbs in between his neck and the rope and with his other hand he held on to the noisy donkey. Staring at the ape man loping towards them he squawked, "I'm dead, I'm dead."

Daniel loosened the rope and hissed, "Run, man, run!" Then with his left hand stroking the aggrieved donkey, he quietened Josh by clicking his fingers twice. Josh looked up – surely this was a mistake. He clicked his fingers again and Josh sat by his feet focusing firmly on the approaching ape.

"Trouble?"

"Nothing much," said Daniel nonchalantly.

"There will be."

Josh growled.

"There needn't be," Daniel said with the merest hint of a grin.

"You reckon?"

"Looks to me like you're the one with the troubles."

The ape took a step forward and Josh crouched and growled.

"You're off to a bad start with Josh too. Any time you wanna start again, you let me know and I'll let Josh know."

The ape flung a few incoherent words at Daniel, turned on his heels and lurched back towards the inn.

"Drunk too much by the looks of him, Josh. That could be useful." He glanced at the improvised reins around Nancy. "We'll take these off you when you're back in the stable. Deal?" Not waiting for an answer (he knew when he was beaten) he gave a slight tug on the reins and the three of them went back to the apology for a stable at the back of the inn. It was little more than a tumbledown shelter but was all that was on offer at the moment. "Sorry, m' beauty. You deserve better." He whipped a small brush out of his pocket and gave her a quick rub down. Without her milk on the journey here, the expedition would have been even worse.

Under a Dark Star

After letting Josh inspect the surroundings of the inn and giving him a good run to the cliff's edge and back, he clicked his fingers and Josh came to heel. Together they walked into the disorderly crowd in the bar which immediately fell into surly silence and he headed up the stairs to his room.

The stew pot had been cleared away and a tankard of ale put in its place on the table. Was that a good sign? Or was Tolly indicating he wasn't wanted in the bar or even in Kaddakay? The dying fire was now revived, just, but together with the lamp he'd taken again from the hook on the landing, he could see his bed had been disturbed. Tolly? Or had someone else been searching the room?

He flung back the two thin blankets and recoiled faster than any blunderbuss.

Under a Dark Star

Chapter Seven
"Akin to the fires of hell"

The following morning, having had little sleep – the floor wasn't at all comfortable – and only a boiled egg and a hunk of stale bread for breakfast, Daniel took his saddlebag and walked out of the inn, passing Tolly at the bar. Josh growled low, expressing his own and Daniel's wariness. The parrot gave an impression of a growl and Josh dashed to the counter, stood on his hind legs and snapped. Polly fluttered, fell off the perch and scrabbled around the bottom of her cage. Tolly could not even look Daniel in the eye. Hardly surprising. For all his slobby bulk, he hadn't a pinch of courage when it came to facing up to that ape. There were two pieces of good news though – when the ape had come after him, no one had followed to back him up. And although someone had been in his room, his saddlebag hadn't been found. He'd resorted to his old trick of nailing it flat to the ceiling behind the door.

He noticed for the first time a short, sturdy woman standing behind the bar washing tankards. "Mrs Tollervey?" he enquired of her.

Tolly responded instantly. "That is."

That is! What a way to refer to your wife. Before closing the door behind him, he nodded genially to Mrs Tollervey and, making sure no malice showed in his voice, he called out, "Good day to you. I'll no doubt see you again." Tolly was probably under orders. One day soon they would be *his* orders.

Under a Dark Star

Frost crunched under his feet. There were no footprints leading up to the inn, at least not to this door. Some led away from it: there'd obviously been late-stayers in the bar last night. There was almost certainly a back entrance too. He wore the same brown jacket he'd travelled in and his old woollen breeches but they were no match for the south-westerly wind whistling round the old inn. He flung his cape around his shoulders and took a deep breath of sea air. Invigorating perhaps on a warmer day, but today it just made him hurry to the stables. Poor Nancy. He must find his cousin fast.

Josh didn't run ahead as he usually did at home. He stayed perilously close to the legs of the donkey. Which way to go? Daniel looked for smoke. It was still early but a few villagers had lit a fire. He'd follow the smoke.

No one had heard of a Tynton, not that they were admitting to anyway, so he led Nancy and Josh towards the church and crossed the track to the parsonage. The parson would surely know.

"Tynton? No. It's not a name I'm familiar with." The parson coughed loudly and begged to be excused.

"I wonder if I might trouble you…" Daniel stopped. In the presence of someone likely to be well educated, he had reverted to being the man he'd become since knowing Lucy. He tried again. "I want to see the parish records. I'm sure me Ma said he lived in Kaddakay."

"You've called at a most inconvenient time," said the exasperated parson. "I haven't unlocked the church yet."

He could smell something cooking. Good to see that at least one person could afford a cooked breakfast. He positioned himself so he could see over the parson's head. And what he saw was a shabby but comfortable parsonage and there were at least two maids visible in the background. "I can wait here as long as it

Under a Dark Star

takes." Daniel indicated the doorstep of the parsonage and Josh sniffed around then took up his place lying across the entrance.

The parson frowned. "I'll take my breakfast first."

Take his breakfast! Pompous little man. Like most of the local inhabitants, he was short, scrawny and inhospitable. Raffles never had to lock his church doors, what sort of a place was this 'back of the Wight'?

"Aye, I'll wait." Using his favoured slip knot, he tethered Nancy to the post and sat down next to Josh. Almost immediately, Josh's nose twitched and he stood alert. Daniel nodded to Josh. "Off you go. I'll be right behind you."

Josh went around the parsonage and lay flat on the ground watching the parson scurrying through his back gate towards the church. Josh followed silently and Daniel followed Josh. The parson carried a bundle of clattering keys tied to his belt and he selected a large one, inserted it in the keyhole and pushed the huge oak door open. While he extracted the key, Josh slipped in unnoticed. The parson closed the door behind him and was about to lock the door from the inside when Josh decided this wasn't allowed. Tugging at his long coat, Josh succeeded in distracting him until Daniel pushed the door open.

"I should have introduced myself," said Daniel standing in the doorway. He was annoyed with himself. He was not sounding like a smuggler; he must try harder. "I'm Daniel Tynton."

The parson did not return his greeting. "I know who you are," he retorted under his breath.

"I see from this board..." Daniel pointed to a polished wooden board listing all the rectors from many years before, "...that you are Rafe Driver?" His intonation gave the parson a chance to correct him if he was wrong.

"What is it you want?"

"Nothing more than what I said. I want to find my cousin." The parson walked away from the door to the other side of the church and Daniel could see why: just inside the main door was an open register. He chose not to follow but laid his hand on the substantial book. "Perhaps there's an answer in here." He began turning the pages. Josh sat between his master and the approaching parson.

"That's not for the likes of you to fumble through."

Daniel had seen a register in Wintergate and he knew just where to look and what he was looking for. His mother had told him that twenty-three years ago his cousin Zeb Tynton was born in Kaddakay. The register showed a marriage of a Tynton a few years earlier but no registered birth of a Tynton. Then Daniel saw the name "Tynlan". Had the parents changed his name or was it a mistake on the part of the person entering the details? "Zeb Tynlan – where does he live?"

Rafe Driver smiled the sort of smile that, once seen, forever haunts. His thin lips revealed many teeth, teeth which looked as if they had been sharpened like stakes. "My predecessor was elderly, past eighty when he relinquished his calling. His eyesight and hearing were, shall we say, not as good as they once were. Young Zeb Tynton's parents were killed when their cottage burned to the ground. Some scandal surrounded their name and he took the orphaned boy to the House of Resolution across the other side of the island. I think he registered him there as Zeb *Tynlan*. And that is what he has been ever since."

"Not your fault then?"

"Indeed no! And young Tynlan was fed, probably better than he eats now; even had beef potage. There's no doubt though that the work was hard. He was indentured to a farmer and it was one of the farmer's daughters that he married. There was a rumpus about it because she had a little money, but the farmer relented on his death bed. They have bought an acre or so, not much more, half a mile the other side of The Ship Inn." The parson hesitated. "Tynton is not a name a person of good repute would wish to bear and your presence here has caused some alarm."

"I've noticed." More information would be useful. "Why is that?"

"There are those here who know of the North Kent Gang."

Daniel wondered if this man could be trusted. Could he become an ally? Perhaps he'd been in Kaddakay too long. Yet he had been helpful. Daniel was undecided so he opened his leather cape and slowly withdrew the body of a weasel, intending to ask its precise meaning. The reaction was immediate and the jagged toothed grimace brought to Daniel's mind the menacing image of a rat smiling.

"Go back to where you came from. Kaddakay is akin to the fires of hell and you should leave well alone."

Under a Dark Star

Chapter Eight
"The Dark Star"

Daniel knocked on the door of Tynlan House and wondered what was on the other side. The sign on the garden gate was impressive but the house was no more than a tiny cottage, at least a hundred years old, and cracks showed in the walls. To *own* the land, though, was unusual. He would accord them the respect that landowners expected. A young woman with unnaturally ruddy cheeks answered the door.

"Oh," she said with a nervous smile, "We were told you'd be coming."

No need for introductions then. His eyes flitted from head to toe and back to focusing on her pretty blue eyes and long eyelashes – were they charcoaled? "I thought you might be." He gave her an engaging grin. "You are Mrs Tynlan, I presume. May I come in? It's cold out here."

"Yes, yes, you must come in."

Now that he knew he'd be admitted, he pulled the saddlebags off Nancy and returned to where Mrs Tynlan stood twirling her hair.

A tall, lanky, dark haired man swaggered to the door and stood behind his wife. "Move aside, Becky, and let my cousin in quick."

Becky Tynlan scuttled back to the hearth in the parlour which allowed Daniel and his dog to get through the small front door leading straight into the room. "Mr Tynlan," despite the lack of space Daniel managed a bow in greeting. "I hope you don't mind

Under a Dark Star

Josh. He seems to be keen to get to know you." Or your warm hearth.

The Tynlans both replied that they loved dogs and insisted that, being family, Daniel should call them Zeb and Becky.

For the moment he thought it better to pay no attention to Nancy who was still tethered to the gate post and braying. Nancy didn't mind the cold but her coat had become sodden with the rain and she clearly hated being wet.

"Here, Becky, take Daniel's cloak and bring us some ale."

Becky obliged with many more nervous smiles and Daniel began to tell his cousin a suitable reason for his visit.

Zeb responded enthusiastically, "I told them I'm one of the legendary Tynton family but they don't believe me."

Daniel wasn't sure 'legendary' would be the word he'd choose but it could be helpful here in Kaddakay.

"Aye, they'll sure know who I am now." Scrawny Zeb puffed out his chest. "So you'd maybe like to stay with us for a while – you having come all this way to find me."

Daniel nodded. "I'd be very pleased to accept your hospitality. I've been on the road for the best part of three weeks. When my father..." he hesitated, "died, Ma said I should come and find you as we'd not heard anything from the island for years. She wanted to make sure you were..." he searched for an acceptable word, "comfortable."

Zeb shouted for Becky who eagerly came and sat down immediately. "No point in you thinking you can sit around with us men, Becky, this here is my cousin," he said with pride.

"I know that," she snapped.

"Well you go and get a proper meal ready for us and be quick about it. Then you can get a bed ready too."

Daniel reckoned a smile might help and she returned his willingly. The windows rattled with the wind and a spattering of sleet could be heard against the panes behind the mismatched curtains. "Have you somewhere I can stable my donkey, Zeb?"

"Course I have." Zeb stood and said, "Follow me."

Daniel decided not to mention the weasel hanging from Nancy's saddlebag.

~

Becky served a meal of turnip and potatoes with a few shredded green herbs scattered on top.

"If only I'd had more notice, I'd have found some eggs, even a chicken maybe."

She didn't sound very certain, and Daniel thought of the meals he'd become used to. He had just that morning commended himself on not thinking too much about Lucy – if he did, he'd 'go soft' and even worse, start wondering if he was doing the right thing coming here.

"You rustled up a very welcome dinner, and I'm feeling very comfortable now." Daniel patted his stomach and smiled at the blushing Becky who quickly cleared the plates to the scullery. Taking the opportunity of her absence, Daniel leaned towards Zeb. "I need some help."

Zeb took a while to think before saying, "Doing what?" His friendly demeanour turned suspicious. "You're not thinking of muscling in on Leon Tridd's trade, are you, 'cos if you are, there isn't a man around here who'll help, no matter what the prize. They've seen what can happen."

"What *does* happen?"

"The parson over at Brigton he preached one sermon too many." Zeb raised an eyebrow and gave a knowing look as best as he could. "All about the wages of sin being death. He didn't dare talk about anyone on the island so he told the story of your father. 'Sydney Tynton,' he said, 'was a farmer who got greedy'. Anyway, the parson was *removed*."

Under a Dark Star

"Not by Leon Tridd?"

"Tridd's violent and he doesn't care who gets killed."

"You mean he *killed* him?"

Zeb shrugged his shoulders. "Can't be proved. The parson was there one day and gone the next. House emptied too. I don't know if he'd been told to leave, or if he was murdered and his house ransacked."

Daniel remembered the days of the North Kent Gang when so-called justice was meted out by those with a trade to protect. His resolve to rid this part of the island from lawlessness grew.

"Surely his disappearance was investigated?"

"There's no law but Tridd's. If anyone breaks ranks – they disappear. Even the revenue men are scared out of their wits!"

Daniel allowed him to gush on; every bit of information about this man who had such a malevolent influence was useful.

"And once he's set his mind to something, he can't be stopped. He lets it be known who's master round here. He's as hard as rock."

It appeared to be a matter of pride to be acquainted with a man like this. A strange, yet familiar mixture of hatred and admiration. Daniel's face showed the merest hint of a smile. "Living so close to the sea you undoubtedly know that even hard rocks become sand."

Zeb perked up. "Especially round here. Crumbling cliffs is what we've got. You take care when you're out with that dog of yours."

Was he being warned of Tridd, or crumbling cliffs? "I can see this man has his own little kingdom," Daniel said as he shifted in the uncomfortable chair, "but his subjects look like they don't get a fair share. Am I right?"

"Too right! But Becky and me, we've got this little bit of land, and we reckon on staying out of his way. We're not scared of him.

And you'll see, I've got plans. This time next year this place will be a palace."

Daniel looked around but said nothing. Leon Tridd had affected everyone in the back of the Wight, it was all too obvious. Yet somehow Zeb's pride was endearing; so much better than just giving in to a bad start in life and a tyrant living not much more than a stone's throw away.

~

Late that evening, in the parlour, Daniel was alone with Becky as Zeb was "out the back".

"I heard what you said to Zeb."

He thought she'd probably been listening; he just had to hope she didn't hear everything, particularly the part where he had leaned forward and all but whispered to Zeb.

"Especially the bit where you were whispering," she said with a touch of triumph.

"Don't get involved in men's business, Becky. From what your husband says, this Tridd fellow is violent when roused."

"He's as cunning as the foxes round here." She thought for a moment then added, "He can be as nice as apple pie when he wants to be."

"Let's hope we see more of the good side."

"That's when he's at his worst. We never know what he's up to but you can be sure that the only one who'll be better off at the end is him." She drew closer to Daniel and whispered, "We girls call him the Dark Star."

"Dark Star? Whatever do you mean?"

"It's as if he is magnetic. He shines like a star in this dreary life – a bright light, drawing us all closer to him with his charm. Then when he's got us where he wants us, he goes back to being his usual self, and controls everyone and everything around him, pulling them into his schemes and no one can resist."

Under a Dark Star

"And the light goes out?"

"Yes, that's it exactly."

Daniel hesitated. He vaguely remembered Raffles talking with Karl about dark stars in the heavens and the pull they exerted on everything around them. Yet how could someone like Becky know? Perhaps her parents were more educated than he'd imagined. He decided she must be thinking of something else. "Because his schemes usually involve dark nights?"

She gave him a conspiratorial look. "You being a Tynton will know about 'a dark'."

Thoughts of successful moonless nights flew through his mind. They'd smuggled goods right underneath the noses of the customs' men in Wintergate. He flashed her a smile. "Aye, I do. But tell me, where does this treacherous star hide?"

"Ain't no secret. Come with me to get some provisions tomorrow and I'll show you."

Josh, who had hardly stirred since arriving, pricked up an ear. "Thanks, Josh." Daniel understood and changed the subject rapidly.

Becky stifled a giggle as Zeb put his head around the door. "You got Danny's bed made up yet?"

Oh no, not *Danny*.

"Course I have," she said, sounding offended before turning to Daniel. "We've not got much wood for a fire in your room, Danny, and only one blanket."

"Don't concern yourself, Becky. I'll throw my cloak on the top and that'll keep out the draughts, and Josh will sleep with me, won't you Josh? He's warmer than any blanket." Josh lifted his head and plodded towards Daniel. Daniel leaned forward and ruffled Josh's coat. He dare not say it aloud, but Josh did not like being here at all.

Becky stood up from the chair near the stove and her husband sat down. "I'll have to get some food in tomorrow, Zeb."

"You'd better! You ought not to let your stocks get so low. You go straight away tomorrow while I show Danny around."

Daniel decided Becky might be more useful than Zeb. Furthermore, in this weather it would take a good twenty minutes to walk to where he'd seen a general store near the inn, and carrying heavy goods back would take even longer. "Have you got a cart of some sort, Zeb?"

"Hand cart. We've got a good hand cart. Take that Becky."

"I could hitch it up to Nancy and come with you and we'll be back much sooner."

Becky was too quick to allow Zeb to say no. It was agreed – if they didn't call him Danny, he'd traipse in with the donkey and cart to get the larder fully stocked.

"Just in case the weather takes a turn for the worse," said Daniel carefully. He mustn't come between husband and wife.

Chapter Nine
"Weasel! We're not eating weasel"

Daniel, Becky, the donkey and the dog arrived at the store near The Ship Inn. He could not trust leaving his saddlebag, so he'd brought it with him. A little money could be used to help his poor relations. Their life, for all Zeb's high-flown talk, was hard, and it was Becky who seemed to pursue her hopes with rather more vigour than her husband.

"You see that grey stone wall up there on Rose's Ridge?"

He glanced up to a steep ridge overlooking Kaddakay and saw a fortified house with a tower, like a small castle, and surrounded by a high wall. "Is that where Tridd lives?"

"Yes. We call it Tridd's Fort. It's best not to stare. He keeps watch and he's bound to be looking out for you."

"Does he live alone?"

Becky lowered her voice. "No. There's a woman who lives with him but she's not been seen for some months now."

"Doesn't she come down to the village?"

"Oh no. He doesn't allow her out except into the grounds of the fort. He has everything delivered to him."

"So what chance is there for anyone to see her anyway?"

Becky lowered her voice even more. "There's another, narrow ridge, a bit further up, and from there you can just about see into the grounds. Some of the men have seen her but Tridd rarely talks about her." She considered for a moment, then added, "Except when he gets drunk. And sometimes he takes her a dress or a shawl."

"But you say she's not been seen for a while?"

"No, but she must be there because she does all the work. He wouldn't manage without her, though there's an old man who lives over the other side of the ridge who looks after the grounds. He goes there most weeks. He's odd, not quite right in the head. And nasty, very nasty."

"Anybody else?"

Becky seemed reluctant to continue at this point but did say, "There's daily women."

Becky was turning out to be so much more useful than he'd expected, far better than his cousin. He turned to look behind him and she walked away. Stacked against the outer wall of the store was some hay and straw. He loaded a bale of each onto the cart leaving only a little room for anything else. There was a rudimentary shelter with a few scrapings of bark on the ground. No wood. Just as he put his foot in the doorway of the store, he overheard Becky.

"He's my cousin."

Daniel raised an eyebrow – she'd claimed him for her own.

"What! Is he staying with you?"

Becky responded quickly. "Course he is."

Another woman's voice joined in. "Is he married?"

"What do you wanna know for? You're married already."

"Yes, but I'd do anything to have a man like that around."

Daniel decided it was time to examine women who'd do anything. He stamped his feet and noisily walked around the corner to where the group of three young women and Becky stood gossiping. "Good morning, ladies." This simple greeting was delivered with the sunniest of smiles, in contrast to the overcast,

Under a Dark Star

windy weather. Having verified that no one could see him, he bowed low.

"This is my... this is *Daniel*." Becky beamed.

Stunned, the little group took a moment to respond, then, one after the other, they all returned his greeting with attempts at elegant bobs. Josh looked up at his master. Were these friends? Daniel introduced them carefully; he did not place his right hand on his left shoulder – the sign of a friend. Josh wagged his tail slowly; he'd got the message.

"I hope to meet you all again," said Daniel.

"Is that your donkey?"

The plan he'd been working on would need adjusting. These young women, so keen to stay and talk, looked tough, tough enough to give him an idea. "Nancy is my donkey, yes. Would you like to get to know her? Give her a pat, she loves it."

They didn't need asking twice. All scuttled over to Nancy and began putting their arms around her neck, patting her and talking to her just like Lucy always did. Why did everyone on this island keep reminding him of his own dear little Freddie and adored wife. Why did all the names end in the letter 'y'? It was hard enough trying not to think of them but the islanders seemingly insisted on reminding him. He must forget them for a while – for their safety.

While Becky spent time with her friends, Daniel went into the store and bought a sack of flour, sugar, a large pat of butter, some carrots, salt, dried apples and four cabbages. He dug around in his pockets pretending money was hard to find. "I have a bale of hay and straw too." The man who looked after the store seemed affable, as well he might. Hardly anybody could buy sugar and not many customers brought a cart because everyone mostly managed with the little they grew themselves. Daniel stepped outside and took his provisions to the cart and carefully placed them under the bales. The fewer people who saw what he'd bought, the better. He called Becky over.

"Flour, carrots, salt, cabbages and apples." He'd leave the sugar as a surprise. "Anything else you need? What about wood?"

"If there's none in the store, sometimes the parson has a good stock. He has it sent over."

The parson. Not good news. "Sent over?"

"Yes, the carter brings it from Brigton forest. He's got lots but he refuses to come to Kaddakay. The parson meets him on the road. Then the parson sells it on to Tolly and Jimmy in the store."

"The Kaddakay parson it is then." He looked across to the three young women and asked, "Do you see your friends often, Becky?"

"In the summer I did. I didn't know anybody when I first came here and Zeb was so kind, he let them come to our cottage sometimes and we would sit in the garden."

"Perhaps they could visit you in the winter too and you could bake some cakes and have tea around a roaring fire in the stove. What do you think?"

She eyed him suspiciously. "They're all married."

"I'm suggesting this because they are, like you, married and it's my guess that while their husbands can meet at The Ship, they rarely leave their sculleries. You could arrange it and I'll make sure Zeb doesn't mind."

"I haven't got much flour for baking, Daniel, and we don't have tea."

"You leave that to me. Just make sure you enjoy the time you can spend with your friends while I'm here. I'll make it up to Zeb." It was the least he could do and maybe they could influence their husbands to join the winning side.

~

"Weasel! We're not eating weasel. Where did you get it from?"

Under a Dark Star

Daniel could see fear, bordering on terror, in Becky's eyes. "Someone gave it to me." He refrained from saying *I found it in my bed with its fresh blood seeping into the lumpy straw.*

"Oh, mighty God," she clasped her fists together and looked up. "What can we do? Zeb will get so mad."

Daniel continued chopping up the body. He had put the skin to one side. Pointing to the fur, he said, "You don't want to use that to make a bonnet or muff, then?"

"How can you stand there and jest about such things?"

"It's a weasel. Its damaged leg tells me it's been caught in a trap, poor thing. You'd eat rabbit, wouldn't you?"

"Oh please don't tell Zeb. You've got to promise me. He's probably out rabbiting now. He'll bring us something."

"I'll need a little salt to cure the skin and I'll hang it in the stable to dry. Nancy won't mind, even if Zeb does."

"I suppose it'll be all right so long as he doesn't go round there."

"Does he need to?"

"Not often, but he keeps a spade and hoe in there."

"I'll make sure he doesn't notice the skin." Daniel thought of the nails in his pocket. He'd dry it flat on the underside of the roof above Nancy. "Now give me a pot and I'll cook this for Josh." Daniel glanced at his hopeful dog. "There's no way he'll go without this good meat. Bring me a pot and I'll put it on the stove. We can tell Zeb it's vermin." It wasn't a lie - weasels were regarded as vermin by most farmers. "Is that why you won't eat it?" How puzzling. Folks in this part of the island were hardly the best fed people.

"Oh no," she answered quickly, then seemed to regret it.

"Why not then?"

She clasped her fists together again. "Zeb knows where they come from."

What did she mean? She'd already been very useful so he decided not to pursue the subject any further. It wouldn't suit his purpose if she thought he was prying. She'd even found out from the parson that the carter was due within a day or two and he now knew this carter was the uncle of the twins he'd met in Ryde. The fact that the carter wasn't keen to become acquainted with people in Kaddakay also commended him. He scraped the chopped meat into the pot, added some water, and put it on the only stove in the house, the one in the parlour. Tynlan House! It was one small room and a scullery downstairs and two small bedrooms upstairs and most of the time the place was freezing.

At dusk, Zeb, stinking of ale, brought a rabbit home. Becky looked more perplexed than cross. "He doesn't usually go to the inn. He tries to stay away."

Had he been plied with drink?

"Was Tridd there, Zeb?" Daniel said as he steered him towards his rocking chair.

"Aye. I bumped into him on the road. Good man that. Well… sometimes." Zeb patted his pocket.

"Generous when he needs something?"

Zeb didn't reply. He didn't need to. Daniel hoped his cousin would regret selling his honour once he'd sobered up. Gainful employment was what he needed. Daniel chuckled a little: he sounded like Raffles.

"What you laughing at?" Zeb wasn't belligerent, only confused.

"Oh, just thinking, just thinking." He took a deep breath. "Perhaps tomorrow, if the weather's fine, you and I can turn over the soil, get it ready for planting, that sort of thing."

Zeb had, in the space of thirty seconds, fallen asleep and was now snoring. Somehow he had to turn this man around. The boat

Under a Dark Star

would be coming in just under three weeks, timed for the next moonless night. Could he get a gang together before then?

Chapter Ten
Ryde, Isle of Wight - Karl
"They failed spectacularly"

Saturday 22nd February

Karl walked into an inn. Any inn. It didn't matter which. Less than two hours ago he, Lucy and screaming baby, Mrs Raffles and Martha, together with mountains of luggage, had all been crammed into or on top of his oldest carriage. Matters were made worse by Midnight and Fiddle who clearly hated the experience of being hitched to a carriage with two other horses and pulling them all. Oh and, of course, there was his coachman. "Let's not forget him," he muttered. The worst part was the difficulty in being conveyed across the heaving Solent in a tin-pot boat. Nevertheless, he could forgive Lucy anything, even though her scheme to be near Daniel had caused such inconvenience.

"What did yer want?" said the surly, scruffy man behind the bar.

Karl shivered which shook some of the rain from his shoulders. "Brandy."

The barman poured a measure of brandy while Karl looked disdainfully around for a comfortable seat. No one else was in the inn. Sensible people. He drank immediately, recognized it was watered down so asked for another much against his better judgment. The bar stank of alcohol; wiping the counter and washing the floor didn't seem to be high on the list of priorities.

Under a Dark Star

Karl hid his thoughts; *list of priorities*, this barman had probably never heard of such a thing. He stank too.

He moved quietly towards a dark corner bench with a threadbare velvet curtain pulled around it. Karl's instinct for finding out why privacy might be needed was rewarded.

A gruff voice snapped, "And all her property?"

"Shut your gob!"

This sounded interesting so, feigning warming himself by the nearby fire, Karl stood, feet apart, brandy in hand, and listened.

A third voice could be heard placating the other two. "Gentlemen, you must be discreet. You know as well as I do, that what you are calling her property is not hers. Now he's six feet under, it reverts to his next of kin, and that's his son. But she needs to be removed from there. It's his son who has devised this..." he coughed quietly, "...this means to remove the mistress without any controversy."

The first man spat out his opinion. "Controversy! Huh! Whoever wins will be doing her a favour. Losing her protector and not being one of us, shall we say, she'd be facing trouble one way or another."

Karl was fascinated. Were they arranging a duel over a woman? Probably not a duel: they didn't sound like gentlemen. He noticed that the surly barman had slunk off to an upholstered chair at the other end of the bar and was snoring.

A fourth man had something to say. "I want you to be clear. If I win, I'll be taking her tonight, and I won't need your help. Except," there was a short silence, "except, you as a..."

"Don't dig me in the ribs, like that!" It was the voice of the peace-lover, but he didn't sound very peace-loving now.

The fourth man resumed, "...you as a *magistrate*, will ensure that there are no..."

The magistrate interrupted tetchily. "There will be no repercussions for any of us, I'll see to that." There was a regular, shuffling sound. "So long as we are all agreed that whoever wins, gets to take her away from the island, then there should be no one to identify her."

"Let's get on with it. Are those cards clean?" said the gruff man.

The fourth man, a younger voice than the rest, snapped, "You saw me ask the barman for a new pack."

"Get on with it! Stop shuffling those cards and start dealing."

"Not 'til you've put your money in my hands. Remember, you are here by my invitation and I'll be the one who has to protect our backs," said the magistrate.

The sound of heavy coins being slapped down on the table, followed.

As stealthily as a stalking cat, Karl moved well away. They were playing cards for a woman. The winner would furtively take her away and no one would bother because no one cared about her now that her protector was dead. Poor creature. He should do something. But if he became involved now, he'd never meet the timetable he and Daniel had agreed. He had just a short while to settle himself in to his new position as Chief Riding Officer along the back of the Wight. He'd use his rank as a former naval Lieutenant to command more respect for law and order than his predecessor. Law and order! And here was a magistrate gambling with ruffians for a woman!

Silently he pushed open the door, taking a last look at the sleeping innkeeper. No point in asking him who the men are, he supposed. He'd just say *dunno*. And he hadn't got time to wait for the end of an undoubtedly fixed card game. He'd make enquiries later as to who'd gone missing – someone would notice a woman who was no longer there.

Under a Dark Star

~

He'd slept well. His hotel was not the best in town, he'd made sure Lucy and her baby, Mrs Raffles and the ever-present Martha were safely ensconced in the most comfortable; his was well away from prying eyes. He must now assume the role of an official in the Customs, and not look like the wealthy landowner that he was.

He'd eaten a good breakfast and the plan was that he should meet Lucy and the others on the road leading to Newport where he had to collect some papers. He spread out his map on the bed and traced the route they would take with his finger. From Newport they'd journey on towards Freshwater. Mrs Raffles' cousin's farm was south of the road and just north of the village of Bruton. "By Jove! It's about eighty acres." He remembered dimly that Emmeline Raffles was the *poor* relation of quite a wealthy family. He'd forgotten the details and the only relevance now was that she had reasonably wealthy, possibly useful connections. He folded up the map and put it in his leather bag. He thought of Daniel crossing the island with only the scribbled plan he'd given him; it wasn't much more than the diamond shape of the island with Ryde, Newport and Kaddakay on it. He took a deep breath; Daniel was, he grudgingly admitted, superior to all the other motley smugglers he'd grown up with and he also seemed to have some sort of inner sense of direction. Like a pigeon, he could always find his way home. Would it be the same on an unfamiliar island?

He pursed his lips, seized his leather bag, paid his bill, and set off towards Newport. He walked up the steep main street and saw the little café Lucy and the parson's wife had visited yesterday and enthusiastically cooed over *little French pastries*. He stopped. There was a note on the inside of the window. "This café is now closed." A reminder to him that it was Sunday. He passed the splendid Ryde church and wished he had time to look inside but he must leave this town behind.

The watery sun could not win against the piercing, biting cold searching out uncovered flesh. He buttoned up his coat and lowered his chin before contemplating aspects of the plan with which he needed to familiarize himself. He must not threaten hanging and gibbeting. Huh! Wreckers! They should be… He decided not to waste time on those thoughts. Being an M.P. gave him power and he had given his word that those apprehended would be transported. It was the fault of Raffles' sermons and Daniel insisting that every man must be granted a chance to repent. *He'd* been saved from the hangman's rope, he'd said. Uncannily true. Karl felt a little uncomfortable when he thought of his threats to rid the county of murdering gangs of smugglers, Daniel's in particular. It was Daniel's father, Sydney Tynton, he'd really hated: the man who'd left his father, a naval Captain, to drown on sinking sands. He'd deserved gibbeting; having his body pecked and eaten by crows was justified. But Daniel could never be caught. Not a single man, and definitely no women, would speak ill of him. And when everyone else had been rounded up on that dark night on the beach at Wintergate, Daniel was safe at Bethlehem Farm – injured. And injured by him – Karl! As Lucy so often said, it was as if it was by the guidance of God that they were now almost friends.

His thoughts were interrupted by the sound of the church bells ringing in the distance and these were accompanied by the rumbling of a carriage approaching.

He glanced over his shoulder. It wasn't a carriage. It was a horse and cart rattling like a beggar's cup.

"Wanna ride with me, friend?" called the carter.

"Most kind of you," responded Karl, "but I am awaiting my horse."

Under a Dark Star

The carter looked puzzled. "Just as you like, sir. But you'd be welcome. No payment necessary. I'd be glad of the company." Karl scrutinized the friendly, respectable-looking man. "I am obliged to you but truly I await my horse." The carter nodded, shook the horse's reins gently and called "Walk on."

"Wait!" Karl caught up with him. "I may have need of your services at some time. How do I contact you?"

"Where are you headed, sir?"

"I am taking up the post of Chief Riding Officer along the back of the Wight. Quartered at Watch House near Rose's Ridge."

"Ah... the naval officer. Yes, I heard there'd be someone new – I thought you might be him. Well, there's some places around there where I don't go. I go to Norwell Farm with provisions from Ryde and along the road back up to Newport but that's all. Sometimes I take wood to the parson over at Kaddakay."

"You go to Kaddakay?"

"Never! The parson meets me on the road. If you need me, it's best to leave a message at Norwell."

"My thanks to you." Karl waved the carter on. "I am glad to have met you." He watched as the large cart, pulled by a great shire horse, trundled away towards Newport.

He'd walked another mile before he heard a sound other than birds singing. At last! It was his own old carriage, jolting and rattling along slowly and pulled by his black stallion, Midnight, and Daniels' faithful Fiddle, and two more from his stable. His coachman, Miller, looked ill at ease trying to control the two spirited horses, Midnight and Fiddle, and they failed spectacularly at being inconspicuous.

"Take your time, don't hurry, Miller. A comfortable journey will be much appreciated." As would sitting close to Lucy; the longer the better.

Chapter Eleven
"More than could be explained"

"Welcome! Welcome to Norwell Farm."

Relief at the journey's end was coupled with regret at leaving Lucy. Nevertheless, Karl leapt out of the carriage. It might be his oldest but it was also his sturdiest and had travelled more than one hundred miles from Kent across some badly rutted roads without even needing a wheel change. He bowed low in greeting and his courtesy was returned with a low curtsey by Mrs Lytton, Emmeline's cousin. Miller helped Lucy, Mrs Raffles and Martha alight.

"Major Lytton, come quickly, my cousin has arrived."

Major Lytton hurried past his wife and bowed low to Karl. "Lieutenant Thorsen, may I extend to you a welcome to the island."

Karl bowed low in response. He might need the respect and trust of this man who presented himself well; clearly a military man. "My thanks to you, sir, for your offer of not just hospitality but also protection for these ladies."

The Lyttons welcomed them not only in words. The well-proportioned stone farmhouse had a lamp in every window and a lamp hanging in the gabled porch. A groom rushed to help with the carriage and horses and soon Lucy, Freddie, Mrs Raffles, Martha, Karl and all the trunks and baggage were inside the generously sized hall. Freddie was the centre of attention and loved it until he felt the need to express some concern at the lack of food.

Joeline Lytton, a slender but pleasingly curvy woman in her late thirties, ushered Lucy into what she called "a snug little sitting room which we have set aside for you and Freddie". Karl watched her carefully and wandered over behind her. He wished he could have seen her face as she saw Daniel also standing inside. "We'll talk later," he called across to Daniel who soon had his arms around Lucy and Freddie with Josh stretched to his full height trying to join in.

Mrs Lytton beamed and called for her servants to attend to the luggage. "Mr and Mrs Tynton and their son have a bedroom at the back of the house. Emmeline, my dear, dear cousin, you have a smaller bedroom at the front, which we fondly call the blue room. Your servant," she looked at Martha, "has a room in the attic. And Emmeline dear, if you wish to send for your maid, Mrs Tynton's too, or the Nanny, there is another, tiny room to spare." Politely, she smiled at Karl. "Lieutenant, we have a large room in which I keep my sewing, but it has a comfortable couch. I hope you will understand?"

"I am grateful to you, Mrs Lytton, and you may be assured that having been a sailor, I can sleep anywhere."

Mrs Lytton bobbed slightly and smiled. "You are most gracious and will always be welcome to stay here should you need to."

Martha had set herself up to be the guardian of the luggage, directing to which bedroom each piece should be taken. Showing her best, nearly toothless grin, she finished with, "And that belongs to Mr Tynton! And don't try and unpack it. You can't. No one can. Not even me. It's his flight trunk."

"Martha!" Karl glared at her. He walked over to her and whispered. "Your gossip could kill a man. Imagine you are back at Watch House in Wintergate. Talk to no one of what you hear or know."

Martha was suitably mortified. "It's another person's flutten trunk, she yelled at the servants." She turned to Karl. "There! That'll get 'em all confussled."

His expression did not reassure her and he reflected on the reasons he had not been able to employ her for long at his country estate despite her undoubted loyal intentions. It had turned out well as Sarah, Lucy's buxom maid at Faefersham Court, had married earlier than expected, and Martha was better suited to the relaxed management at Bethlehem Farm. He'd speak to Lucy about reminding her of the dangers of loose talk.

While coats were being removed and the ladies shown to the drawing room, Major Lytton was closing the curtains and removing the lamps from the windows downstairs. "Can't be too careful," he explained.

"Very wise, Major Lytton, very wise." Karl eyed him from top to toe – he certainly didn't go without food and why should he? His wisdom probably extended to how to run a good farm. Satisfied that the Lyttons were sensible people for Lucy to be staying with, he wondered if they could be called upon for help, should the need arise. "You have a fine company of servants, Major Lytton." It wasn't exactly what he thought but it was courteous. "How many men are needed to farm this acreage?" Karl hadn't time to be anything but direct.

"Depends on the season, Lieutenant Thorsen." He might have left it at that but Karl continued to await a further response. "Are you wondering what the men do in the winter?"

"I'm aware that there are certain jobs…" he thought of his own estate and back to the time when Daniel's escaping father desperately hid from him in a ditch, "…ditches to be maintained and so forth, but how do they make a living in the winter months?"

Under a Dark Star

"Ah. I see why you ask." Major Lytton stroked his chin. "Are any of my farm hands in need of supplementing their income?"

Karl was pleased to be speaking with someone who understood his need to ask such questions. "Indeed."

"This farm provides sufficient for our household throughout the year and there are surpluses which sell well, particularly in Newport, Cowes and Ryde. We also keep emergency rations for those of our workers who find themselves in difficulty. I tolerate no involvement in evil deeds. We are a God-fearing family and those who work for me are required to maintain the highest of moral standards." George Lytton had not stopped for breath and held Karl's stare throughout.

Karl could not believe how very fortunate it was to find that Mrs Raffles' relation was a man of such forthright probity. "Emergency rations." He turned the phrase over in his mind. "You are not only God-fearing, you must surely be considered a Godsend to many."

Major Lytton lowered his voice. "Sir, I request you refrain from the use of the word 'godsend'. A little further along the coast, where you will be quartered, a 'godsend' is a shipwreck."

Karl's face fell. Of course, from the point of view of those who plunder the ship, it could be seen...his thoughts stopped. "As I understand it, most wrecks are not an act of God."

"Let us resume this discussion after dinner as I believe Daniel has information for you."

"My apologies, Major Lytton. I am constantly short of time and hurry into situations conducive to gathering evidence." 'Burst' was a more accurate description than hurry but Karl felt he could excuse himself.

Major Lytton led the way into an extremely comfortable drawing room where the ladies were now acquainting themselves with their hostess. It could not be considered fashionable but seemed to exude warmth and encourage relaxation. Cream and raspberry-red flock wallpaper gave it a cosy feel. Karl sat against one of the softest cushions he had ever felt. He picked it up and examined it. Had it been on the mainland, it would have undoubtedly been made of silk, but this was a cotton tapestry of a sailing ship. "Such skill," he said and Joeline Lytton flushed a little. "So soft," he added.

"Goose down," said Mrs Lytton. "We use it for our bedding too."

Major Lytton, having sat himself close to Karl, leaned across and whispered, "Geese make good guards too. You'd think all hell had broken loose."

"Could you sell me some?"

"You'd need to keep them penned. I offered a couple to Daniel but he reckons Nancy and Josh do the guarding."

Karl allowed himself a grin. "Fortuitous," said Karl. "For if both he and I arrived with geese, we might look suspicious."

"On another matter," George Lytton was also not slow to extract information, "I am concerned that Emmeline has left her husband alone. Does he have sufficient support?"

Karl hid his own concerns. "He is an extraordinary man of God. I don't think his parishioners will allow him to go without. He has a cook and one or two other servants." Karl could almost hear Raffles' voice saying that Daniel had insisted on more help for the parsonage. Strange that Daniel…he gave up thinking. He knew he was missing a piece of information and that he might never find out what bound Daniel and the parson so closely. "I have to say that we, that is Daniel and I in particular, were not in favour of Emmeline and Mrs Tynton coming to the island."

"Does he have a curate?"

"No, I'm afraid not."

Under a Dark Star

"When you say he is extraordinary, what exactly do you mean?"

Karl furrowed his brow. How could one describe Raffles in a few words? He decided upon, "He seems to have God on his side." He paused. "In all things." That was the briefest way to explain more than could be explained.

Immediately Major Lytton grasped Karl's arm. "Our church has had no one to give guidance since the parson mysteriously disappeared. Do you suppose he could be prevailed upon to be our parson? If Emmeline likes it here on the island, they could find it, if not a rich living, then perhaps one where they are decidedly needed." He squeezed Karl's arm then removed his hand quickly upon seeing Karl's reaction.

"I cannot answer that for you. I am not well versed in matters of ecclesiastical law. His living in Wintergate has been sufficient for his needs. In whose gift is the living of your parish?"

"Sir Richard Moorcroft of Fresham Manor, west of here. Elderly, no sons, and somewhat impoverished. I believe I could ensure that your parson would be given the living of Brigton if you think he would come?"

Karl decided no. To take Raffles out of his current living would be needlessly cruel. Far better to work towards returning Mrs Raffles to Wintergate as soon as possible.

He frowned but was saved from having to voice his dissention when a servant announced that dinner was ready.

Under a Dark Star

Chapter Twelve
"Lord of the Manor"

The following morning, after a hearty breakfast, yet still under the cover of darkness, Karl mounted Midnight and rode towards Watch House near Rose's Ridge. He left his carriage and most of his luggage at the farm. He'd rather arrive unencumbered. Miller, his good coachman, would drive over tonight.

 He took the coastal road, that way he would be certain not to miss his destination. He might also spot anyone on watch for the new Chief Riding Officer. The chance of his arrival being a secret was slim. He passed through sleepy Brigton, a picturesque village of thatched cottages with white ashlar chalk walls. There was a baker, one or two other shops and a blacksmith. He thought of his conversation with Major Lytton the previous evening. Despite Brigton appearing to be a little bit of English heaven, he was sure he was acting in the best interests of Raffles and his wife in not agreeing that Raffles should be approached to come to the island. Daniel also considered it a needless disruption and decidedly unsafe. He was undoubtedly right for, as he paused to look carefully, there were signs of decline and it was appalling that the twelfth century church should find itself without a spiritual leader of any sort. Daniel's tale of the disappearing parson sounded like something out of the Middle Ages. They could not invite Raffles to the Brigton church, even with a *hundred* geese to guard him.

 Karl rode towards the east where the pink and grey sky anticipated the rising sun. He passed the bay where he'd observed

Under a Dark Star

the wrecking and tossed those inspirational words around his head: all that it takes for evil to triumph is for good men to do nothing. He was doing something and he flung a look at the sky as if to say *and don't blame me if it all goes wrong.* He smiled: he knew it wouldn't.

When he reached Kaddakay, an anaemic orb appeared above the horizon, promising little in the way of warmth. He avoided the road where the Tynlan's lived which allowed him to assess The Ship Inn and the small general store. He noticed a few scrubby bushes dotted here and there along the cliff top – might be useful, some were big enough to hide a man or two. Kaddakay was far too remote; worse than Wintergate, no doubt about that. No wonder they were a law unto themselves. At least Midnight seemed more like his lively self, despite his arduous journey from Kent. "You won't have to pull that carriage for a good, long time now." He patted his spirited black horse as he crossed the lower slopes of the ridge leading to Watch House. He refrained from saying that the other two horses had made a better job of pulling than either Midnight or Fiddle. "Not what you're bred for, is it?"

A large, stone circular tower, reminiscent of a medieval folly, loomed up before him. He held his mount to a walk as the land levelled out, then drew him to a halt. He pursed his lips and sighed. It was, he decided, a badly designed building, unsuitable for its purpose and probably yet another building with the hearth set against an outside wall. So much heat lost. A folly indeed. He focused on the task ahead and took a closer look at his quarters. There was the ground floor and then another three storeys with a castellated flat roof on top. A trace of a smile crept over his face as he remembered Watch House in Wintergate and how Lucy had turned the roof into a garden. He must get a grip. There'd be little time to dream of this woman who lit a room like the sun lights the sky. He took control and a thought flickered through his mind: the roof would make a good place for a warning fire or from which to signal.

He dismounted. The frost crunched as he walked Midnight around the back to some outhouses – for security they should be enclosed with the tower, perhaps he'd find time to attend to it. He patted Midnight. "Your stable, I suspect." Close by, on a small promontory, there were three terraced cottages. They'd be the Customs' cottages. They looked drab, but occupied. The two Riding Officers were likely living there. And the third cottage? Was he supposed to live there? Well he wouldn't.

He rapped on the stout Gothic style door with the heavy iron knocker. No answer. He tried the handle. Locked. He rapped again. "By Jove! This'll wake the whole of the Wight." He turned to see a man running from one of the cottages and another attempting to get into a uniform jacket and stumbling towards him. His fervent hope was that the men of the Preventive Waterguard were more reliable than these so-called Riding Officers. He reminded himself that the term 'Coast Guard' was creeping across the country and the land and water services were combining. Progress, long-drawn-out, but he must bring the new terms into use.

The slower man, still straightening his jacket, held out a key. "You'll require this, sir."

Karl did not take it. "Do you give your key to anyone who hammers on the door?"

"No sir, no. But you are expected."

"If I am expected, why weren't you here?"

"Well sir, we heard you were coming from Newport today. We thought you would be arriving much later."

"If a man arrives unexpectedly, and isn't wearing the uniform of a Riding Officer, you offer him your key, do you?"

The man looked sheepish. "Sir, I…"

Under a Dark Star

"By thunder! Are you going to stand there all day excusing your inexcusable behaviour? Open the door!" Owing to the overwhelming smell of damp, his next order on entering the tower was, "Light a fire!" Contrary to his expectation, the stove was in the middle of the room with a chimney leading straight up through the ceiling. He then turned on the other man. "So you are in receipt of information which leads you to incorrectly assess my arrival time. I hope you can assess the tides better." They thought he'd ridden from Newport. Who in Newport had informed on him? Not the carter. It would not be him. More likely someone who saw him when he stopped at that hotel for refreshment before going to the Custom House. They had assumed he would stay overnight. He was extremely glad he had taken the precaution of eating separately from the rest of the party and boarding his carriage well away from prying eyes. "Who was your informant?"

There was some hesitation before the officer replied, almost in a whisper as if that were common practice, "Tridd, sir."

He should have known. Daniel had warned him that nothing happened without Tridd knowing. "And who is this Tridd? And why did he keep you informed of my arrival? Is he one of your usual informants? Can he be relied upon?" As Karl knew the answers to these questions, he would be able to tell a lot from the answers he received.

The man in front of him, shuffled a bit and looked over his shoulder to his fellow officer who had hurriedly lit a fire in the stove. It was this man who spoke.

"Tridd, sir, is," he faltered, "well, he's like the Lord of the Manor. He lives…well, I'll show you later, sir. Well…"

"Get on with it man, I want no more 'wells'."

"Well, er sorry sir, he's not like a proper Lord of the Manor, he just behaves as if he is. He's quite violent."

Karl was becoming more annoyed. Lord of the Manor! By thunder! "How violent?"

"Well…"

"Get on with it, man." What a dozy duo.

"Yes sir. He's vicious; he has men who work for him…" If his own work wasn't so important, it would be comical. Karl grinned mockingly and taunted, "Servants you mean?"

"No sir. It's like the whole village works for him. If he wants something done, he just makes someone do it. If he wants wood for the fire, he sends someone to bring a cart load up to the fort. And he doesn't often pay for what he gets. Well, not, er sorry, he doesn't pay in money. He'll let them have something more when a ship comes in. More than the others."

"Other wreckers?" Both men decided to be silent. "You'll be Buckby, I take it?" Karl stared at the talkative one who nodded. "So you are Tomkins." The quieter one nodded. "Don't you think you should have identified yourselves when I first arrived?" They both stared at the floor. "And what do *you* do for Tridd?" Still they remained silent. Thumping the nearby table, Karl thundered, "That is the last time you will refuse to answer my questions!" Karl did not allow them time to agree or disagree. "Tomkins! Bring in my saddlebags, stable my horse, brush him down and feed him. Make sure he likes you." He did not say why: he hoped the implicit threat was understood. "Buckby, you can show me around. Are there beds in that third cottage?"

"Yes sir, but there's not a lot else."

"Next job for you then is to clean the cottage and prepare the bedrooms and provide some fresh linens, make the beds comfortable and dry." He could tell from the look on Buckby's face that this would not be an easy order to follow. Just as he expected, they had not even prepared somewhere for him to sleep. "I want that cottage spick-and-span. If there's no bedding, use yours and Tomkins. Clean! Understand, clean! Two senior officers will be arriving shortly, so it's in your best interests to welcome them correctly."

Unexpectedly, Buckby looked pleased with the news of two more officers and said, "Two! That'll be a big help, sir."

"I'll sleep here." Safer, much safer.

~

By the time his coachman arrived in the carriage just before midnight, Karl had settled himself into the top floor. He was grateful to receive a few home comforts packed into his trunk together with his all-important new uniform: two pairs of cream breeches, two more shirts, another pair of boots, the short blue coat with epaulettes on the shoulders, and a peaked blue cap. There was no bed yet, but that could be arranged and in the meantime he would sleep on the old leather armchair and put his feet up on the trunk. The centrally sited stove on the ground floor met with his approval as the iron chimney threaded up through to the roof and warmed each storey, if only a little. His quarters had been swept and cleaned from the top floor to the bottom. He was amused to hear Buckby complaining loudly whenever he thought Karl would not be able to hear. These men had a lot to learn in a short time. Providing incentives would help, so Buckby's wife was appointed cook. He thought he might as well spend his Parliamentary salary on keeping the poor honest so he made the terms for this service sufficiently attractive for Buckby to overcome his visible objections.

No sooner had his coachman departed for Newport, than two smartly dressed Riding Officers rode up to Watch House. Karl, in his uniform, was at the door to meet them.

"Gentlemen." Karl supposed, correctly, that they were not used to being addressed as such but he'd need them on his side. "I am Lieutenant Thorsen. Welcome to your new appointment."

Much would depend on these two hand-picked good men from the north of the island.

Having loosely tethered their horses to the post, both men stood to attention and saluted. Karl returned their salute. "Your names?"

"Lieutenant Thorsen, I am William Tutte."

"And I am Thomas Flowers, sir."

Tutte and Flowers were tall and well-built and Karl eyed them as if they were prize bulls. "Were you seen?"

Tutte replied, "I doubt we were seen, sir, even though the moon is bright, but it is known, even as far north as Cowes, that nothing gets past Tridd."

"Until now," Karl said with a broad grin. "I'm sure he would like a surprise from time to time." He rubbed his hands together then said, "At ease." The two men relaxed. Karl pointed to the stables. "Flowers, you look like you're good with horses. How are you with geese?"

"Geese sir? They love me!"

That was the spirit he liked to hear. He could only hope it was true. "They've not arrived yet but to avoid the stables being vulnerable to attack, as well as Watch House, of course, there'll be a delivery of as many as can successfully be transported. They will be arriving in a day or so. In the meantime, be aware that my stallion doesn't take well to surprises, so stable your horses but go carefully. Tomkins is already nursing a bruised leg. He's lucky it isn't broken."

While Flowers unloaded the saddlebags and led the horses away, Karl turned to Tutte. "Come on in and I'll show you what we've got. Or rather what we haven't got."

"We're both relishing some action, sir."

"I promise you plenty."

Under a Dark Star

Within an hour, both Tutte and Flowers had seen the small, rudimentary gaol on the floor above, and the view from the top of the tower where the full moon shone across the sea onto the craggy rocks leading into deep water. The waves lapped around this eerie, treacherous landmark and there, right on the tip, was the mast of the latest wreck. No one spoke but each focused on the tell-tale mark of the tragic loss of life. And on moonless nights that mast and those rocks would be invisible.

"Sleep! That is undoubtedly what you need. Here is the key to the third cottage, nearest the sea, which is yours to share until I can arrange something better. At least you'll have a bed. There's little else of comfort either here or in the cottage." He raced down the circular stone stairs and called out to the following men, "Sun-up, I want to hear you banging on the door and I'll introduce you to your fellow Riding Officers who are, I hope, fast asleep in the other two cottages."

As he slammed the big door shut behind them, he drew in a deep breath, pursed his lips, then let it out slowly. He'd defeated the gangs in Wintergate, he could do it again.

Chapter Thirteen
Norwell Farm - Daniel
"A date was set"

Tuesday 25th February
"I want to take you for a walk on one of the wild beaches, find a cave and hide from the world." Daniel stood behind Lucy who was gazing out of the snug little sitting room window towards the sea and wrapped his arms around her.

"I wish we could." Lucy looked over her shoulder and he bent forward and kissed her neck then spun her around so that she could respond.

"I'm glad you came but I hope you will return immediately if…" he hesitated.

"If things turn violent, I will put the safety of little Freddie first. You must trust me on that."

"Stay away from Kaddakay. Nearly everyone on the island is involved in either smuggling, wrecking or trying to prevent them. Some people are involved in all three!"

Lucy laughed. "All three?"

"Yes, hard to imagine, I know, but it appears that some of the Revenue Officers are very happy to be bribed on a regular basis."

"Did that happen in Wintergate?"

"It did before Karl arrived."

"Oh Daniel! How naïve I was."

"It was a good way of sharing the money around. Nobody had more than they needed." He thought for a moment then added,

Under a Dark Star

"Except for when Karl arrived, of course. His money, paying the Riding Officers extra, ensured their loyalty."

"Karl was very generous to Martha and me too."

Daniel shook his head. "Don't remind me of those awful days when you turned up to work in torrential rain and received so little pay from my ma."

"Don't feel bad, Daniel, I know it was your pa drinking and gambling it away."

He kissed the top of her head and toyed with her hair as a thought ran through his mind: Karl had improved the lives of so many around that coast, including his, just by being stubbornly incorruptible. Not that Karl intended it to be the outcome but a series of consequences had made it so.

He must fight to defend his wonderful wife. It was going to be very hard making sure they were never seen together. If only he could show her some of the beautiful scenery, the high, multicoloured sandstone cliffs so different from the white chalky ones towards Freshwater. "I'd love to take you to see the little thatched cottages in Brigton but someone else will have to do that." He was unable to stop a sigh and he hugged her closer. "Mrs Lytton tells me the carter who comes by here regularly will deliver messages but you are not to send any to me at all. If you need to contact me, have Mrs Lytton send a message to… not Karl, or the smugglers will think she is in league with them, send it to…Damn! Pardon me, Lucy. I cannot think of anyone I can trust or who will trust me. I shall give this some more thought. I'll let you know if I am close by whistling the song of the linnet."

Despite her worried frown, the remembrance of their old signal brought a smile to Lucy's face. "I love you so much, Daniel. Do you recall when you had injured your leg and I was on the rooftop at Watch House in Wintergate? And you sent an arrow with a message attached, remember?"

"I do, I remember every moment I spent with you or tried to spend with you."

"I peered over the parapet but couldn't see anyone; but I heard the melodious sound of a linnet and I knew you were close."

"Not close enough!" Daniel whistled their special signal and Josh, who had been lying in front of the fire looking like a rumpled hearth rug, opened one eye and raised one ear. Daniel picked up Lucy and twirled her around while they laughed. Josh closed his eye and let his ear fall.

~

Only the thought that his absence from Kaddakay probably seemed suspicious made him attempt to hurry away from Lucy and Freddie. He must put them both out of his mind, but how could he? Freddie could now crawl around the floor so Lucy had scooped him up for Daniel to kiss goodbye and Freddie had smiled and then chuckled. Oh he was adorable. That thought made him ache for Lucy. She should never have come. The temptation to ride over just to see her, to be with her, to spend a night with her would, he knew, grow in him until he'd have to give in.

Daniel stayed as long as possible but left as the sun was going down. It was so good to be astride Fiddle once more. He glanced down at Josh. "Towing Nancy slows us, eh Josh? Ambling is about all we can do." Josh wagged his tail. He liked these conversations. His master rarely chatted to the donkey, probably because it never listened. "Yes, I know what you're thinking, Josh. Did Nancy have to come? Yes. She carried me from Kaddakay to the Lyttons and she gives us her milk." Josh looked unimpressed. "And she's carrying my trunk." He refrained from saying *which is more than you could do.* Josh, though, read his master's mind and felt unappreciated and padded alongside with his tail trailing low.

Daniel took the path by the edge of the forest. This way he was unlikely to be seen and he could perhaps pick up a few logs for the fire. Suddenly Josh dashed ahead and bounded into the trees. Minutes later he came out with a weasel in his jaws and placed it in front of Fiddle. Fiddle was none too pleased and Nancy was agitated so Daniel dismounted, scooped up the bloodied animal and fondled and hugged Josh. "If you could talk, I know exactly what you'd be saying. *The donkey can't catch a weasel for dinner.* Right?"

Daniel reached Tynlan House and stabled Fiddle and Nancy. He knew he'd need to build more protection from the weather for Fiddle otherwise on wet nights they'd be fighting over the driest place in the corner. The back of the cottage formed one wall and the adjoining scullery formed the other. It would be easy to add a further two walls and a door and maybe Zeb would enjoy doing some work for a change. He'd need some money for materials though.

Daniel pushed open the door at the back of the house. Chatter in the parlour stopped. He'd prefer to get his trunk unseen into his room so without saying hello, he took the small but heavy trunk up the dark stairs. He'd left the weasel nailed to the stable ceiling; he'd deal with that tomorrow.

He became aware that there were several female voices coming from the parlour so he might not have to explain to Zeb and Becky where he'd been. As he came down the stairs, the chatter resumed momentarily then stopped again. He turned into the parlour and there he saw Becky with the three friends he'd met at the store. Every smiling face was turned on him.

"Good evening, ladies." Daniel bowed.

The four friends leapt up and curtseyed, some wobbling more than others.

"Where's Zeb?"

"They're all at The Ship," Becky said.

"All?"

Becky grinned. "The men told us they were *all* going down to The Ship. Leon Tridd's sent round the call, so we said that if they could get together, then we could too."

Daniel was surprised. "So your husbands said they welcomed the idea of you visiting Becky?"

The young women giggled. "They don't know we're here!"

"How does he send round the call?"

Becky laughed. "Oh it's a very loud owl hooting away. Saves time knocking on doors."

"It's a real emergency if anyone knocks on doors," said one of the women.

Daniel grabbed a wooden chair and took it from the table to nearer the stove – the only warm spot in the house. A tin of little cakes stood warming on top.

"Have a fresh cake, Daniel," said Becky. "Janey made them."

Daniel took one, being careful not to take the biggest. "Thank you. They smell delicious. Would anyone else like one?"

All nodded enthusiastically and Daniel thought of Lucy. Lucy would fetch plates but he just picked up the stove cloth and passed the tin around. Josh squeezed through to be in the warm and near the possibility of cake. He was rewarded by everyone. He'd have to wait for the weasel.

"I don't know your names yet."

Janey, Ruthie and Ellen introduced themselves.

"And who are you married to?"

Janey and Ruthie told him but Ellen needed a little encouragement before she said, "My husband is Ricardo Brantiani." She hung her head then flung it up and looked Daniel straight in the eye. "His brother, Jim, is…"

"Daniel's a good man, Ellen. He's one of us. He was the most successful and famous smuggler in Kent!" Becky's creative description of Daniel was exactly what was needed.

Under a Dark Star

Ellen stated clearly, "His brother Jim isn't what anyone would call successful but he is a man to be feared."

Becky explained. "He is one of Leon Tridd's spies."

So Becky trusted him and the women would too.

"Do you often slip away without your husbands knowing?"

They all nodded their heads.

"And how will you get home before your men?"

Ellen spoke. "They're usually too drunk to notice if we're there or not. Anyway it'll only take a short time if we hurry and the moon is quite bright tonight."

He must take the plunge into these waters while they were warm.

"Could you slip away on a moonless night?"

Each girl looked at the other. "Who are you asking?" said Becky looking slighted.

Daniel pulled a small packet of tea from his pocket. "Any or all of you – if you'd like some of this."

"Just tea?" said Ellen.

Becky leapt up. "See, I told you he'd bring us some tea. I'll put a kettle of water on."

Becky brought a kettle and set it on top of the stove.

Daniel noted that there was not even a proper hot drink on this cold night before he responded to Ellen. "No, not just tea. Bales of cotton too." He watched as their eyes widened. Four women, not much more than girls, all dressed in clothes that reminded him of Lucy's when, completely impoverished, she had worked on his parent's farm. Rags. And each clutching a shawl around her thin shoulders. "Some silk," he added, "which can be sold."

Before the water had boiled on the stove, the wives of the smugglers of Kaddakay had gathered tightly around Daniel and a date was set.

Chapter Fourteen
Karl
"By thunder! What goes on here?"

Saturday 8th March
Karl slithered down the rocky path to the beach at Attenfold, feeling pleased that he'd put on his *old* uniform breeches. He'd left Tutte on watch at the top of the cliff holding the two horses loosely, thereby allowing them to nibble the patchy grass. Time should be used well. He was keen to take a closer look at the rocks that were often exploited to wreck passing boats. So this was where twenty-four Americans and all the crew had lost their lives. Needlessly. What good had it done this part of the island? He'd never come across such impoverished people. Tridd. He was the reason. Sitting up there in his fortress on the ridge overlooking Kaddakay. Strange sort of man. With something resembling a small castle, any other man would have servants living in. A butler and footmen. Not him. There was a single groundsman, another crippled man who tended his two horses, and two daily women. Then, of course, he did have a woman up there. Though when he'd arrived there was a rumour he'd got rid of her. But he'd definitely seen a beautiful, dark-haired woman at one of the windows. Country folks' rumours usually had a measure of truth in them, so this was odd.

He reached the bottom and looked more puzzled. Someone had created a circle out of chalk rocks and within was a five-pointed star. What did it mean? Even odder was the dead weasel

Under a Dark Star

in the middle in some sort of cage. His stomach turned over. There was mischief of some sort here. He peered over his shoulder and made his way back up the path leading to the top of the cliff.

"Tutte."

"Yes sir?"

"What do you know of signs left on the beach?" Karl explained what he'd seen.

"You have to crack the code, sir. They all mean something. One will mean there's a landing imminent, another warns that it's moved somewhere else."

"And you know the code?"

"Of course, sir," Tutte said with a huge grin and a wink. "William Tutte's good with codes."

"Very glad to hear it. So tell me, what does this sign mean?" Karl took the reins of Midnight and mounted. Tutte followed behind straining to hear Karl's words whipped away by the wind.

"Did you say there was a *weasel* in the middle?"

"I did."

"That's not good news, sir. Not good news at all and best not spoken of lightly, nor out in the open. You never know who's listening. You didn't disturb the sign, did you?"

"Didn't touch it. It was somehow sinister."

Once in the relative warmth of Watch House, Karl gathered his men around the large table on the ground floor and Tomkins placed a jug of ale and five tankards in the centre.

Karl sat at the head. "Progress report. I've been on this island three weeks now and you've all been here a lifetime." Karl pointed to the ale. "Help yourself." Karl toyed with the idea of allowing Buckby and Tomkins to speak for themselves and then thought better of it. "Right, Buckby, you've enlarged the gaol above us," he indicated the stone steps, "and made it so that it will accommodate as many as eight in single cells?"

"Well, up to sixteen if we shove two in together, sir."

Karl decided to overlook yet another *well*. "Excellent work, Buckby. And have you shut yourself in each cell and tried to get out?" Buckby's proud grin fell and was replaced by a lot of lip chewing. "Imagine you have Tridd in a cell. Can he, bearing in mind his strength, can he force his way out?"

"I'll test it, sir, right away."

"You do that, and take Flowers with you. If anyone can find a way out, he will." Buckby stood up. "Not yet, man! Wait until I've finished."

Karl reeled off the progress of each man. Buckby had hauled bricks, stones, wood and iron bars and turned almost all of the next floor into a gaol. Tomkins had improved the end cottage for Flowers and Tutte to share while they were here. He'd also assisted Flowers in connecting the stables to the tower thus enlarging them, enough for the stabling of six horses and room for a cart. Furthermore, they had built an enclosure around the tower and the stables for the sixteen geese which had been transported from Norwell Farm.

Karl looked thoughtful. He was thinking of Daniel and the way he whistled like a bird to signal to Josh. And Lucy. He pursed his lips. At least he'd found that out, if somewhat late. "Tutte," Karl thumped the table with his fist in satisfaction; he'd worked out a way to use and modernize these old ways. "You say you have devised a simple yet effective code for the five of us to communicate with each other over a distance. Are you at the point where we can take a few minutes to learn it?"

Tutte, a man who by nature chose to use as few words as were strictly necessary, nodded. He handed around a whistle and a set of instructions to each man and told them that the whistles, on thick string, were not to be worn around their necks but were to be sewn into the inside of their uniform jackets. He picked up his

Under a Dark Star

whistle and demonstrated what he meant by a short trill and then a long trill. "I believe Tridd has his own method of communicating with his gang. Or perhaps the owls around here are very noisy."

"I've thought the same," said Karl with an appreciative grin. He stared at Tomkins and Buckby who failed to volunteer any information so he turned back to Tutte and said, "Do you think you can crack their code?"

"Already started. There's not much to it."

Karl moved on to commending Flowers for stocking up on food and other essential supplies now stored on the floor above the gaol.

"And your surveillance? Is there anyone who can be trusted?"

"No sir, I wouldn't trust any of the men around here. Not one. Though I think the innkeeper disapproves of much of what goes on." Flowers glanced across to Buckby and Tomkins.

Karl understood and grasped his chin. Weak links in his chain. He could only hope that the Coast Guard were honest and reliable. They'd certainly be needed. Buckby, puffed out his chest and Karl deduced that he was a man who would side with the strongest. It also seemed he was finding a sense of pride at last. Was pride enough?

Karl took a moment to down some ale. "This morning, on the shore at Attenfold rocks, I saw a sign." He took a large sheet of paper and drew a star with a circle around it. Then he marked the centre with an X. "The X is a dead weasel."

Tomkins choked on his ale and pushed his chair back from the table. Buckby went rigid. Flowers glanced at Tutte who nodded.

"Tutte. Explain."

"The upside down star denotes witchcraft, sir."

"Witchcraft? What's that got to do with smuggling and Tridd?"

Tutte shifted in his seat. "It's like I told you, sir. It's a sign. And with a weasel in the middle it is the strongest warning to keep well away from that area."

"Because something is going to happen?"

"Most probably, sir."

"How can you tell it's inverted? Surely it depends on where you're standing."

Tutte grinned. "Everyone just takes a look from the top of the cliff."

Then Buckby found a trickle of courage. "Well sir, Tridd sends someone to the beach to remove the stones and the weasel just before the gang need to unload the boats. No one will go near until that sign is removed. Then they know when it'll be happening."

Karl drew a deep breath. "So everyone has to keep watch?"

Buckby responded, "Yes sir. Usually just a few of us keep watch and then pass the message around."

"You're telling me that you and Tomkins not only know how to interpret the signs but you also keep watch?"

"But what can we do about it?" Buckby appeared fearful.

Karl was beginning to understand why. "So Tridd places the sign…"

Buckby interrupted. "No sir. The witches' coven does that. They put a curse on anyone going near."

"Witches coven! By thunder, what goes on here?"

Chapter Fifteen
"You underestimate the devil"

Sunday 9th March
All night, and alone, Karl kept watch over the rocks at Attenfold. There was nothing to be seen, not even a passing ship, nor anyone tampering with the message on the beach. All he heard was the sound of waves rolling in, crashing on the rocky shore and receding with a hiss. Having defied the sleep-inducing sounds of the sea, just before dawn he decided to return to Watch House to get some much needed rest. He hurried up the steep pathway and darted across to where he'd hidden Midnight. Fatigue struck him but he resolved to see if there was a message. Dressed all in black, Karl rode Midnight to the base of Rose's Ridge. He'd reconnoitred some routes and found two were protected from prying eyes, particularly those of Tridd. He dismounted and, keeping close to the steep overhang, searched for the boulder that he and Daniel had agreed upon. Feeling around he finally located the heavy stone and picked up a squashed scroll of paper from underneath. He tried and failed to read it in the dark. To lessen the chance of being seen, he stood between Midnight and the towering slope of Rose's Ridge, then lit his spout lantern and directed the light towards the paper.

By Jove! What's Raffles up to? Karl continued to read the coded message and, being well practised in codes from his early days at school and in the Royal Navy, he grasped the news immediately. Raffles was now the parson at Brigton. And Daniel was asking him to go on Sunday. Today!

~

Karl and Tutte, in full uniform, arrived at the church in Brigton to find the doors open. He entered quietly and stood in awe. This was a very fine building; somewhat neglected now, but even he was conscious of the many centuries of worship this church would have witnessed. Parson Raffles was the only person inside.

Karl gave the briefest of bows. "Mr Raffles, have you taken leave of your senses?"

Looking every inch, and he had many, the picture of a country parson, Raffles greeted Karl with enthusiasm. "Lieutenant Thorsen, how good it is to see you."

Karl inclined his head towards Tutte. "This is Mr William Tutte, a good man who can be relied upon."

"Perhaps Mr Tutte would stand at the door and alert us to any parishioners wishing to attend." Tutte looked at Karl who nodded. Raffles waited until Tutte was in position. "I received news, extremely good news." He strode to the front of the church, well away from the doors. "Mrs Raffles is expecting our first child!"

Karl was astonished. "By Jupiter!"

"Is that all you can say?"

"I ask your pardon, Mr Raffles. I do, of course, offer you my heartiest congratulations."

"You thought I had come to interfere?"

Karl was still recovering from the news but managed, "No. Not interfere. But now that you are here…" Karl could think of no one better to deal with the shock of the previous day. This good man's very name, Emmanuel, had the meaning of 'God with us' and his presence declared that the back of the Wight was not the God-forsaken place he had come to believe.

Under a Dark Star

Raffles encouraged Karl to continue. "Now that I am here, you think I could be useful?"

Karl was not known for his sensitivity which he demonstrated yet again by announcing, "Witches. What do you know about witchcraft?"

It was now the parson's turn to look astounded. "Witchcraft! It is to be avoided."

"Is it all nonsense?"

"Oh you underestimate the devil if you call it that. Remember, he has the powers of an archangel."

Karl looked puzzled. "It's a way of ruling by fear, surely?"

Raffles rocked his head from side to side and pursed his lips. "Yes and no. The main point to remember is that God is the strongest spirit."

A sneeze from the back of the church called the discussion to a halt, but Karl had one more question to ask. "Where are you to live? With your wife or at the ransacked parsonage?"

"Mrs Raffles will come to me. We cannot be separated at this time. The Lytton's are being exceptionally kind and will be providing us with all we need." Raffles took a step closer to the stove at the side of the church and warmed his hands over it and Karl swiftly followed, rubbing his hands vigorously. "I must not be seen to be in league with anybody in this locality. From now on, Karl, I shall treat you as I would any other visitor to this parish."

They need not have worried for the first person through the door was Emmeline, rapidly followed by Mr and Mrs Lytton and Lucy. Within seconds Emmeline had hurled herself into her husband's outstretched arms.

"Oh Emmanuel, I have missed you so very much."

"My love, I have missed you far more than I could ever have imagined. You shall come to live with me at the parsonage as soon as it is fit for a mother in waiting." He had to bend quite low to plant a loving kiss on her upturned lips. "How clever of you to give me the excuse of impending fatherhood to draw me here."

Emmeline's eye sometimes twitched when she was nervous or excited, and not only was it twitching now but she was also blushing. She placed her hands across the front of her thick woollen cloak, patting her stomach. "You are the clever one, arranging to come to Brigton is nothing short of a miracle."

"If that is so, my dear, then it is our Lord who has performed it, and it may be that he has specific work for me to do." He drew her into his arms and stroked her upturned face.

Karl contemplated this sweet love. So devoted. And all wrapped up in their love of God.

He wandered towards the Lyttons. Another couple happy in each other's company. Why had love eluded *him*? He contemplated Lucy, hiding behind them. She had almost been his. Almost. "Lucy, it's so good to see you looking well and content."

She was wearing a rich blue velvet gown with a grey cloak, edged in fur, and a bonnet trimmed to match. She curtseyed to Karl then pulled the cloak tightly around her. "I suspect the congregation will be very small. Fear rules around here, I'm told."

"You're safe, are you?"

"Oh yes, thank you. Major Lytton knows how to defend the farm. I think he must have been a formidable soldier."

Parson Raffles, towing his wife in his right hand, strode over to the little group. He bowed then immediately said, "If the parishioners don't come to us, then I will go to them!"

Karl raised his eyebrows. "How?"

Raffles smiled broadly. "On the way here, I stayed with the Bishop of Portsmouth and he told me all I need to know."

Under his breath, Karl said, "I doubt it."

Under a Dark Star

"And anything he couldn't tell me, I shall learn from you, Daniel and good Major Lytton. For the moment though, may I ask you to *choose* a *pew*?" He smiled broadly. "There are plenty to select from but I shall conduct the service on this side." He pointed to the stove. "I must go and ring the bells. I haven't done that in years." He rubbed his hands in glee and went to the bell tower. Karl followed. "Most kind, Karl, most kind. You pull one and I'll pull two and together we can make a joyful noise."

They did. For five minutes three bells rang out, and when they stopped Karl whipped out a hip flask of brandy from his pocket and each took a sip.

"Very thoughtful, Lieutenant." Then almost as a reminder to himself he said quietly, "I must call you that from now on." Raising his voice again, he said, "Lieutenant, you have drawn my attention to the need for warmth in this bitterly cold winter weather. The outdated stove is near the front and I have enough wood to throw out a good heat, but I will soon run short. I think if we can provide comfort and if I can persuade my dear wife to do some of her baking – not too much in her condition, of course – and maybe I can borrow Martha sometimes…"

Karl could not wait for Raffles to go on thinking aloud. "A warm place, and maybe gather around the stove afterwards for tea and cakes? Are you suggesting that?"

"Yes, but don't tell the Bishop."

~

After a short service, Karl escorted Lucy to the Lytton's sturdy and comfortable carriage with its black velvet curtains and leather upholstery. "How is Freddie? I presume Martha is looking after him?"

"She's trying. She's having to fight off Mrs Lytton's maid and housemaid. It seems they've fallen in love with him too." Lucy laughed but soon became serious again. "How is Daniel?"

Under a Dark Star

Karl caught sight of three shabby looking men leaning against a wall some distance away on the opposite side of the road. His gaze flashed back to Lucy. "He is in good health. I can say no more. We are being watched and I don't want you to be seen with me more than is strictly necessary."

Lucy's eyes grew large. "I understand, but please take my love to Daniel. I shall come to the service every Sunday – tell him that."

"Lucy, you must be very careful." Karl walked away without looking back.

"Tutte!" William Tutte came immediately to his side. "We are being watched or it could be the parson they are interested in. Follow me and we'll follow them."

It was indeed the parson they were intent upon and as he closed the church door, put on his hat and strolled towards the once-imposing and sizeable parsonage, the men roused themselves and picked up three wooden clubs. Once the parson had gone inside, they moved swiftly to the gate. One stayed watching and the other two stood on the doorstep. Moments later they knocked on the door.

Parson Raffles, smiling broadly, opened the door. "Good day to you, gentlemen." He flung his arms wide as if in greeting, seized their heads and banged them together. They dropped to the ground. The third man raised his wooden club then thought better of it, he turned and ran – straight into the arms of Karl.

Raffles picked up the stunned men by the scruffs of their necks, which ripped their flimsy coats, dragged them inside the doorway and deposited them on the bare floor of the empty drawing room. Karl and Tutte pushed their captive ahead of them and shoved him on top of his now stirring comrades.

"Tutte, is there a gaol nearby?"

Raffles did not give Tutte the chance to reply. "Lieutenant, I think these men were bringing me an offering of firewood. It is clear to me that they are hoping to benefit from a good fire in next Sunday's service."

Tutte whispered in Karl's ear. "They'll be too afraid to attend if Tridd is behind this."

Karl could not restrain himself. "Afraid! Then it's the town gaol for them."

Tutte leant towards Karl. "The magistrate is also afraid."

"Then it's *my* gaol they'll be kept in until we replace these lily-livered magistrates!"

"Replacing them isn't easy, sir. They are put there to do the will of those who have made their fortunes through what they call free-trading."

"And I call smuggling!" barked Karl.

Raffles coughed slightly. "I cannot interfere with the workings of the law," he drew in a deep breath and unobtrusively winked at Karl, "so I must bow to your decision but I ask that they be escorted to my church service each Sunday they remain in your custody."

The three felons, all now standing, flinched as their captors debated their fate, their faces reflecting the fear and confusion they felt.

Karl inclined his head. Of course he would oblige his friend and make them attend, but he must not be seen to give in too easily. "Watch House is not in the parish of Brigton, Mr Raffles."

Raffles was quick to step forward and insist. "It is to my church that these men brought their firewood." He held up the wooden clubs.

Karl was enjoying playing along with Raffles' ruse to turn the tide of evil. "You are complicating matters."

"Where do you live?" asked Raffles of the bewildered men.

The man who'd stayed back by the gate doffed his shabby cap. "Oh, sir, it is in your parish we live, down by the marsh."

His comrade chipped in. "That's why *we* were told to…"
Raffles interrupted, "Bring the firewood?"
"Well… yes, sir."
They were scruffy and poor and needed guidance which was best left in the competent hands of Raffles.
"Right!" Karl's lack of sleep was telling on him. "I'm not spending my time arguing with a country parson and felons. Tutte! Get the rope. You three are coming on a six mile trot behind our horses."
"And I shall expect you next Sunday," called Raffles after them.

~

That night, when the waning crescent moon shed minimal light, Tridd led forty men down to Kaddakay Bay and landed enough cargo to keep eight donkeys busy all night.

Under a Dark Star

Chapter Sixteen
Kaddakay Beach - Daniel
"Get this dog off me"

Wednesday 12th March

Not one man! These four women, not much more than excited girls, his dog Josh, and trusty Nancy were all he could safely muster for the landing. Fortunately, it would only be a small cargo; he'd made that very clear to his French contacts before he'd even left Wintergate. But it was still too much for these women and a donkey to handle. He'd brought some weights and markers – he'd have to sink some of the barrels and collect them later.

His brave little band nestled in to the side of the cliffs and were under strict instructions not to talk and to be as still as a hunted mouse. It was fortuitous too that Tridd had chosen to do a run a couple of days earlier. It would have been grim if they'd met on the beach. Tridd brazenly ignored Karl and the increased presence of Riding Officers. Daniel approved of Karl's plan to let Tridd get away with a successful landing - it would embolden Tridd to continue as usual.

When he'd exchanged coded notes with Karl, Karl had said he'd wanted to appear all bluff and bluster but not very good at stopping even a minor landing. Tridd had been king pin for too long to be intimidated by the arrival of a few Riding Officers. The idea was to tempt Tridd into the spoils of a wreck and catch him with blood on his hands.

Under a Dark Star

Daniel rubbed his hands together; this was a particularly cold and clear night. The girls were quiet and all stared out to sea, so his mind could wander and plan. Karl knew about his boat coming in tonight and was no doubt on watch; he'd promised to ensure Tridd didn't come near. Daniel frowned at the thought of Karl opposing Tridd.

To keep warm on this bitterly cold, moonless March night, Becky clutched Daniel on one side and Ellen snuggled up to him on the other. Janey and Ruthie didn't look too pleased so Daniel suggested to Josh that he keep them warm, and himself too. He was apprehensive about Ellen. Being married to Ricardo Brantiani, brother of Tridd's right hand man, she could be a liability. But she was strong of heart and biddable. An unappreciated treasure. They were all sure their men were at the inn, they'd carefully enticed them into a long night out with a tale about new, unadulterated brandy which was almost true. Daniel had made sure of that. Even so, this escapade was fraught with danger. He tried to recall the Biblical quotation Raffles had mentioned, something about if God be for us, who can be against us? These women, along with the rest of the village, didn't seem to care about God. Kaddakay's cowering parson must have the smallest congregation in the country. Or perhaps Raffles could claim that award in Brigton now.

Gossipy girls asked to keep quiet – how long could they manage? He cast a glance at Becky. Even for this wild, midnight foray, she had rouged her cheeks, charcoaled her eyebrows and lashes, and made a black mob cap to hide her hair. A quick peek at the rest of his gang showed they had all made black mob caps and had ruby red lips. He rested his head on his knees – what a contrast with the old days when his tough men wielded bats. Here, Tridd ruled through fear and his tentacles reached far wider than he'd anticipated. Now all he'd got was a group of ill-clad,

Under a Dark Star

shivering wives seeking excitement. Their tough hearts would have to be enough. But when their husbands found out – what then?

They were quiet and the only sound was that of the choppy sea and the wailing wind as it navigated its way up the steep cliffs. It was far too cold for romantic dreaming but, nevertheless, Lucy was in his thoughts. A smile crept slowly across his face as he relived his ride to the Lytton's farm on Sunday night. He'd taken some daffodils he'd seen in the forest and on Fiddle, being so much faster than Nancy, it took a little over half an hour, so he'd had time to spend with her. Freddie was asleep in his cradle. Her soft warmth... his thoughts exploded.

Becky nudged him. "Daniel, look!"

He was annoyed with himself for missing the first sign of the boat that had made it all the way from the coast of France in the winter seas. He took out his telescope which was a particularly fine brass and leather one, and lay flat. Becky must have good eyesight because the only way to catch the outline of the red sails was as they hid the distant stars on this clear night. "Yes, it's here. This is the lugger." He felt around for the spout lanterns. He had five. He organized the girls into formation. "No talking!" he hissed. He added, "Please." He gave them a weak smile. "Don't forget the training. This has to be done stealthily; remember?"

Wearing their husbands' breeches, held up by string, and feeling immensely important, they crept a few paces forward then spread out, two paces between each of them. They lit their lamps which were enclosed on all sides so light only escaped through the long spout. They pointed the spouts out towards the sea. Daniel trained the telescope until he could gauge the angle needed for the beam to be seen. "Hold it like this," he said. Then, in unison, they all raised their lamps. One by one they slowly lowered them before putting their hands in front to cut off the glow. They went through this sequence five times. The lugger responded with five quick flashes.

Silently, well almost, as Ruthie nervously giggled, they each undertook to get the equipment needed to the shoreline directly opposite the chine. Becky took Nancy loaded with ropes, and Josh herded them to where Daniel led. Their excitement was practically tangible. Daniel wasn't sure if he was embarrassed to have such a motley gang or proud to have gathered a very loyal band of followers. He decided on the latter; these women deserved a little excitement and reward. They had done what their men would not. Protecting them was a priority.

The square rigged lugger came close, its dark red sails keeping it almost invisible. Daniel showed two quick flashes of light, then took an arrow from his quiver and shot it at the boat. Attached to the arrow was a thin twine which the sailors carefully pulled in because the twine was attached to a hefty rope.

The women looked amazed. Such skill, such a clever strategy. Unfortunately, there wasn't time for basking in their admiration and he disguised his surprise at only needing the one shot. The sailors tied five barrels to a rudimentary raft and a rope to pull it back to them once unloaded. Daniel hauled in his rope, released the cargo and floated the raft back out to sea after he had secured weights, markers and a small but heavy, tarred box to it. The box carried a note and gold sovereigns. Karl's sovereigns. Daniel hadn't any goods to exchange and by not coming in too close, the lugger had successfully avoided rocks or the danger of an ambush.

The captain of the lugger had been advised that the Preventive Waterguard would not be doing any preventing, courtesy of Lieutenant Thorsen, who also would not be doing any preventing that night. But his little gang did not know that. They needed to believe this was a real landing. Because the women could not carry the barrels on their shoulders, Daniel loaded them onto a flat

Under a Dark Star

sledge he'd constructed and hidden. Becky held Nancy who, with a little temptation of a somewhat soft carrot on a stick, pulled the heavy sledge with assistance from Daniel pushing the sledge from behind. The others tidied up the shore, until not even a footprint was visible. Josh, with his bright white patches, was given the task of leading the way up the slope. In the old days, when every gang member could find his way along the Kent shoreline in the dark as if he were a bat, Josh had been "sooted up" to enable him to do his work unseen. But tonight it didn't matter: they were safe from discovery.

Towards the top of the chine, Josh turned to face them and stood his ground. Daniel whistled quietly.

Josh lay down with his paws outstretched and answered, growling low, just a quiet, short rumble. Daniel signalled for everyone to stand back and be on their guard. Flattened against the steep side of the chine, Daniel watched in horror as two men crept towards them. No cutlasses, no bats – that was the first thing he ascertained. They might be carrying knives though. Their faces were covered by kerchiefs.

The chine was particularly steep and one of the men tripped then slipped. Drunk. The other bent to pick him up. Daniel leapt out and Josh followed. With one swift swipe on the back of the neck, Daniel disabled the man trying to assist. The one on the ground had his arm firmly held in Josh's jaws. Daniel pulled down the kerchief. "And you are...?"

There followed a stream of curses and finally, "Dammit man! Get this dog off me." The man tried to smash his other fist into Josh who was well practised at dodging thrashing limbs. Daniel put his heavy boot on the man's flailing arm. "Davies. That's me." The defeated man's speech was slow and slightly slurred.

"Husband of Ruthie?"

Davies swore profusely and finished with, "I'll have your balls for this. She's not at home where she should be. And I know you're behind all these women and their crazy ideas."

The other fellow stirred and Ellen rushed over with a rock in her hand, raised it then, alarmed, she dropped it. "And this is my husband, Ricardo Brantiani."

"When Tridd hears of this, he'll…" Brantiani lifted his arm to cuff her.

Chapter Seventeen
"There is a third condition"

As Brantiani raised his hand, Daniel caught it in the loop at the end of the rope hanging from his belt. He swiftly twisted Brantiani around and tied his hands together behind his back. Next he tied Davies's free hand to the one Josh held tightly in his jaw.

"Chewing my arm, he is." Davies stared hard at Josh. "You won't be wagging your tail once Tridd finds out."

"Tridd isn't going to find out." Daniel was sure of that; not yet anyway. "Calm yourself and I'll call Josh off."

He ensured no one else was around before, with a quick double clap, he told Josh to let go. Josh was not convinced this was wise but obeyed and circled the two men with his head low, ready to pounce if required.

The women gathered round the men once they were sitting, hands tied and cross legged, beside each other. Ellen couldn't resist the obvious comment. "Too much drink has robbed you of your wits." She received a grunt, as if from a rooting pig, in response.

"And them's my breeches you've got on," shouted Davies to his wife.

Brantiani joined in as he realized Ellen had *his* breeches on. "Get them off, you slut!"

Daniel smashed his fist into the side of Brantiani's face and Josh nipped Davies's arm again. "Shut your mouths, or you'll be needing to disappear. The sea's not far away." He turned to Josh. "On guard!"

The four women's eyes shone with respect like the old days when everyone looked at him like that.

He led Nancy pulling the sledge into a hollow where slippage had occurred and been swept away. He began breaking into the barrels. "Who'd like to inspect the booty?" The women abandoned their humbled men. "Quiet – not a sound!" He turned to the two men. "You can come too if you keep your mouths shut." Josh padded behind them, giving his master a look that told of his disapproval. Daniel rubbed Josh's ears; his faithful dog was getting old and would rather be in front of a roaring fire instead of out in this biting cold with rogues that his master shouldn't be trusting.

In the first barrel were four sacks of tea. "This is real tea – not the smouch you've been selling." Daniel watched the two men as their eyes flickered from side to side. "You'll not find any elder or ash leaves mixed in." He lifted a heavy sack out and laid it at the feet of Brantiani. "As you're here, you can carry this straight home." Brantiani, his hands still tied, looked unimpressed. Daniel did the same to Ruthie's husband. He'd planned to take the tea back to Tynlan House and distribute it later, but this way would save time. "Janey and Becky, I'll leave yours in the barrel.

In the second barrel were five bolts of cotton. He chose one for Lucy. The women eyed him suspiciously and Becky blurted out, "Ain't for a fancy woman, it's for his mother." She then turned to Daniel and said quietly, "That's right isn't it?"

"No fancy woman," and gave her a lopsided smile. "You'd better choose one each before I claim the lot." They were not slow to obey. "Can you carry yours home, Janey?" Janey grinned enthusiastically.

Under a Dark Star

The next barrel was filled with silk, buttons, cotton reels, lace and ribbons. "I'm taking these back with Becky and me on the sledge and I'll let you have some later." The women gasped as they peered into the dark cask and twittered about pink silk dresses and contrasting ribbons. "We need to hurry in case anyone else comes looking for you ladies." He put his fingers to his lips and they quietened immediately though their eyes still glowed with dreams of fine living.

The two brandy barrels presented a problem. He'd planned to take the barrels himself, sell them and share the money amongst his little gang. Now that two husbands had turned up, perhaps this was actually an opportunity. If he could make it worth their while to trust him, he might even get in on the next run or wrecking. He looked at the men. "What do you usually do with the brandy?" Huh! As if he didn't know.

Brantiani croaked, "Tridd has all the brandy, then he sells it."

Davies chipped in. "He sells some to the landlord." He nodded in the direction of The Ship Inn.

"And what do you get out of it?" This run was insignificant for a smuggling gang from Kaddakay of perhaps twenty or more men and Tridd's landings were much bigger, probably thirty or forty barrels.

"Oh we're well paid, all right. Well paid." Ricardo Brantiani was loyal, if not too bright.

Daniel looked into Davies's eyes, their sorrowful look told a different tale. Daniel had been here long enough to know that the only one who was well paid was Tridd. "So if I said to you that you could take one of those barrels and sell it, would you?"

The men exchanged anxious glances and Brantiani explained in his croaky voice. "If Tridd found out he'd cut our throats."

"So you don't want me to give you a barrel each for you to sell and keep the money?"

Under a Dark Star

This was a hard choice. A barrel of brandy would fetch enough to keep a man's family in comfort for several weeks. Brantiani spoke with exaggerated care. "Could you take them and mind them for us? We'll get over to you later."

Davies joined in. "I've got a hand cart. We could get the barrels to one of the inns on the other side of Newport."

"I'll take the brandy then and you collect it in a day or two." With the tea and cotton – all for no work at all – this might win him some influence. "I have some conditions. One is that your wives take half of each bolt of cotton for themselves and half of the tea. The rest you can sell." The two men exchanged glances. Half a bolt of cotton would be worth a fair bit in Newport, enough for a good slab of beef and mutton and a few luxuries. Their eyes began to shine.

Janey Fawcett whispered, "What about my husband?"

"The second condition is that you *persuade* Mr Fawcett to keep his mouth shut, because he'll want to know why you've all got spoils and he hasn't."

The men exchanged conspiratorial looks, then nodded. "It'll take some doing. Fawcett's not going to like being left out," rasped Brantiani.

Daniel glared. "He won't be. Mrs Fawcett will let him sell some tea and cloth, won't you?" The look in his eye told Janey what her answer must be, and she nodded. "And every time you are in The Ship, you are to pay for Fawcett's drinks." He noticed Brantiani struggling to think of a retort. "At least for a month, not forever, and not so anyone suspects." His eyes held daggers as he stared at Brantiani. This was not like his old North Kent Gang, these men still needed to learn who was in command. "And you, Brantiani, you are to see Mrs Fawcett gets home safely. Got that?"

Brantiani snapped, "I'll see she gets there."

"There is a third condition. I want to be a part of the next Tridd operation."

This time the men looked alarmed. Davies spoke up. "Not going to be a run for a while now."

"I know," said Daniel.

"You know?" Brantiani looked anxious. "How do you know?"

"You don't think our family led the North Kent Gang for all those years without being able to nose out a run do you?" He raised an eyebrow. "But the March winds will bring a few storms and storms mean opportunities, don't they?

Into Davies's eyes crept respect followed by caution. "But Tridd doesn't like incomers."

"Well he can have an incomer who'll steal his men and his trade or he can take on an extra man." He watched fear reflect in their faces. "My horse isn't…" he hesitated. He'd rather not resort to lying; he'd turned away from those ways, but in this company it was all too easy to slip back. "Horses don't come cheap."

"Yah! We've seen your horse. You gotta pay for it. Thought it was a bit, well…" Brantiani wasn't too good with words.

So Daniel jumped in. "Expensive."

"That's the word I was thinking of!" And Brantiani gave a croaky laugh until Ellen raised her finger to her mouth. He kicked out at her but kept quiet.

"Now you make sure Tridd gets that message. Remind him I have a donkey." He took a step closer to Brantiani, turned him around, and untied the rope on his hands. Back home he'd have brandished his knife and slit it, but here there might not be too much rope going spare. "If you touch Ellen, it will be for the last time. Understand?" Brantiani rubbed his wrists and grunted. "I want more than a grunt." Daniel reached for his knife and wiped the blade on the sleeve of his coat.

Brantiani grudgingly responded, "Aye, I understand."

Daniel let out a loud whistle and Josh turned, put his head down and waited for his master. "Wasn't for you, Josh," he whispered as he ruffled his ears.

They took their share and staggered up the steep slope of the chine with Josh sniffing the heels of the two unsteady men.

Daniel made no mention of the ten barrels of brandy sunk in the shallow waters which he'd collect tomorrow night.

Chapter Eighteen
Karl
"An orange glow"

On that same dark night, near the inn, Karl was reflecting on what Buckby and Tomkins had told him. They reckoned there was no way he'd get near enough to Tridd's place to gain entrance uninvited. Those two were scared of everything; they'd flapped like sails in a whirlwind when he'd told them he was first going to The Ship to see if Tridd was there and they were coming with him. All they had to do now was patrol on horseback to deter men from leaving the inn by way of the cliffs to guarantee secrecy for Daniel and his band of women. Reliable Flowers was patrolling the clifftop already and would join Buckby and Tomkins when Daniel whistled to him to ensure the path was clear. All would be well so long as Tridd remained in his lair with his woman.

Behind the inn were some empty barrels and he thought he saw one of them move. He lifted the lid and inside were two terrified faces anxiously looking up at him. For a moment he couldn't grasp why they were there, then the awful truth crept over him. They had nowhere else to go. These were the two little urchins he'd seen on the refuse tip outside the village, turning it over and picking scraps up and eating them. Good Lord in Heaven above! This was no way for a child to live and they wouldn't live long like this. His stomach, not given to weakness, turned over. From his pocket he took some dried apple pieces and handed them down to them with a smile. He had nothing more to offer except a little hope. He put his finger to his lips and whispered, "Tomorrow night you'll find some cheese." He strode over to Midnight and murmured, "You and I will just have to go without our snack tonight." He did something unusual: he sighed aloud. He was damned lonely. Even those little urchins had each other; all he had was his horse to talk to. He wished Lucy hadn't come to the island; it made it harder to forget her.

With his Riding Officers keeping an eye on Kaddakay, he galloped towards Watch House until in the shelter of the steep sides of Rose's Ridge he met with Tutte, also dressed in black.

"Is Mrs Buckby all right?" Karl was concerned: she was alone in the cottage near Watch House.

"Yes sir. She'll not be by herself for long. The Officers at Ventnor have signalled: the lugger has been sighted. With the wind in her sails, she'll be off the bay within the hour."

"In code was it? I don't want that madman monitoring our actions."

"Though I say it myself, sir, my code is working well."

"I've told Buckby he can go home when Flowers joins them." Karl took a deep breath and said, "We need to hurry. I don't want Tridd nosing around tonight."

They tied their horses to a useful rock and began climbing the steep rise until they were on the ridge overlooking the square tower of Tridd's Fort. They lay flat on the sparse tufty grass and took out their telescopes.

"By Jove! Tutte, take a look at that window at the top of the tower."

Tutte shifted to get himself comfortable and trained his telescope on the window. "Interesting." He sniffed. "Yes, attractive, but more importantly, she's still there. There's been some rumours that he got rid of her somehow."

Under a Dark Star

Karl was riveted. "No wonder he doesn't let her out. She's exquisite." Tutte did not reply; he seemed troubled. "She must be sitting on a window seat and she's reading by the light of a candle. I'm going to see if I can attract her attention."

"Sir!"

"If she's not allowed out, she's little more than a prisoner or slave and that cannot be permitted." Karl lit his spout lantern and turned the beam towards the window and swung it slowly from side to side. His thoughts went to William Wilberforce's campaign against slavery. His intent to break Tridd hardened.

"Shall I keep watch on the rest of the fort, sir?" Tutte's tone implied his concern that the purpose of the surveillance was being forgotten.

"Yes. Ensure Tridd doesn't go out. I'll work on making contact with the woman." With his right hand holding the telescope and his left steadily swinging the lamp, his patience paid off. "She's seen the signal! By Jove, she's beautiful. Long, dark wavy hair." He reasoned that if she was anything but a prisoner, she would by now have alerted Tridd. And she hadn't: she was opening the window and waving a handkerchief.

Karl grasped his grappling hook and skidded down the hill to the fort. Although he had muffled the top parts of the claws, they still clanged as they caught the stone wall. He scaled the barrier, sat on the top and rearranged the hook so that the rope hung on the inside. He jumped down and rolled over before dashing to below the open window. Suddenly it was slammed shut and this beautiful woman spun around and moved away. Someone had come into the room. He flattened himself against the wall around the corner of the tower. He heard the window open again and he imagined Tridd peering into the dark night.

"There's someone out there, isn't there?" Tridd snarled, "Who is it? Tell me or you know what will happen."

Karl could not hear if the woman replied but he heard the window slam. He was annoyed he couldn't stay to challenge this brute. As he was without his sword, it might be better if he lived to fight another day.

A crumpled white paper showed up against the dark ground beneath the window. When all was quiet, he snatched at it and dashed to the rope hanging over the wall. He had just jumped down on the outside and removed his grappling hook when he heard barking, deep and loud. No one had mentioned dogs!

"Over here, sir!" Tutte called out and they fled together. If Tridd let those creatures out they'd not reach the horses in time.

Much to his relief, the dogs remained inside the walls. They sat astride their horses and Karl fingered the paper in his pocket. He'd have to wait to read it: not wise to use the lamp at the moment. By happy accident, their mission – to ensure Tridd was not likely to thwart Daniel's escapade – had been accomplished; he'd been disturbed and would watch over his fort tonight. "We'll move round to the front and from there we can see both Tridd's gate and The Ship Inn."

They turned their steeds to face the sea and saw, to their horror, an orange glow and heard a distant screeching and honking.

"Watch House!" shouted Karl. "Those three villains are still locked up inside." With as much speed as they could muster on the difficult terrain, they galloped towards the glow and the increasing din of aggravated geese attacking a man attempting to climb into their enclosure. He was flinging oil soaked rags at the doors but the geese succeeded in impeding his aim and the rags fell short.

Whoever he was, he took flight at the sound of galloping horses and Karl and Tutte headed straight towards the source of the glow – the nearby cottages. Buckby was outside his own, beating down the flames with the remnants of a rag rug and screaming profanities as he did so. Karl leapt off Midnight and dragged Buckby away.

"My wife! My wife's in there!"

Chapter Nineteen
Raffles
"A curious crowd"

Sunday 16th March
Early on Sunday morning, Parson Raffles stood inside his cold church and praised the Lord for sending sunshine on the day he had decided to hold the service outside. A confirmation from on high that he was doing the right thing.

 He reluctantly lit the fire in the stove. There was so little wood and it would probably be warmer outside than in, but a small fire might tempt some to come inside and would keep the eight tins of Emmeline's and Martha's cakes warm. At least a hundred little finger cakes in all. Such faith these ladies have. His first service, held inside the church, proved one thing – there was no residual congregation from the previous parson's time. Putting aside his own home comforts – none had arrived yet anyway – he had visited every house in the parish. Some greeted him cordially, others stared at his feet, no one invited him inside; all refused or ignored his invitation to come to the service. So he would hold it *outside* the church. Karl should be bringing the three miscreants who had tried to scare him away. George Lytton would bring his fiddle, as well as two carriages with his wife, Emmeline, Lucy, Martha, and three of his house servants. Together with the coach drivers, the congregation would total fourteen. If no one else came, there'd be almost seven cakes each. The parson beamed before he remembered that Easter was only two weeks away. He

Under a Dark Star

flung a little prayer upwards: "Forgive this extravagance during this time of penitence, dear Lord." His mind flooded with the memory of the time he'd tried to reduce his weight. He'd fasted on two days a week, just like the Pharisees. He'd allowed himself only water and, when feeling faint, boiled cabbage. It had been torture, sheer torture, so he'd stopped. And now he was just as heavy as before. Perhaps the short time away from the delights of a household run by his beloved Emmeline would be good for him. But today there would be cake. Another year he would observe Lent rather better and give something up but this year there wasn't anything to give up. Except perhaps the cake? No. He would have a little finger and if no one else attended, he'd have seven. There might not be much dinner.

He set up some of the vestry's wooden chairs outside. He thought he would stand within the confines of the porch as it would make an attractive frame. Presentation was important. Then he realized that this would severely hamper his delivery of God's word; he could think better if allowed to pace up and down as usual. Besides, the villagers would not be able to see or hear what his congregation was listening to. So he moved the chairs to the grass on the side of the bell tower that faced the street. There were only five but that would accommodate the ladies and George Lytton. He erected a sign on a post near the gate stating that today's service would be held outside in the warm sunshine then returned inside to ring the bells.

As the effort of ringing two bells was more than he could manage today, he rang one most of the time and occasionally pulled the second. He got into a good rhythm and found he enjoyed the exercise. After a few minutes, he stopped, exhausted, and went outside in time to see the Lytton party arrive, bringing his dear Emmeline holding another tin of delicious somethings. They alighted and walked alongside the church wall towards the gate. Karl stood there with one of his Riding Officers. The three prisoners tied to the gate post, huddled together, and seemed more terrified than tired despite their six mile walk. The cause of this terror became apparent. Karl was standing on the pathway and he'd stopped in front of a chalked inverted star and in the middle was a dead weasel.

"I'll clear this away for you, Mr Raffles."

Raffles held his arms wide, his palms lifted to heaven. "No! It must be left for all to see." He walked to the edge of the star and looked down. From his viewpoint it was not inverted, just an ordinary star with the one point at the top – no longer a symbol of witchcraft. Whoever had chalked it there had intended to frighten those approaching the church on the pathway from the gate. With the two points of the five-point star at the top, it would scream 'evil' to anyone intending to come inside. "Almighty Father, the moon and the stars belong to you, no one else can claim them. No one. In the name of Jesus who conquered death and rose again I reclaim this ground for you. I ask for your protection. Surround us all with your love and drive all evil away."

He stood for a moment, then lowered his arms and marched across the star with a confident smile on his face. He beckoned his congregation inside the gate. "Chairs for the ladies…" Right beside the star. He escorted Emmeline to a seat directly in front of where he intended to stand.

Karl escorted Lucy and Martha, and George Lytton escorted his wife and sat beside her. Karl returned to where Tutte stood wide-eyed. Raffles guessed the reason for everyone's baffled faces and he chuckled at the peculiar happenings in this once beautiful village of thatched cottages, a few fine houses and a twelfth century church with a parson conducting a service outside and standing in the middle of a symbol of devil worship. What a peculiar sight he must be.

Under a Dark Star

When all were seated on chairs, the wall, or the grass, Parson Raffles lifted his eyes to the sky. His feet straddled the weasel. He began his own version of the liturgy with a prayer. With his head held high, as if absorbing the rays of the sun, he clasped his hands together in entreaty and claimed the mighty power of the creator with a faith that made it his.

He bent down and lifted the weasel with both hands so very gently it might have been a beloved pet dog.

Curtains twitched on the other side of the road and two smocked farm labourers hurried past then stopped to listen from what they regarded as a safe distance.

"This creature was designed and crafted by Almighty God. The chalk that drew a sign of the devil was also created by God. The skin will become one of many stitched to make a warm cover and the rest of this animal will be used for the purpose of feeding the poor."

One of the three prisoners drew in his breath so sharply that he started coughing. He received a swift kick from Tutte's boot to remind him to act with propriety.

Raffles put the unfortunate dead weasel around the corner behind the porch where it could no longer draw attention.

"Major Lytton has brought his fiddle and will accompany our singing of the hymn "Soldiers of Christ arise." As some of his growing congregation would be unable to read, he read aloud the words of each verse and as he did so he paced to and fro, back and forth and even round and round so that all had a chance to hear. When it came to the singing, Major Lytton stood to scrape the fiddle, those with seats also stood, and Raffles boomed until he got close to the end of each verse when only his eyebrows aimed for the top notes. A curious crowd gathered in the road. Martha's face shone and by the second verse she started clapping out the rhythm, although this was not quite the rhythm the tune was built upon.

Raffles had no doubt that the hymn was a resounding success as an offering to God but had some reservations as to whether it was enjoyed by those with a musical ear.

He indicated that all should sit. "There is a verse in the short epistle of James which I should like to read to you." Caring too much about the message, he forgot the verse while he expounded on the responsibility of *everyone* to contribute something for the eternal good. He went on to mention "The boy King Edward died at the untimely age of sixteen, yet had overseen so many improvements in the lives of his subjects. He established three institutions." He raised his index finger each time he counted out the achievements. "One a school." Then he paced back and forth with his arms behind his back. "One hospital for the sick." More pacing gave the congregation time to dwell on his words. "And one for homeless children. And…" he added with a huge grin, "it was during his short reign that the clergy were finally allowed to marry!" Emmeline shone. "A brief life, yet it changed so much for the better. You might be very young or old and frail, and not being a king, you feel unable to do much. Wrong! You can encourage and you can pray and you can set a fine example of courage in the face of evil." Completely unaware, in the eyes of those watching, Parson Raffles was doing exactly that.

He realized his sermon had become convoluted and it wasn't at all what he'd planned to say, so he hurriedly finished by saying, "We can all do something to improve our small part of the world, even if we have little time left to us, and what we do might affect *generations* to come, just as the boy King did."

Quite the opposite of his last intention, he didn't finish there. He remembered that he had not read from the Bible. He gave an endearing chuckle. "The verse! You are all waiting to hear the

Under a Dark Star

verse." Perhaps they weren't? He looked around – good, they were all eyes and ears. He marched round and round, bellowing his next words slowly and clearly. "James chapter one and verse twenty-two says, 'Be ye doers of the word, and not hearers only'." Hmm. Perhaps there were too few hearers. Faith. He took in a deep breath and launched into the tale of a friend who galloped up to a house one day and declared, "All that it takes for evil to triumph is for good men to do nothing." He drew in another deep breath and repeated it slowly facing those now gathering by the gate. "Is this not what James is saying? Don't just listen – stand up and do something!"

Martha could contain herself no longer and leapt up, clapping wildly until she caught sight of Karl giving her what she called "one of his damnifying looks". Chastened, she sat down and smoothed her best green, dimity cotton dress.

Parson Raffles wondered if the open air service was a good idea. It was losing all dignity. He vowed never again to speak without notes. Then immediately retracted it as one of the bystanders crept forward and shouted, "Look! The star has gone!"

The onlookers across the road tentatively approached then others rushed over to see, and it was true. There was chalk on the bottom of the parson's shoes but the path no longer had the mark of witchcraft upon it.

No good man of God would fail to grasp this opportunity. He stood in the centre of what had been a symbol of the devil and bellowed, "And from the book of Deuteronomy we are told, 'Don't try to use any kind of magic or witchcraft to tell fortunes or to *cast spells* or to talk with spirits of the dead.'" He lowered his voice and smiled, "You see my good people, the Lord God Almighty is the strongest power."

A ripple of applause from the villagers culminated in a hearty cheer from all, except for three women standing by the gate. But the parson knew who and what they were, eyes being the windows of the soul.

~

One hundred and seventeen men, women and children enjoyed cake and a few sips of mead made by the Lyttons. Not all came inside, but all who listened went away with more than cake and sweet honey drink. Even Raffles learnt more than he'd expected. As he served one of the roped prisoners by the gate with cake, water and a little mead, he was told, "That there weasel ain't fit t'eat. Ain't no sign of it bein' trapped. Likely it's been poisoned."

Those who talk, don't know and those who know, won't talk. That spell was now broken.

Under a Dark Star

Chapter Twenty
Karl
"A malevolent, swirling fog"

The following morning, a cold, wet and windy Monday, Karl propped himself up in bed and reached for The Note. He'd read it at least a dozen times and once more wouldn't hurt. The handwriting was exquisite, just like her, but the wording was strange. There was a clue in this and he was missing it. Worse still, she hadn't had time to finish and had scrunched it up and thrown it out of the window before completing a proper message. Tutte and Flowers certainly didn't need to know.

Tutte, Flowers, Buckby and Tomkins were now all living at Watch House and sleeping on the floor below, between Karl and the prisoners who hardly seemed like villains now. They'd saved a few lives by enlightening Raffles to the poisoned weasel. Furthermore, they were trying to be helpful yet keen to stay in gaol. Couldn't blame them for that. Safe, good food, they were warm – warmer than most.

He'd moved the two little urchins into the end cottage, too badly smoke damaged for Tutte and Flowers, but an improvement on a barrel for the boys. They'd be knocking on the door soon.

He examined the note again. "Sir," it began, "I beg of you to help me. I am captive." That much he'd worked out without the need for words.

Under a Dark Star

Noises from below floated up the spiral staircase. He stuffed the note in his coat pocket before reaching for his shirt and breeches.

Dressed, he dashed down the steps to the stirring Riding Officers. "Up, up! We've work to do." He didn't stop other than to shout at the prisoners to shift their lazy bones, but went on down to the ground floor where a week ago, Mrs Buckby would have been preparing breakfast for them all. In her place he'd appointed Tomkins in charge of household chores and he'd been trying to train the boys who, by the sound of the geese, were now approaching.

He peeked through the spy hole, flung the door open and ushered them in quickly.

"Got yer some eggs, sir," said the one who'd had curly brown hair. "Them geese is fierce but they like us now we're giving them their oats."

"How many eggs?"

Their eager eyes shone. They were holding out their hands to show six big goose eggs which they placed in a bowl on the table. At least they were clean now that he'd dunked them in the sea, soaped them and rinsed them under the pump. He'd shaved their hair to rid them of the lice and now they had only a hint of soft fuzz. They didn't know how old they were; they looked about eight or nine but perhaps that was due to stunted growth. He told them they were ten and at the beginning of each new year they were to add a year to their age. They'd looked mystified but after whispering together they'd thanked him. "And your names? What are they?" The boys huddled together and whispered. "Speak up!"

"Please sir, we don't like our names."

"What are they?" Karl's patience was being tried but he was charmed by their upturned faces with the expression in their eyes fluctuating between fear and hope.

"I just call him 'you'," said one pointing at the other.

"And I call him..." said the other who seemed to find it difficult to continue. He stared at Karl, then with his eyes welling with tears, he turned and clutched his friend and they hugged each other.

Immediately Karl squatted and put his arms around them. "We'll find you some good names. Ones you'll like." He stood up, with his arms still around their bony shoulders. "And you'll have a home and good food too."

Tomkins had been into Newport for provisions late on Saturday and, on instruction, had bought them boots, breeches, two shirts and a coat each. All second hand, or perhaps even third hand, but definitely not lice or flea infested. Poor little lads, they'd got bites all over their scrawny bodies.

Tomkins leapt down the steps and collected the eggs, then collared one to light a fire and the other to lay the table with bread, butter and the sweet conserves he'd bought in Newport.

Their young lives had improved even by moving them into a near derelict, burnt out building, yet he allowed himself a growing smile: Tomkins was taking them under his wing. All they needed now were names. He'd let Tomkins name them, or should it be Buckby? And one day perhaps they'd feel secure enough to tell him their story.

Karl ate to live rather than lived to eat like other members of his privileged class, which was just as well with the lowly positions he kept taking. After a frugal breakfast, he told Tomkins to take the prisoners something no less than they'd had themselves. No sooner had Tomkins carried out that order than Karl was giving him another. "Get yourself down here and train these lads to make something of a feast for a midday meal. Do you hear?"

"Yes sir!" Tomkins said as he raced down the steps.

Under a Dark Star

Karl watched Buckby's desolate face. He put a hand on his shoulder. His wife's funeral had taken place on the Saturday before and she'd been buried in Kaddakay's graveyard. He had stood some way back from the dozen or so mourners, waiting to see who had the courage to come. More specifically, he'd been watching for the arsonist. Sitting motionless on the lower slopes of Rose's Ridge was a single man visible only to Karl's trained eye.

Karl squeezed Buckby's shoulder and remembered the loss of his own father.

"She was carrying my child. My unborn child! She'd only just told me."

He pulled out a chair from the table and gently pushed the rigid Buckby down.

"I did everything he told me. I didn't do a thing to stop his free-trading nor his wrecking." His eyes flickered up to Karl before staring at the floor. "I needed the money. Yet look what he's done to me." He leant forward and, with his elbows on the table, he propped his head in his hands. "No wife, no child, no home. I'll get him if it's the last thing I do."

Karl watched as hatred dug a home in his heart.

After his men had eaten breakfast and the lads had fetched the water and boiled some for brewing tea, he called them to the table which they immediately tried to clear of dishes. "No, bring the tea and cups and two tin mugs and then sit down," he pointed to the empty bench between the wall and the table. The tin teapot was large and heavy but with the assistance of a cloth, one staggered to the table and the other carried the cups. Being so thin, they had no difficulty squeezing themselves onto the low bench but their bright little faces only just topped the edge of the table. "You've been with us now for a couple of days."

Under a Dark Star

The two boys nodded and fear flashed across their eyes. "Please sir, we..."

Karl held up his hand. "So long as you serve us well and are loyal." He paused and scrutinized each boy. "Do you understand the meaning of 'loyal'?" The boys gawped. They plainly had no idea. "Buckby, as a King's man you know the meaning of loyalty to the service and the importance of not being bribed nor afraid, don't you?" He knew he was hitting Buckby hard. The disloyal Riding Officer had learnt his lesson too late yet now he was the best person to teach these boys the cost of disloyalty. "While we drink our tea – you tell them."

Buckby did. The boys' eyes grew larger and they huddled together as he thumped the table and repeated himself several times until Karl could see that the lads were quite clear on the virtues of loyalty and the consequences of disloyalty to your comrades.

Karl nodded to Tomkins to pour some tea for Buckby then turned to interrogate the boys. "What were you doing in the churchyard on Saturday?"

"Please sir, we didn't mean no 'arm," said the boy that he thought of as 'Curly'.

"Answer the question!"

Tutte raised his eyebrows and pointed upwards. "The boys might be afraid the prisoners hear, sir."

The other boy answered Karl in a whisper. "We sometimes sleep there, sir, when there's no empty barrels."

"In the church?" He remembered Daniel telling him how the parson carried a bunch of keys with him and kept the door to the church locked. "In the porch?"

"No sir. In the graveyard."

He tried picturing the graveyard. As far as he could recall there was no shelter within those low walls. "Where in the graveyard?"

Silence. Had they not been such pitiful children, he would by now have spelt out the harsh consequences of not co-operating.

"Are you telling me you slept in the grave dug for Mrs Buckby?"

Buckby slammed his cup down, broke the handle and tea spilt all over the table. Karl was furious with himself. Why did he have to be so very straightforward?

Curly appeared to spare Buckby's shredded emotions. "Oh no sir! We wouldn't do that." Then spoilt it. "There'd be no roof, see?"

Tomkins mopped up the tea, picked up the broken cup and brought another.

"So where *do* you sleep?"

"In the graves, sir." There was a moment's silence before he added, "'tis 'ard, sir, but some of the slabs slide back so Tridd can keep his stuff in there."

Like a malevolent, swirling fog, horror engulfed the table. "And the bodies?" Karl asked quietly.

"Oh there's no bodies. They dig them up and throw them out to sea."

"What!" Karl thundered.

Immediately the response came. "Old bodies, not the new ones!" The boys' eyes swivelled towards Buckby. "And mostly they leave them, 'cos there's enough room on top if they're in coffins."

"So you push back the flat slab on top of the grave?"

"The two of us can push 'ard, sir. We only use the ones that Tridd's used, they're easiest. We don't touch the others and we only need a little gap to slide through. Keeps us out of the wind and rain." Curly shook his head and tried a glimmer of a smile. "Tain't a bad place."

The other boy, shorter and with darker hair, started to giggle nervously. "We know about it 'cos one morning an ol' woman was putting flowers on her 'usband's grave and we were waiting to take them, we sell 'em you see. She nearly died of fright when the slab next to her moved and this 'ead popped up."

Tomkins gritted his teeth and sighed loudly. "So that's how the rumour started."

Buckby enlightened everyone. "That old woman swore she saw the dead rising."

Tomkins snatched his tale back. "Spread like gangrene." Karl looked mystified. "Tittle tattle. At first it was just a little local gossip that no one took any notice of. Then another old woman swore she'd seen it too. It wasn't long before all the village heard. It became unstoppable and now the whole of the back of the Wight reckons Kaddakay's dead rise up and haunt us all."

It explained a lot.

Buckby finished the tale. "Well, there's a witches' coven that meets on a beach bit further along towards Brigton and they claimed it was their doing. Of course, we didn't believe it, did we, Tomkins?"

Tomkins stared at the ground before answering. "Course not!"

Karl stood up. "Thanks to these two lads, we now know the truth." He strode backwards and forwards. "So what happened to the man who got up from the grave? Do we know who he was?"

Curly's eyes grew large. "I don't know who he was, sir, but he ain't no more."

He sat down in front of Curly and hoped the boy didn't mean what Karl thought he meant. "Do you mean he is dead?"

"Dead as the nails in the coffins, sir."

"Tridd?" The boys took a quick peek at each other but said nothing. They didn't need to. The fright on their faces told its own story. "It's imperative we catch this Tridd. He exploits everyone for miles around; his behaviour is immoral; he craves riches at any price; he…" Karl stopped, clenched his fists and muttered, "And enslaves."

Buckby had put his elbows on the table with his hands over his ears but now raised his fist and said between gritted teeth, "I'll get him! If it's the last thing I do, I'll get him!"

"And bring him to justice," Karl reminded him.

Buckby glared. A sympathetic silence surrounded him; what else could anyone offer? Tears spilled from his eyes. "My son. We wanted a son."

The two boys leapt up with one accord and shouted, "I'll be your son, sir!"

Under a Dark Star

Chapter Twenty-One
"The scent of her"

That evening, Karl wondered what Daniel would be doing. Relaxing before tomorrow's big night? Yes, he'd be sitting by the fire next to Josh, with Becky fussing around him, cooking rabbits perhaps. It didn't matter what circumstances he found himself in, that man was never short of female company. Nearly s*even o'clock*. Yes, he'd be having dinner, knowing that nothing would be happening on this treacherous night. Karl, however, always had something to do even on a stormy night, and this time a woman was the draw.

Having removed his uniform cap and hung it on the saddle, and climbed over the stone wall, he squatted beneath what he now called Her Window and turned over in his mind the words of the note. "I beg of you to help me. I am captive. Come Monday at the time for the dinner, dogs inside, window open..." This was Monday, and he consulted his watch again. Just past seven o' clock, probably the right time, or did Tridd have his dinner earlier in the day? Dark clouds overhead defeated the twilight. The leaded light window was only ajar. He'd thrown a handful of gravel at it but there'd been no response. He made an excuse for her: the window was barely open because of the torrential rain and fierce winds. How could he get a grappling iron into the room? Perhaps he could dislodge the fastener holding it ajar without making too much noise. He collected several stones then took off his leather riding cloak and folded it as small as possible and threw it over the wall near where Midnight was tethered. Useful as it was to keep dry, it hampered his movements. He took careful aim and, throwing underarm, he missed the casement window arm. Nevertheless, the pebble had come back to him, he'd made no noise and he'd got the measure of the task: he needed a larger stone. So, taking into account the twenty-five feet gap he had to cover, he dislodged the arm, and the window slammed open against the grey stone wall at exactly the same time as a distant flash of lightning and roll of thunder sounded. He hoped the threatening storm might explain the dogs howling.

He threw the grappling iron expertly and shinned up the rope and hauled himself into her bedroom, dragging the rope in too. She wasn't there. He pulled the window closed. He groped around in the dark and found a small bed with fancy hangings and a chest at the bottom. A flash of lightning revealed a velvet padded chair and a dresser. The bare stone floor was covered by several sheepskin rugs. This was not Tridd's room. He'd wait, at least for a short while.

But he couldn't. This was such an exceptional chance to explore that he could not resist carefully opening the bedroom door. He'd told Tutte where he was, so if anything went wrong, they would rescue him. He grinned. Rescue! Tridd never took prisoners! From his pocket he pulled out a crushed, small bunch of primroses. He straightened it out and laid it on her pillow. If he couldn't find her, at least she'd know he'd been. An image of Tridd seeing the flowers flashed into his head so he lifted the white satin bed cover and put the little yellow flowers underneath. As he did so, he savoured the scent of her. Why was there never any time for a woman in his life?

A stone staircase led down past another door which he could only just discern. This room must be in permanent darkness as he'd seen only the one window in the tower. Maybe for storage?

Under a Dark Star

He listened, then turned the handle. Locked. A prison? He noticed three bolts and drew them back. The door groaned on its rusty hinges. He daren't open it further so he peered through the gap. Black as the womb, cold as a tomb. He pulled the groaning door closed. He crept down to the base of the steps where a row of three candle sconces lit the way along a short corridor with a heavy oak door at the end. If he were to be caught here, there was nowhere to hide. Should he give the ring handle a twist and see what happens? What about the dogs? Where were they?

He decided there was little point in getting this far then turning back. His hand patted his knife. He'd not had to use it on a man since he'd saved Lucy's life from the smuggler bent on killing her. He chided himself for yet again thinking of the one woman he'd ever loved. He gripped the handle and very cautiously turned it. No dogs barked. He slowly pushed the door ajar. It creaked. He drew in his breath and squeezed through the narrow opening, right hand on his knife.

The vast, high ceilinged and cold room befitted a castle or fort. The huge fireplace was empty. A stout, lit candle glowed inside a glass lamp on a side table against the wall on the right, close to another huge door. On his left, and straight ahead were two large leaded glass windows. He took a keener look in case he needed to escape. They had bars on the outside. In the centre of the room stood a long oak table with sturdy wooden chairs around it and an unlit, ornate silver, seven branch candelabrum occupied a central place. The high sideboard on the far side of the other door might prove useful to hide behind if necessary. Hung on the walls were figureheads taken from the prows of ships – wrecked ships, no doubt. He counted twenty-two. Where other men had reminders of days hunting deer for food, this man celebrated human death and destruction. Yet one wall was devoted to oil paintings. Perhaps a dozen, both large and small, and all of them featured the sea. How surprising that Tridd was a collector of works of art. He walked towards the door and stood so that if it opened he would be hidden. He listened. Not a sound. He turned the handle slightly and waited. Surely the dogs would be picking up his scent or sounds. He opened the door. It began to creak so he squeezed through. Ah. This was where the day-to-day living started.

His eyes, as was his custom, took in every detail instantly, including the woman seated before a blazing fire. He raised his hand; she saw him and her eyes lit up. Only his training stopped him from hastening to her. She was wearing a deep red dress and a black velvet spencer. She put a finger to her perfectly shaped lips and pointed at another door. He beckoned her to come with him and she tiptoed towards him. Almost immediately, voices and footsteps alerted them to danger and she turned and fled back to her chair and he squeezed back through the doorway.

Tridd stomped in and growled, "You're sure?"

He had to listen hard to hear what the second man said. His was an educated, soft voice. "I've just been informed. It's making its way to the island."

"What's the cargo?"

"No news on that, only that there's a brigantine, with a mast down, in trouble, and limping along our coast. Probably looking to anchor somewhere and ride out the storm."

Tridd swore profusely about the lightning possibly showing up the rocks, then made a decision. "Right! Let's go! I'm expecting a ship tomorrow, but this is a godsend." He turned to the woman. "Flo, get your arse out there and clear up those dishes."

Flo did not move. Without another word, Tridd grabbed her by the arm and dragged her towards the other room. Karl's thoughts raced. He yearned to challenge this monster but who else was in the fort? Where were the dogs? He had no doubts he could defeat Tridd but if he did, he'd not be able to bring *all* those responsible for wrecking to justice. He must wait.

Through the crack between the door and doorway, he could see the slight figure of the parson of Kaddakay. Tridd, still holding Flo's wrist hard, yelled at him. "I want that ship brought into the bay – the rocks." He flung Flo through the door and Karl heard her gasp then hastily clear some dishes. Tridd came back to the parson and switched from angry to smug. "Usual trap - we'll get them thinking it's a safe harbour. Where's that swaggering Lieutenant?"

"He was seen riding away from Watch House about an hour ago."

"I don't want to know where he was, I want to know where he is! Where is he *now*?"

Parson Driver sounded anguished; he coughed, and spluttered, "On the way to Brigton. There's a woman, staying with relatives at Norwell Farm. I think she's taken his fancy."

"Well damn well see he stays there! Get them crones out on the road to Norwell and make sure he doesn't come back."

"Do you mean…?"

"Nah – not him. Not yet. I don't want to complicate matters. There's others to deal with tonight."

At first the parson sounded relieved. "Of course, Mr Tridd." Then his eyes betrayed his growing awareness of Karl's ultimate fate.

"His faint-hearted layabouts won't do anything without him, so just keep him out of the way until I get time to stick him good and proper."

The parson seized the opportunity to say something soothing. "They won't even know. If they know anything, which I doubt, they'll be thinking it's later this week. And who wants to patrol the cliffs in this weather if you don't have to?"

Under a Dark Star

Karl watched as the parson tentatively smiled; he was exactly as Daniel said, like a menacing rat. Lightning cracked over their heads. An explosion of thunder swiftly followed. Dogs barked, but where were they?

"Stay here; I haven't finished with you." Tridd stomped off and suddenly the barking grew louder. Within a matter of minutes, he returned with two scuffling, growling brutes on leads.

The parson moved back towards the other door, coughing a little. "Have they been fed?"

"I'll feed them when their work is done and not before." Tridd swore foully at the dogs and they quietened, though still straining at their leashes, sniffing the air.

Karl felt the sweat at the back of his neck. His best hope was for Tridd to tie them to something while he continued issuing his instructions. He needed to hear all he could.

"I want to see you running, none of this parsony gliding. Rouse Jim Brantiani. Tell him to round up everyone. Spout lanterns, donkeys, ropes, the lot. Understood?"

"Of course, Mr Tridd, of course."

Tridd took a knife out of his belt. "Now get going while I see what these overheated creatures are smelling. Whatever it is, it'll likely be a leg short by tomorrow." He pointed to the door. "Don't stand around, man, get everyone down to the star and its weasel and you, *you* shift the weasel – and if you can find any spare hags, get them on the beach calling up the wind and the rain until I tell 'em to stop."

"I'll do that, Mr Tridd, but I thought you didn't believe…"

"Never you mind what I believe. It's what the peasants believe that matters. We don't want them thinking the clouds might be clearin' and the moon shinin'!" He waved his arm at the parson, "Don't just stand there, move yourself. I've got to get Flo locked up again, and let the rest of the dogs out of the cellar. I want to see

Under a Dark Star

everyone, and I mean every able bodied man ready and waiting, including Zeb and his lodger – say we need his donkey. Got that?" Tridd turned away. He didn't wait for an answer; he'd finished with this phoney man of God.

"Yes, the more men, the quicker…" but the parson, trying to maintain a measure of control yet appear obliging, was cut short.

Tridd spun around and shouted, "Get out!" The parson scuttled away and Tridd's thoughts turned to someone who'd got under his skin. "Thinks he can rule with just a bunch of skinny women to back him up. Huh! He doesn't know who he's up against." He punched his fist in the air and announced, "There'll be one over-rated piece of slime not returning home tonight."

Karl raced towards the door leading to the corridor and the steps to the tower. He had barely reached it when he knew he should have left earlier.

"Touch that handle and I'll release the dogs." Tridd didn't shout, he snarled like one of his dogs guarding its meat. Nevertheless, Karl slipped through the gap, slammed the door and raced to the steps. A crack of thunder rent the air and the dogs went wild, hurling themselves at the barrier to their quarry. Swearing worse than any smuggler Karl had ever heard, Tridd was dragged through the opened door by the two rampaging animals. Karl was half way up the steps when the dogs were released.

He'd no hope of reaching the woman's room and shinning down the rope without serious injury, so he took the only option and dashed into the blackness of the room halfway up the steps. He pushed the groaning door shut behind him just as they reached it. He didn't need to hold the door firmly closed – he heard the discordant screech of the bolts as they rammed home. Standing in his wet uniform, he sneezed loudly as if expressing his anger.

Chapter Twenty-Two
Daniel
"A real godsend"

Monday 17th March
Josh appeared a little happier living on the island now that Zeb supplied a regular rabbit, supplemented occasionally by chasing and catching his own weasel. Zeb, influenced by Daniel, encouraged this, saying weasels were nest robbers and it was only fair to give the fledglings a chance now that spring approached. Josh was also allowed a warm spot of his own in front of the stove. Daniel gave him an affectionate hug as he nuzzled up to his master sitting in the comfortable chair he'd bought. Sometimes at night, on Daniel's bed, Josh whined pitiably, especially after they'd stolen an hour or two with Lucy and Freddie.

Still, tomorrow, would likely bring matters to a head because a ship was expected to be sailing towards London from America with a cargo of rum, sugar and cotton. If the cloud cover persisted, and the ship stayed on course to pass the south of the island at night, Tridd might put his plans into operation and Daniel would be a witness to murder or attempted murder. Furthermore, he should be able to save the lives of most of the crew. Thankfully, Daniel knew about this as Tridd had told his right hand man, Jim Brantiani, who'd told his brother, Ellen's husband, and Ellen had told Becky. Becky had been thrilled to prove herself useful in passing on the news to Daniel and she could even tell him he was to be included. He, of course, left a message for Karl, and their long-hatched plan might at last be put into action.

Perhaps he, Josh and Fiddle could finish their work within a month and be home with Lucy to greet their visitors. So many livelihoods depended on those spending their vacations at Bethlehem Farm, it really would be untimely to be so far away at the start of the season. Lucy always charmed the gentlemen of the county, and beyond. And the lady wives clucked and cooed over their new-born son. Everything had been going so well and then Karl arrived. Yet there was work to do here which Raffles declared to be God-given and akin to freeing the Israelite slaves in Egypt! Dear Raffles. He and Karl would win enthusiasm competitions, if ever there were to be such a thing.

He took his pocket watch out and saw it said *seven o'clock*. A Monday evening of peace lay ahead and tomorrow's dirty work was twenty-four hours away. He glanced around. Becky was a good home-maker and had already been into Newport and sold some of her bolt of cotton to buy heavier fabric for making new curtains for the parlour. The old mismatched ones currently adorned Daniel's room and that was an improvement on none. She now sat opposite him sewing some lace curtains by the light of two candles.

"There! I've nearly finished these. Do you like them?"

"Aye, I do. Are they for here?" Daniel pointed at the window.

"Of course," she smiled, "I'm going to have my window looking just like the ones I've seen in Ryde. I shall draw them back with some of your red velvet ribbon."

He smiled broadly to encourage her and show he was impressed. A great pity Zeb was not so industrious, though, to be fair, he was now outside chopping some wood. He stretched his feet out onto "Josh's rug" which Becky had bought second hand.

"Spoilt, you are, Josh." He was relieved that Josh could not reply.

With the income from the barrels of brandy he'd retrieved from the sea, he knew he could afford to buy this impoverished couple a few discreet luxuries. Karl had insisted that he should finance this expedition but Daniel didn't need or want any help for his part. For a brief moment he again wondered how the work on his own Bethlehem Farm was faring without him. His thoughts were interrupted by the blast of icy air as Zeb stumbled through the scullery door with an armful of logs. Daniel leapt up to shut the door behind him.

"Damned cold and wet outside!" Zeb said as he let the logs drop in the hearth beside the stove. As if to confirm his statement, the window panes rattled with the force of the wind and rain against them. "Looks like there be a storm brewing too."

"At least we got some ploughing done this afternoon."

"Aye, we did, we did."

Daniel wondered if he should leave Nancy for them when he finally went home. She'd pulled the plough – just. She wasn't very happy being yoked but Becky kept her sweet with some old soft carrots. Becky doted on her and it just might work until Zeb could afford an ox. He'd think about it. "It's Nancy we have to thank. She's not been asked to pull a plough before."

"Asked?" Zeb laughed. "You and your animals!"

Becky put her sewing aside while she lit another candle and set it down by her husband's chair. "It's nice to be able to afford three every evening – one each!"

Josh sat up to allow Becky to stir the stewing rabbits. His nose twitched, his eyes never left the steaming pot and his tail wagged excitedly.

"That stew ready yet?" Zeb was also watching the longed-for dinner.

Under a Dark Star

"By the time I've warmed the bread through, it will be."

They were half way through their meal when the wind dropped momentarily and the sound of galloping hooves broke into the cosy mood. Zeb and Becky exchanged worried looks: it could only be bad news. Zeb peered in vain through the window. He went to the door, Daniel stood behind him and Josh backed him up. A gust of wind meant that he only needed to release the latch for it to fly open and reveal Janey Fawcett's husband. Zeb grabbed hold of him and pulled him through the door.

"Come in, man, and be quick about it."

"It's you whats gotta be quick, Tynlan." Fawcett, dressed as always in a shabby old brown coat, wrapped it closer around him. "Tomorrow's still on, if the cloud gives us cover, but there's one in trouble offshore *tonight*. A real godsend. Tridd wants us all out, including you Tynton. Ready or not, you're to get down to the rocks. Bring your spouts, ropes and your donkey. Tridd says that's the only reason you're allowed to come."

Privately thinking this was just a pretext, Daniel answered immediately. "We'll be there."

"Don't bring that dog of yours. Tridd's taking his two manglers. I gotta go. Gotta get round another nine houses."

"Need any help with that?" said Daniel.

"Nah. You'd better get yourself down to the star."

"Manglers," repeated Daniel quietly. He doubted there was such a word, but it did its job.

Chapter Twenty-Three
"A stink of dogs"

Daniel's thoughts whirled. He must get a message to Karl. If this ship were to be wrecked tonight and the cargo was substantial, Tridd might not need to attempt another wrecking tomorrow night and that's when Karl planned to surprise the wreckers. The customs' men needed to be there *tonight* to witness a wrecking. Daniel's testimony alone might be outweighed by the gang's denial and lack of proof.

Zeb fussed around. "Tridd always told me I didn't have to do any wrecking. All I'm supposed to do is store stuff. Us being that bit out of the village and on a good road to the rest of the island makes it easy for…" he stopped, shook his head slowly from side to side, then added resentfully, "I don't like wrecking. 'Tain't right."

Becky rushed over and put her arms round him. "We ain't supposed to be treated like the others, Daniel. Tridd *owes* Zeb and he shouldn't be called out."

Buried truths were surfacing and he'd love to find out more but he held his curiosity in check. He grasped Zeb's shoulder. "I'll do my best to see you come to no harm." There were several things he could warn his cousin about. "Don't take any kind of weapon. Don't go into the sea. Find yourself a job near the cliff face."

"Not sure I'll get to do any choosing, Daniel. You don't know what he's like; he'll set the dogs on me if I dis…disobey. And *you're* just there for your donkey!"

Under a Dark Star

Daniel felt his blood rising but knew he must act his chosen part. This was not the moment to provoke a rebellion.

As Zeb stomped up the stairs, Daniel's thoughts turned to how to alert Karl. He'd probably be preparing his men for the expected wrecking tomorrow. Since arriving on the island, Josh had learned to take messages to Lucy and that worked very well. He would come bounding back with a note inside the tiny woollen pouch attached to a collar. His long hair hid it well. Could he be relied upon to get to Karl? Josh knew Karl's name but it would help if he could sniff something belonging to Karl. His mind rummaged but nothing surfaced. Nevertheless, he prepared a warning note and put Josh's rope collar on. Many a dog would have resented such a restraint but Josh liked to be useful and rushed to the door with his tail wagging briskly. "Wait, Josh, wait, and I'll take you halfway to *Karl*." Josh sat down while Daniel dashed upstairs with Becky close behind him.

She tugged at Daniel's coat and said desperately, "He can't swim! You will look after him, won't you?" She attempted a smile. "Much of the time he doesn't know where he's supposed to be going or how to get there."

Daniel spun round and kissed her forehead. The map! The map of the diamond-shaped island that Karl had drawn for him – that might still have the smell of Karl on it. "Don't you worry about that good husband of yours. He'll be home safe in no time at all. Get a good fire ready to warm us and a bowl of hot broth too."

When Daniel came down the stairs, Zeb and Becky were embracing by the front door as if parting for years instead of just a few hours.

"Got your spout lantern, Zeb?"

Zeb's face fell. "Ah. It's round the back in the stable."

Daniel put his arm around Zeb's shoulders. "Come with me to get Nancy and we'll pick it up."

Becky looked at Daniel with an expression which said *I told you so.*

~

When they were as close to Watch House as Daniel dared go, Josh took a good sniff at the scrappy map. Daniel knelt beside him and pointed in the direction of where Karl should be. "Karl – find Karl."

Josh did not set off at the lively pace Daniel hoped for. He sniffed around the earth and trotted along slowly to get a scent. Nothing. His master turned and ran back to Zeb and that donkey, leaving him on his own. But he'd soon show who was number two in the pack. He sniffed the air, then put his nose to the ground again. No scent of Karl. He headed towards the base of Kaddakay Ridge. Some minutes passed before he wagged his tail. Fiddle had been here but his scent was overpowered by a stronger one. He sniffed the air again. This horse was close by. Nose to the ground, he then picked up Karl's scent. It was strong; he'd been here very recently. He followed the trail to the base of the wall and reached up on his hind legs, sniffing. Defeated, he trotted around the outside. A stink of dogs trailed inside the gate. Josh trotted back to pick up the scent of the other horse. That'd be Midnight. He remembered the time he'd once nipped at him. Things had changed. Both masters now seemed to be friends but they'd fallen on hard times, no doubt about that.

He trotted over to Midnight who anxiously pawed the ground. Karl must be inside those walls but there was no way in, so Josh followed Midnight's trail back to Watch House. Perhaps he could fetch help.

Under a Dark Star

He was met by some very unfriendly geese making a terrible rumpus. Flapping, honking and waddling all over the place. Probably good for eating – if you could get near one.

High up on the wall a window opened and Flowers peered out. "It's a dog! Harrying the geese, it is. I'll send it away." On his way to the door, he picked up one of the stout clubs hanging from a peg.

Josh heard him coming and barked. Midnight's scent ended here and Karl's began again. The geese increased their honking and flapping and Flowers cleared a way through them. Josh barked meaningfully; this man must be a friend and might need to be alerted to danger and maybe he'd come with him to fetch Karl. To show he meant no harm to these honking flappers, Josh sat down and wagged his tail. Encouraged, Flowers went through the gate and bent down to pat this friendly-looking dog, but Josh ran. There was no way this man was coming near the precious pouch around his neck and he clutched a big stick. He ran a few yards, turned and barked twice, then ran a little way again, but the man did not follow. Several times he returned to the man, barked, then turned and ran a few paces. But the man did not understand. He was a stranger. He'd go back to his master.

There was a problem with this plan. The man whom his master had indicated was an enemy was patrolling the top of the cliffs. Not that Josh couldn't topple him with a leap and a well-aimed bite but he'd got two of those vicious stinkers protecting him and they'd picked up his scent. They were both straining at their leashes. Fat, squat things, with mighty jaws. He could outrun them if he needed to, so he went around the man and barked. Perhaps his master would hear? He did! There was the whistle!

In response, Tridd released one of the slobbering dogs. Josh stood his ground, head lowered, paws wide.

Chapter Twenty-Four
Brigton Parsonage - Raffles
"There must be more cake"

Meanwhile, Raffles sank into the only comfortable chair in the parsonage and took out his pocket watch. It was *seven o'clock*! The carter was late but in this stormy weather, it was to be expected. He surveyed the parlour. Never in all his life had he lived so frugally and he certainly would not have asked Emmeline to come and live with him if it hadn't been for the generosity of the Lyttons. They were cheerfully furnishing the main rooms and supplementing the living for six months. And dear Lucy, she'd insisted that Martha should stay with them to help Emmeline with the household duties until a daily maid was found. But he'd been fortunate; after his service held in the open air, a woman came forward to offer her assistance as a cook and her friend readily agreed to be a daily maid. He'd accepted gratefully, of course. He chuckled and patted his stomach. "Much diminished these last few weeks," he said to it. He sighed as he reflected that one of the best ways of appreciating God's gifts is to go without them for a while. "Not too long, I hope," he said looking upwards. Then, respectfully, he smiled: what a surprise he'd get if, one day when he looked up, God was looking down.

Raffles glanced at his watch again then settled back to await the delivery of the furniture. The rickety table in the window, piled high with books and papers, was serviceable but really belonged in a kitchen. If it hadn't been for the kindness of the grocer, he

Under a Dark Star

would have neither the table nor his bed. Life here on the south west of the island was undoubtedly gruelling. Brigton had obviously been a thriving village at one time but the tedious routine and endless hard labour for little reward had worn down the inhabitants' spirit. He must make Sundays very special for them. The cakes had been received well. There must be more cake and ale, and no unnecessary work on the Lord's Day. A small improvement to their lives until this stranglehold by Tridd was broken. A broad smile stayed on his face for at least a minute while he imagined his parishioners' delight at attending future Sunday services. It was banished by a crunching of heavy wheels on the dirt road alerting him to the arrival of the carter. He took a deep breath, stood up, and opened the door. Like a furious phantom, the wind howled as it rushed through the opening and blew the parson's black woollen cloak almost horizontal.

The carter jumped down from the overloaded cart. "I hope yer'll excuse my tardiness. Them Lyttons, practically gentry they are, and generous too. Took me and my girls a while to load up and the poor horse here," he patted his shire, "he's getting on and in this terrible weather, well..."

Raffles beamed as he interrupted. "Do not concern yourself, my good man, about being late. Let me assist you in unloading..."

It was the carter's turn to interrupt. "Aw! I couldn't allow yer to do that, sir. I've brought my nieces with me to help."

~

It took an hour to unload and take a little hot refreshment but Raffles, the carter and his twin nieces were finally on the road back to the Lyttons. The twins sat in the empty cart and huddled underneath a heavy tarpaulin and Raffles sat at the front on the right of the carter. His cloak was soaked and the water was seeping through the many layers he was wearing for the journey.

Under a Dark Star

"Here, lay this over your knees," said the carter as he heaved a partially tarred canvas cover towards the parson.

Raffles pulled it up as high as he could and hunched beneath the smelly shield. His oldest and largest hat was strapped on his head with a red scarf and he closed his eyes to protect them from the whipping wind.

They had travelled about two thirds of the way when a strange sound managed to find his ears. It sounded as if the wind was wailing, then grumbling and coming to a crescendo with a roar. The carter called his agitated horse to a halt and Raffles peered towards the sound. It was directly ahead of them, only fifty or so yards away. In the middle of the road was a fire and prancing around it were macabre silhouettes, hands held high and howling at the dark sky, then flinging themselves to the ground and moaning louder than any wind.

"Someone doesn't want us to reach Norwell Farm tonight," said Raffles resignedly.

"I knew I shouldn't come this end of the island. I knew it! 'Tain't safe."

The twins peeped out from beneath the tarpaulin and, hiding behind the carter and Raffles, one of them said, "It's those witches!"

The other whispered, "Let's get ourselves some good, heavy clubs," and they crawled back under the tarpaulin and jumped off the cart at the back and ran into the woods.

"Can't we just go around them?" said Raffles.

"'Tain't wise to do that. This road's rutted enough. Get these wheels on the soggy, rough earth and they'd get stuck and likely come off!"

Raffles heaved himself down onto the ground just as a flash of black and white hurtled past him barking loudly at the witches.

"Here boy! Come here!" *What good timing.*

Under a Dark Star

Without any change in pace, Josh circled back to Raffles and jumped up at him barking desperately.

Raffles bent down to reassure him. "Are those witches making you afraid?" He thought of other times when he'd noticed how animals were more aware of things unseen by the human eye. Raffles sat on the step of the cart and patted his lap for Josh to jump on. Placing one arm around the quivering dog and raising the other high, he said, "Let us pray." Oblivious of the carter slipping rapidly away to the refuge of the woods, he began his prayer. "Almighty God, creator, preserver and governor of all things on earth, under the earth and above the earth, seen and unseen, I ask for your almighty love to surround and protect me and this good creature here." He stroked Josh and ruffled his hair. "Jesus, conqueror of all evil, be with me as I, and this good dog, approach these dark forces." There was so much more he wanted to say but 'one thing at a time' had stood him in good stead over his increasing years and, firm in his faith, he stood slowly then, summoning his courage, he marched towards the now shrieking silhouettes. Josh followed reluctantly behind him.

As he came closer to the fire, he could see the steam from the steadily falling rain, and the hissing as it hit the flames added to the eerie scene. He could now distinguish four women and two men, all dressed in long black robes. The men had covered their faces in mud which was streaked as the rain washed it down; they clutched fiery torches.

Never before in his life had he been so grateful for a loud voice. He thought he'd start with *Children of God, cease your babbling*, but their reply might be that they were *Children of the Devil*, so he took a huge breath and boomed, "I come in the name of Jesus and command you to cease this babbling."

The women cackled; the men drew closer, torches in hand.

Under a Dark Star

Into his mind came Karl's quotation. *All that it takes for evil to triumph is for good men to do nothing.* He bent down to the fire, picked up a log and hurled it further along the dirt road. Then flung another. The two men brandished their torches in front of his face. The women sounded as if they were attempting to put some curse on him. He refused to listen. "If you are Children of the Devil then you must know, as does the Devil himself, that Almighty God is the most powerful spirit, and nothing you say can harm me."

The men snarled but backed away.

Emboldened by this welcome appearance of weakness, Josh crept round in front of Raffles and turned to face the men. One commenced what appeared to be some sort of dance and the other shook his torch at him. Josh saw his chance and his jaws closed around the man's wrist, shaking it wildly until he dropped the torch. Raffles bent down and hurled the flaming log into the puddles along the road. The man appeared insensible and unaware of the blood dripping from his wrist, but the women weren't. They redoubled their efforts at cursing the good parson but Josh was losing patience with these ragtag ne'er-do-wells and he rushed at them, barking furiously. As if pursued by a pack of wolves, they fled.

The two men were not so easily defeated. Both now seemed to have come out of their trance-like state and decided that a good fist fight was the way to deal with this troublesome parson.

Raffles held his arms wide as they approached with maniacal grins on their faces and threatening fists in front of their chests. He smacked their heads together and they dropped to the ground. Josh, who'd rushed over to assist, looked as bewildered as any dog could look. He sat down next to the triumphant parson who turned to him and said, "I didn't think I'd get away with that trick yet again!" Josh wagged his tail and Raffles added, "I suppose it helps to be very tall." He didn't mention his girth.

Under a Dark Star

From the edge of the woods, the twins and the carter approached slowly and without a word, dispersed the remaining logs on the fire and put out the flames. Raffles easily hauled the scrawny men out of the path of the horse and cart and propped them up under the shelter of a tree.

With the road now clear, all four climbed aboard the cart.

"Now yer know why I didn't wanna come," said the carter. "It was them twins that made me. They wanted to find out what happened to some young fella who left Ryde and went to Kaddakay. I ask you, all this trouble because of these silly girls! Know anything about the man?"

How could Raffles answer? "I've never been to Kaddakay and I'm not sure I want to." That would have to suffice. He moved across to make room for Josh and looked down at him. "My, you're a soggy doggy! Are you coming up?" Josh barked once and dashed off towards Norwell Farm.

"Fine dog that," said the carter.

"Indeed, indeed. He could easily have cut across country but he's not one to shy away from his duty." Then he remembered that he was not supposed to know Josh. "Well, so it seems."

"Been chased by Tridd's hell-hounds, I reckon."

Raffles tucked himself under the canvas, ensured that the twins were behind him then said, "I'll be glad when today is over."

"There's more troublemakers scattered around Norwell. Something's up. Yer mark my words. I nearly turned back. 'Tain't safe, I said to myself, 'tain't safe." He peered across to the hunched parson to see if he could hear. The parson screwed up his face against the cruel elements, glanced at the carter and nodded. The carter seemed to be anxious to make him aware of further strange happenings. "Thunder and lightning, there was, over Kaddakay. Somebody up there," the carter pointed to the sky, "don't like them, that's for sure."

Raffles decided this was not the time to point out the error in this line of thinking and sat quietly until they arrived at the farm, where pandemonium had broken out.

Chapter Twenty-Five
Daniel
"Dark, shifting shadow"

Daniel looked around the windswept, wet sandy beach. It was quite different from Wintergate Bay. Both had sheer cliffs, but this bay's were three times as high and not the beautiful white chalky ones of home. These were a mucky yellow sandstone, much of which had slipped onto the beach. In the dark it was difficult to tell which was which. He led Nancy to a nook in the cliffs which provided a little shelter. He rubbed her sodden forehead. "It's easing up now, old girl. The rain will soon stop."

"Who you talking to?" Jim Brantiani demanded.

"My donkey, of course. She hates the rain." Brantiani scoffed. As he was known to be one of Tridd's enforcers, Daniel added, "We'll be ready as soon as the ship is sighted." No point in teasing a bear.

"You'd better be."

Daniel showed no sign of his dislike for both the man and his mission and allowed the meaner of the Brantiani brothers to have the last word. His eyes were taking in the slack organization of this wrecking with men becoming increasingly anxious and hostile to each other. Where was Tridd? Being here would be in vain if Tridd wasn't seen to be involved.

Daniel, wearing his leather cape and a woollen muffler knitted by Becky, watched the waves leaping onto the rocks which led out from the shore for about a hundred yards. In high tides many boats could safely pass over them but the tide was quite low – very much in Tridd's favour. And the crashing white heads of the waves, which usually alerted sailors to the danger, were lost in the swell. Worse still, the wind was blowing from the south-west – straight onto the shore.

Then he heard a dog bark: Josh. Instantly he whistled and when Josh didn't appear, he whistled again. The wind should carry the sound but there was no sign of Josh. And when Tridd sauntered down onto the beach he'd only got one dog. Where was the other he'd seen earlier?

"I told you not to bring that mangy dog of yours." Tridd's eyes were narrow and his voice measured. "Don't expect a share of tonight's plunder."

Daniel tried to look aggrieved whereas he was relieved – relieved that Tridd thought he might need ill-gotten booty; he clearly hadn't worked out Daniel's objective, and that was reassuring. "Aye, he'll be in for a beating; he's meant to be with Becky."

Daniel concealed his surprise when Tridd said, "They can be beggars, these dogs. Don't let it happen again." When Tridd attempted a smile, Daniel was unnerved rather than reassured.

Everything depended on Josh having alerted Karl. Josh never failed but had he been confronted, silenced even, by one of Tridd's manglers? No. Josh knew when to run. Karl and sufficient Riding Officers would turn up – enough to stop the brigantine being wrecked and the crew killed. Mutterings that it was Portuguese and heading for London continued, and no sympathy was shown for the sailors forced to hug the deceptive shore.

From the top of the cliff, to the west, came the sound of a distant owl hooting. Then an owl hooted closer. Those 'owls' probably hooted every fifty yards all the way along the coast. No feathery owl intent on living would be out in winds like this. Tridd was smart enough to know this, he just didn't need to care.

At last Tridd strode around marshalling his troops, enjoying shouting instructions like an enraged sergeant. Three with spout lanterns were stationed in line with the rocks that jutted out into the sea. Another three were on the other side of the rocks. Tridd did not seem to be expecting the forces of law and order, though if any foolhardy customs' men did come down to the beach he'd made sure there'd be plenty of men with clubs to greet them. Thirty more men who had been squeezed under tarpaulins close to the opening of the chine came running towards Tridd.

Tridd turned to Daniel and said, "Get that donkey down to the shore line. Remember – no man works with me, you all work *for* me, but play your part and I'll see you get a fair share."

Such a changeable man! A strange way to command. "I'm no shirker, Mr Tridd." It stuck in his throat to call this violent, crass man "Mr" but it served the purpose well so long as he didn't have to say it again. His tactics of being tough enough to attract Tridd's attention, but not tough enough to do without him, had worked. A chill went down his spine and it had more to do with the twisted smile Tridd gave him than the bitterly cold wind.

Daniel stood on the water's edge and watched as those with the spout lanterns performed a strange rhythmic dance. As the three by the rocks held their spouts high towards the sea, allowing a thin shaft of light to be seen from the south west, the others held theirs low. In time to the rhythm of the waves they alternated up and down. The approaching brigantine, looking for a harbour or a sheltered cove, would be deceived into thinking that two ships had found such a haven and it would attempt to come close to calmer waters. Unbidden, tender thoughts seeped into his mind. Within a few weeks this sordid life would come to an end and he'd return to Lucy's soft warmth and the welcome challenge of Bethlehem Farm and a son to dote on and guide.

A whole host of unlikely owls hooted and from then on no one spoke and they all hunched against the dark sandstone cliffs. Where was Karl? He should be here now, waving flares from the top of the cliffs to alert the approaching ship. He should be mounting guard at the top of the chine. He should have men posted. Even if he could only manage five officers initially, reinforcements should be close behind. But there was only the sound of the crashing waves, and the force of the wind whipping his face and whistling past his ears. The thunder and lightning had passed so there was little hope that the stricken ship would see her fate. Dark clouds were in league with the dark star. And Daniel, for once in his life, became one of those who felt powerless.

Then he saw her. Limping directly towards him came the brigantine. The shouts of the crew could just be heard as they wrestled with the billowing and flapping of the partially reefed, torn sails still attached to the one mast left standing. They fought desperately to slow her progress into shore and the bravest sailors clung to the masts as they attempted to reef the sails fully. But it was too late. Lured too close into what they'd hoped was a safe haven, a mighty crash and terrible splintering of wood was met by a cheer from the men on the shore. The Brig keeled over, decks facing the shore, and cargo was snatched by the grasping waves.

As soon as the first casks washed ashore, the mob surged forward lighting their torches and staking them in the sand to form a guide up to the chine. Daniel took the chance to peek at his pocket watch: twenty minutes to eleven o'clock. Men filled empty sacks with anything that washed up from broken containers. Wood of any sort was prized for fires but flung in a heap for later pickings. Mules, old ponies and donkeys laden with port wine, cocoa, salt, tea and cork, struggled up and down as barrels and boxes were loaded onto anything with legs or wheels. Fishermen's old nets were tossed from the shore and outcrops of rocks and a roar of victorious laughter went up when several barrels of sardines were netted. On the cliff top, women joined in to help push overladen hand carts. A tense excitement filled the air. What bounty!

Teeming rain impeded visibility but from his assigned place on the sinking sand of the sea's edge, Daniel could see one of the sailors struggling to the beach. He watched in horror as Tridd knifed him and pushed him back into the sea.

Showing no emotion, Tridd waded out to another and meted out the same gory death. Then he climbed onto the rocks to deal with any who tried scrambling across.

For a few seconds Daniel stopped rolling in the barrels and watched, horrified to see that Tridd enjoyed killing; he had reserved this task for himself. No one else came near. Exhausted sailors were easy prey.

Most of the crew were still clinging to the sinking ship. Broken masts made poor floats with all the ropes and sails attached, but they served to reach one of the small boats still tied to the part of the deck above water. Several men hacked away at the ropes and freed a boat. They clambered in just as a wave washed it into the current which swirled the small boat, like a matchstick, to the far side of the bay and smashed it against the cliff.

Daniel took off his leather cape and flung it over Nancy. Wintergate Bay's rocks were small in comparison with those he now clambered across, racing to get to Tridd before he killed any more survivors. He ensured his knife was strapped to his boot and prepared to kill this fiend if he must. "That's enough, Tridd," all semblance of courtesy abandoned. He glanced over his shoulder and saw Zeb desperately hanging on to Nancy who'd bolted once

Daniel forsook her to chase Tridd. Good. That would keep Zeb away from this dangerous maniac.

A huge wave crashed against the rock and flowed across the top, drenching their boots. Tridd kicked some seaweed away from his feet, then turned and faced Daniel. "You think you're the clever one around here? You ain't. Say goodbye, '*Mr* Tynton,'" he mocked.

Daniel grasped his knife just as this insane killer charged towards him across the large flat rock. He stepped aside within the second that Tridd reached him and kicked the back of his knee. Tridd was up in a flash slowly waving his dagger from side to side.

"Tridd, you don't need to kill the crew."

"I knew it! You know nothing! Nothing! If you think I'm gonna leave any witnesses, you're mad. Mad!" Then he continued with a sickening grin, "And that includes you."

Had Daniel been able to spare a glance at the beach, he might have seen that only Zeb watched the evil on the rocks, but Tridd was circling him like a shark, keeping one eye on the stricken ship and the other on the enemy within his ranks and Daniel's attention was focused on this dark, shifting shadow. He spared just a second to hope in vain that Karl was on his way down the chine.

"Put the knife down, Tridd."

Tridd let out a raucous laugh and, inch by inch, he closed in on Daniel. "You won't win, country boy. I'm tellin' you, nobody ever does!"

Daniel wondered if he could make his way closer to the ship but this was the last visible rock; surging waves hid the danger from hereon.

Sickened by the thought that he could be about to kill a man, he slowly eased back from his approaching foe. He must now stand his ground and try to disable this man. Aware that he was close to the edge of this great rock, still facing Tridd, he kicked back to clear some slippery seaweed out of the way. His foot went straight into the prepared trap – a deep hole. Tridd flung himself, knife held high, and thrust it towards Daniel who, unbalanced, was toppling backwards. Daniel seized the arm with the knife and hurled Tridd over onto the edge of the rocks where the knife clanged then was washed into the sea. He staggered to his feet and took in the sight of Tridd lying flat on his back, waves washing over him, cursing and swearing in his pain. Daniel backed away to watch if Tridd would recover. If he didn't then Daniel need only escort and warn any fleeing sailors.

Five escaping sailors, clutching each other for safety, waded towards Tridd. The captain held out his hand and hauled Tridd upright. Words were exchanged and three of them approached Daniel.

Daniel was wary. What had been said? Nevertheless he declared, "You're safe now." He knew that Tridd could not take on the six of them. But the brawniest struck him hard.

"Safe! With you and your knife? We know what you're about."

Daniel held his hands high, still clutching his knife. "I'm no threat to you, I've come to save you from *him*."

"We saw what you did to the unarmed man who tried to save you from cracking your head open!" All three leapt on Daniel and bashed his head against a seaweed-covered rock.

"Leave him to me," yelled Tridd. "I'll hold him back while you get yourselves to safety."

The sailors needed no further encouragement and continued their struggle to safety. Tridd dragged the unconscious Daniel across the rocks, into the sea and to the ship. Ignoring the danger to himself, he pushed Daniel under the water and through a gaping hole into the partially submerged hull.

"I told you you wouldn't win." Tridd swam back to the rocks and muttered, "It's your own fault you'll die slowly – you shouldn't have knocked my knife in the sea." Tridd smirked at the thought of Daniel never regaining consciousness but if he did, he'd certainly freeze to death in the icy cold incoming tide in a pitch black broken hull. He enjoyed that thought; either way, he was dead.

He retraced his steps, all the time buffeted by the waves, and reached the shore and the dead bodies of the captain and his crew members. "All five, Brantiani! You're worthy of a bigger share of the spoils." A thin curl of a satisfied smile momentarily lit his face as he nodded at his accomplice and took his bloodied knife.

Zeb, having retreated with Nancy further along the bay, stared at the slaughter in horror and seeing only Tridd return, knew he would never see Daniel again. He rushed towards two boxes of oranges and strapped them to Nancy and led her towards the chine.

An arm came round his throat and a knife spiked his neck. "Can I trust you, Zeb?"

"Course you can, Leon. We've always looked out for each other, eh?"

"Aye, you're a good man, Zeb, but I've got to do it. I'll look after Becky for you."

Zeb pleaded, "Leon, I've never told what I've seen."

"What did you see?"

"Nothing. I saw nothing."

"You won't be seeing anything at all now." Leon Tridd slit the throat of the only man who'd ever trusted him.

Under a Dark Star

Chapter Twenty-Six
Karl
"Someone to come home to"

The door was solid oak, old oak, and probably timber from a wreck. Karl felt his way around the door. Now was not the time to examine how he could have done things better, so he set his mind to getting out. Could the bolts be forced? Doubtful. He took his knife from his belt. Perhaps he could find a gap and work out where the bolts are and then chisel the wood away sufficiently to remove the screws? He started chiselling at the easiest – where the middle one might be. His knife scraped against metal! A screw.

His shoulder ached, he suspected blisters were forming on his hands, but he did not stop until the bolt was rendered useless. He listened: footsteps. He stood beside the door. If anyone came in, they'd regret it.

The bolt at the top of the door squeaked as it was pulled back. The bolt at the bottom was drawn back too. The door did not open. Instead there was a knock. Was this some poor servant wondering why the door was damaged? No harm in seeing who it was. "Come in," called Karl as if he were sitting in his drawing room at Whitchester Manor.

The door opened slowly. He was still hidden by it. No one came in. In a flash he seized the door, pulled it wide and cautiously looked out. There was nothing to be seen.

"You must be very quick and follow me."

He did not need to be told twice. It was the voice of the woman called 'Flo' who was already standing on the staircase leading up to her room. He pulled the door closed, pushed the bolts across and dashed up the stairs to her room. "Thank you," was all he said as he rushed towards the window and threw out the rope attached to the grappling iron he'd left in her bedroom.

"No, no."

She too, it seemed, was a person of few words.

"Yes, you must come with me." Karl had no time for a woman to have second thoughts.

"No! First I go to kitchen and feed dogs."

Her way of speaking puzzled him. "There's no time."

"Dogs are outside. I must bring them in with meat. We escape when I return."

"Ah!" Now he understood. "Together we shall go to kitchen." He groaned quietly: he was speaking like her and he didn't have time to spend playing games even with this very delightful woman. He switched back to being Karl, he of the Viking blood. "First to the kitchen, deal with the dogs, then follow me!"

~

The ride had been slow. Midnight had taken longer than usual to negotiate the steep slope down from Tridd's fort. It was only to be expected, of course, for he was carrying two people. Trotting was the fastest they could manage in the dark and torrential rain. Now, having escorted her past the honking geese, he hammered non-stop on the door.

"Thank God! You've taken your time Flowers."

"My apologies, sir." Flowers glanced at the bedraggled woman standing behind Karl but made no comment. "We were concerned about you. I believe something unexpected is happening."

Under a Dark Star

"Indeed, indeed." Karl pulled his rescued lady through the doorway. He now knew her name was 'Flo'. He was thoroughly wet with water dripping from the peak of his uniform cap and off the tips of his fingers. "Attend to Midnight. He'll be needed within ten minutes."

It was obvious to Flowers that the Lieutenant expected more than was possible in such a short time. "Sir, we have much to tell you."

"And I have much to tell you," said Karl.

The boys, who had not yet returned to their dilapidated cottage scuttled towards him with upturned little faces and pleading eyes. "We'll take Midnight, sir. He'll come with us – he likes us!"

"Back in ten minutes, understand?" They nodded and he wondered if they'd ever learnt how long ten minutes was.

Riding astride on Midnight behind Karl with her head tucked against his back, Flo had fared slightly better than he had. Karl had tied his leather cloak around her but she still shivered in the draught from the open door, so he ushered her to the comparative warmth of a fireside seat. Next he dashed up the stairs and returned in another set of uniform clothes and he also brought a clean nightshirt for Flo. "Tomkins, take this lady to my room where she can change into this." He held out his striped cotton nightshirt to Flo and said, "My apologies. This is the most suitable garment I can find." He allowed himself an apologetic look before reverting to his more usual authoritarian style. "Show the lady my room and wait for her and escort her back past the prisoners." Seeing Buckby putting a kettle of water on the stove, he said, "Good man. Tea – and fast!"

Flo's eyes betrayed her thoughts on the nightshirt but, in keeping with the need to move fast, she took the long shirt and swiftly followed Tomkins up the stairs to Karl's room.

Flowers saw his chance at last. "Sir, I must tell you..."

"Be quick about it and then be ready for action." Karl glanced at his pocket watch. It was nearly eleven o'clock.

Flowers beckoned Tutte over and they all sat around the table. "Sir…"

"Hurry man, get on with it."

Tutte took over. "The geese were making a terrible racket. Flowers investigated. A black and white dog, possibly Tynton's, was barking for attention. The dog sat down and appeared friendly, as if it wanted something. Flowers spotted a pouch tied around its neck but the dog ran when he tried to retrieve it."

Flowers took his story back. "It's my belief that the dog was carrying a message."

Karl pursed his lips and thumped his fists on the table. "Damn!" Most certainly Josh had been carrying a message. No doubt a warning about the planned wrecking. There was no time to ponder further. "Right! This is what we're doing now!" He paused to watch Tomkins escort Flo down the stairs. Even in that shapeless garment and with damp hair she was the most exotically beautiful woman he'd ever seen. The interruption to his concentration did not go unnoticed by Tutte and Flowers who exchanged knowing glances. Only once she was seated by the fire and Tomkins and Buckby had joined them at the table did Karl begin again. "Right! A ship is to be wrecked tonight." He anticipated the question on Buckby's parted lips. "Yes, *tonight*. If at all possible we must stop this. Tridd is calling out every able-bodied man and we five have no hope whatsoever of catching them all. I want you, Buckby – you're the fastest – to ride over to Laurie's Point. Call them all out; every Riding Officer available, and I want them back here within the hour. Furthermore, I want a cutter launched, with instructions to pick up any wrecked sailors or passengers and they are to land as many men as possible to help their comrades on shore. " He scribbled a note for Buckby to take

Under a Dark Star

and he surprised himself by remembering to call the Riding Officers by their new name – The Coast Guard.

Out of the corner of his eye, Karl watched Flo search for cups. "Mugs!" he yelled. "They're on hooks above the sink. Milk is under it. Tea is in the caddy above the mugs." He paused, and the men observed him watching her. "Tomkins, as soon as we're finished here, light the rooftop fire brazier."

"Yes sir!"

"Get the boys to maintain it – remind them it's the signal for the Coast Guard. We have to hope they'll see it through this foul weather and be forewarned and ready by the time you get there, Buckby. If it can be seen out to sea, it might also alert the unfortunate ship to the proximity of the land."

The two boys rushed in through the door and shouted. "All done! He's munching now."

"Shut the door!" yelled Buckby.

"Have you got names for them yet?" Karl turned to Tomkins.

"Not yet, sir. We…" he turned to Buckby who nodded, "we wanted to talk to you about that."

"Later."

Flo brought four mugs of milky tea to the table. Two little faces looked longingly at her. "I make you some tea," she said, "come with me." And she ushered the boys away from the table.

That was a French accent. Surely not. Karl pursed his lips. "Tomkins, take the boys up to the rooftop now and get that fire alight. They can have their tea once it's blazing. Then get down here fast, in uniform. I want you back in two minutes. Got that?"

Tomkins leapt up and pulled the boys back from Flo's shepherding. "Yes sir." He wasn't going without his tea though and took a gulp.

The boys had heard and were ready for action. "The rain's stopped, sir. That'll be good for the fire."

"And us," muttered Buckby.

Karl downed his tea. What chaos. Only the methodical Tutte and the inventive Flowers sat silently waiting for orders. "You three, get your uniforms on. If we move fast, we may be able to stop a wrecking. Maybe save some lives. If not, then the best we can do is to make as many arrests as we can. Tridd is to be brought to me alive if possible." He stood up, grabbed Buckby's mug before he had a chance to finish it, and shouted, "Out, Buckby! Bring every man you can."

Karl strode over to Flo who was watching the kettle. "Tomorrow I hope to learn how you got out of your room."

"I have a key."

She had a key? She'd tricked Tridd?

"And here is key to big gates in the wall. I don't have key to main door."

He wanted to know more but he must concentrate on arresting her captor. "All you need do is keep this fire burning in here and keep an eye on the boys and their blaze on the roof."

"You should take some meat with you."

He looked at her with respect. "For the dogs! Of course."

She handed him a chunk. "I have found this." She pointed to a cupboard above the sink.

Karl grabbed a leather pouch and she dropped it in before he pulled the strings tight. "Thank you." They'd make a good team.

She nodded with just a trace of a smile and Karl allowed himself the luxury of a couple of seconds to return it. With all this turmoil around her, she was astute, calm and considerate. Someone to come home to.

Please, God, don't let her be French, not the old enemy.

Chapter Twenty-Seven
"Permanently thwarted"

The torrential rain had eased and the clouds parted enough to reveal a misty moon. Karl wished it were brighter so he could see the time on his pocket watch. It would probably be Tuesday morning now. Lying flat, the scrubby gorse just hid him and also Flowers and Tutte. Tomkins was posted as lookout at the inn so that the Riding Officers could leave their horses and not alert the wreckers. He wondered how much longer he'd have to wait for reinforcements. Being a poorly paid Riding Officer or Coast Guard was rarely regarded as a full-time occupation. Understandably, most spent much of their time attempting to make money in some other manner too and, when needed urgently, they'd be hard to find. Karl looked over his shoulder just in case they were particularly good at sneaking up on people.

"Don't bother attempting to write down any more names, Flowers. We might as well say the whole population of Kaddakay is stripping that brigantine, even of its figurehead."

"Except the innkeeper, Tolly, and his wife, sir."

"And the parrot, don't forget the parrot!" Karl grinned at Flowers. They'd agreed with the very anxious Tolly that if he took care of the horses, he'd be paid two sovereigns. When Karl slapped a gold coin on the counter to encourage him to agree, the parrot had announced *And one for Polly*.

Now he looked down at his once white breeches. He needed to wear this smart yet impractical uniform if he was going to make arrests. The fact that they had become covered in mud was to his advantage. Tomkins and Buckby had warned him several times that the wreckers knew they were acting illegally and some would kill to protect the trade. It was not illegal to take away the cargo of accidentally wrecked ships but there were too few of those. As Buckby never tired of saying, *how else were the villagers supposed to survive in cold, wet winters?* Impatient for action, he sighed. Unbidden, but not unwanted, another thought stole his attention. Flo's luscious dark hair – how he'd love to bury his head in her neck. He'd always long for Lucy; there was no denying it, but what was the point? There was no future for them. He'd agonized for too long.

Buckby, scrambling towards them, broke the spell. The reinforcements had arrived: only five, and Tomkins and Buckby. "A cutter's on its way, sir," said Tomkins.

Karl wasted no time in explaining his strategy. "I'm interested in only one man. Tridd is our priority. I'm sure you men from along the coast know of him?" They nodded. "If we capture him, this abominable wrecking will stop. No arrests are to be made yet other than Tridd's." There was silence as the men absorbed the fact that they were not ten against more than a hundred, but ten against one. However, that one was Tridd. With dogs. "We shall therefore watch for Tridd. He is likely to stay on the beach until everyone else has gone."

Buckby interrupted. "Sir, Jim Brantiani always stays with him, guarding his back."

"Then we'll arrest him too."

"Sir," Buckby's fear led him to continue. "He usually ties two or three dogs to stakes when he is on the beach but he holds the leads as he comes up the chine."

Karl felt an overwhelming sense of pity for the two permanently thwarted Riding Officers detailed to stop smuggling and wrecking on this forsaken part of the island. "Tonight, Buckby, you will be the hero." Karl grinned. Buckby looked alarmed. "Here, take this." He handed him the leather pouch. "Sling that at the dogs and I have it on good authority they'll very much appreciate a thick chunk of meat. With only the one piece, they'll probably fight over it – to the death maybe." He noticed Buckby's anxious expression so added, "We're downwind, they can't smell it yet."

There was a flaw in this plan and Karl knew it.

He was also watching for Daniel but though over a hundred villagers trekked up and down the chine pushing or pulling donkeys, ponies and hand carts, not one of them was Daniel. He was only fifty yards away from the path that led away from the chine and he would certainly have spotted the way he walked: confidently, easily; not like the panting villagers. Neither could he see him amongst those ferrying the goods towards the church, nor could he see Zeb Tynlan, his scrawny cousin.

Tutte nudged him and hissed, "The cutter!"

One of the men from the Coast Guard at Laurie's Point whispered, "It's fitted with three swivel guns, sir."

This became immediately obvious as it drew level with the beach, signalled its intentions, then fired. The light cannons were not powerful enough to destroy vast areas, rather they peppered grape shot designed to injure or scatter an enemy. Their effectiveness began to show as donkeys broke loose and brayed, ponies bolted up the chine and men fled to the safety of the edge of the cliffs, just out of range. When the cutter turned, came in closer, rolled its guns to the shore side of the deck and began firing again, every man, woman and child escaped up the chine, clutching whatever they could manage. A dog howled and then tore up the steep slope, weaving in and out of the terrified villagers, dragging a wooden stake behind it. When it got to the top it stood still, sniffed the air then lowered its snarling head and trotted towards the group of customs' men who were now standing, watching the fleeing wreckers.

"Chuck that meat, Buckby!" Karl roared. "Throw it a good distance and make sure we're still down wind. Your life may depend upon it."

Buckby had hurled the pouch the moment he'd heard the word 'chuck'. "It'll take him a while to get his teeth through the leather and that should keep him occupied."

Karl picked up an abandoned two-pronged pitchfork used for raking in barrels from the sea. He circled round to the back of the ravenous dog and caught its lowered neck between the prongs. "Buckby! Here. Hold this dog down. Tomkins, you come too and bring that abandoned barrel. Tie it up and shove it in the barrel for the moment. I can't waste my ammunition on it." Karl handed them some nails he always kept in his pocket. "Make sure the lid is secure."

The flaw in the plan had been overcome. Tridd had not trained the dog to refuse food from all others except himself. Flo's actions once again contributed to the success of this night. Success? They'd been too late to stop the wrecking, Tridd was loose and Daniel was nowhere to be seen. He must turn this situation around.

Karl glanced at his men. They were clearly very cold and the gale-force wind chilled their damp clothes. The looks on the faces of those Buckby had brought over from Laurie's Point said one thing – *why are we here in this hopeless situation?* He must get them moving.

First he got them to search the beach. He grabbed one of the abandoned torches and swung it in a circle – the sign for the cutter to recognize friend from foe and stand off. They would patrol the bay, searching for survivors and be ready for action should it be required. There was no point in them sending men ashore here, not now. He glanced at his pocket watch, it was nearly one in the morning. Karl began the search for Tridd. He'd not come up the chine, unless he was extremely well disguised. That was a possibility. Perhaps that's why the dog had bolted up to the clifftop – to follow its master; but why was there only one dog?

Flo's management of the dogs crept into his mind and from there it was a short step to the room full of ships' figureheads. Surely Tridd wasn't out in this weather sawing off another trophy? He handed the torch to Buckby and told him to light any other torches the men had brought or seize one of the abandoned ones. Then he walked towards the rocks leading out to the wreck. With the clouds now parting, perhaps he could see a little further. He took out his telescope from his inside coat pocket and held it to his eye as he edged closer. He could just discern the bow being lapped by white-tipped waves. No the figurehead was still there. Then he focused on the stern. The Brig must have been tacking towards the shore because the bow was facing the wrong way for a passage to London and was supported by the submerged rocks. The stern had collapsed into the sea. No need to search for Tridd in that direction.

He turned around and all but tripped over bodies. Five of them. All knifed. All dead.

"Sir, there's another one here." Buckby sounded distraught. The rest of the men approached slowly.

Karl retrieved the torch from Buckby. Zeb lay several yards away with his throat cut. Rage flooded over Karl. "I want you all to comb this beach for any injured or dying wreckers or sailors." He breathed deeply in an attempt to control his fury. He must keep his thoughts focused on the mission he'd come so far to achieve. "Put them on one of these dozen or so abandoned carts. Wheel them up to the inn." Momentarily, he wondered how many had died from the gunshot. His stomach churned – had Daniel been caught in the fire? No, he'd have known to look out for the Coast Guard. He continued with his instructions. "Then remove the dead and lay them outside at the back of the inn."

As he spoke he saw their horror and revulsion turning to fear. They were right, of course. There were enough villagers to ambush them once they were out of gunshot distance. He must keep them moving. "In particular I am looking for Daniel Tynton." Then he noticed one of his men was missing. "Where's Tutte?" Tutte was running towards him from some distance away and when he got close, Karl knew it wasn't good news.

"Sir, there's footprints leading to the edge of the cliff. I suspect Tridd's escaped up a staked rope."

Chapter Twenty-Eight
Daniel
"The sound of hope"

A dark hand clutched Daniel's shoulder. It gripped tightly and pulled him up enough for another to reach under his arm and haul him out of the water. Two men cradled his body between theirs and something dry was laid over him. Rough hands began patting his face but attempts to revive him failed. The men rolled him on his side and began to moan loudly and others joined in.

Daniel stirred. The moaning stopped. He could hear only the slopping of the sea as it surged against the inside of the damaged hull. Where was he? A faint memory returned: Tridd sneering; men attacking. He put his hand up to the back of his head and felt a large bump. That's right, he'd been smashed against the rocks. But where was he now? He looked around and could see nothing, it was black as pitch. Whose palms were these patting his face? Whose strange voices?

Hands propped him up on what appeared to be a sloping bench and held him there. Like a primitive musical instrument, the sound of the whistling wind drew his attention to a hole ahead of him. And through the top part of the hole he caught sight of grey clouds scudding past, tipped with white as they passed the silvery crescent moon. He put his hand up to his sore head. No sticky blood, just a painful bump. He shivered. He glanced sideways and saw two eyes. Then teeth – a smile! A whole row of eyes appeared and acquired toothy smiles. The man next to him spoke. It sounded like "hausa".

Recognizing that it was probably some sort of greeting, Daniel said, "Hello," and the man responded with a broad smile. A feeling of heartfelt gratitude flooded over him. "Thank you." It was all he could manage.

The eyes and teeth continued to smile and then a whole torrent of noises poured forth. There was another noise. Clanging. These were Africans in chains. Slaves! Something Karl never stopped talking about.

His astonishment turned to outrage. Had they been deserted by the crew? Those very men he'd risked his life to save and who had turned and attacked him, had they abandoned these men to their fate? Death by drowning, or freezing. His anger warmed his blood. His wet clothing was stealing what little warmth his reviving body might generate. He took off the top half of his clothes and threw them on the bench and wrapped what he now realized was a thin blanket around his shoulders. With his fingers he felt the face of the man next to him who, mercifully, didn't object. Around his neck hung some kind of metal tag; he ran his hand across the surface – despite his fingers becoming numb, with his nails he discerned that something was engraved upon it. He moved on to trace down to his hand. The man was wearing an iron cuff linked to the next man by a chain. From there he went to his knees and down to his feet. More chains. He gave the blanket back and cautiously slipped back into the water and felt his feet touch boards. He made his way to the end of the row following the chains the men held up. Excited chatter burbled along the row and began to spread to what must be another chamber full of slaves. The sound of hope.

The end of the chain was not padlocked but secured to an iron ring. The padlock must be at the other end. Anyway, he had no key. The only good news was that the chains were quite light and possibly could be forced open.

He warily crossed to the hole and waited for an opportunity to push out into the open sea then swam to the nearest rock which was visible only when white-tipped waves surged over it then drained away. He clambered up, and stood ankle deep in water. If he shouted, it might be Tridd who heard. So he whistled. Josh might be the only one to hear. Please God, let him hear. He peered towards the cliff. He could pick out very little and all was quiet. Two rows of torches lit the beach – one flickered out as he watched. Was that movement he saw at the base of the chine? Yes, someone was walking up the chine and carrying a torch. This might be his only chance. He shouted. The crashing waves and whistling wind were too much competition. An orange glow could be seen some distance away to the right. Could that be a fire on the roof of Watch House? Yes. Someone was signalling. So Josh must have got through to Karl. Good. Had Karl and his men cleared the beach and taken Tridd captive? He thought for a moment. Dear God, he must have been unconscious for some long time. A great wave crashed across the rock and knocked him over. He was cold; he must act fast. The best course of action eluded him. How could he get some help to these poor men? He struggled to his feet. He must shout again and again. And whistle with all his might. The wind whisked his voice away towards the shore but there was no answer. And there was no sign of Josh. Would he be drowned or die of the cold before he could return to the slaves? He picked up a few small stones and a couple of larger ones and swam, slowed not only by fatigue and the cold but also by the weight he carried in his pockets. He threw a few pebbles away, a small sacrifice to keep the hope in those eyes alive.

Under a Dark Star

A huge wave surged and slammed him back onto the rocks as if he were a wooden puppet. Blood seeped into the water as he slid into the rising tide.

Under a Dark Star

Chapter Twenty-Nine
Norwell Farm - Lucy
"The plan was simple"

Monday 17th March
The wind howled, drowning all other sounds of the night except the geese honking. George Lytton put a couple of large logs on the fire. "It's a raw night, indeed it is." He rubbed his hands together and peered out of the window. "Perhaps I should make a quick inspection of 'The Goose House'." He turned to smile at Lucy, "Grand name for a shelter, don't you think?" Before Lucy could reply, he made a decision. "I'll wait until the rain stops."

Emmeline wrung her hands. "My poor, dear Mr Raffles. He shouldn't be out in this weather. Do you think he will have had the good sense to postpone coming?"

Lucy raised her eyebrows. "Nothing stops our parson when he has something important to do." She wondered if that was good news or bad for Emmeline as the parson's arrival this very evening was eagerly anticipated. He was coming to fetch his expectant wife to take her to the comparatively ill-furnished parsonage the following day.

The clock in the hall chimed nine and Emmeline looked out of the window. "Oh!" Scrambling over the garden gate was a squirming, wet animal. "I do believe it's Josh! What can he be doing here?"

Josh stood on the doorstep, paws apart, and barked frantically.

Under a Dark Star

Lucy leapt up and ran towards the door with Major Lytton overtaking her at the last second. He unbolted the door, put out his hand in an attempt to keep the dirty, wet dog from running all over the house, but failed to catch him. Josh rushed to Lucy, stood with his paws wide and barked again. Lucy put her arms around him and tried to calm him. "Shush, Josh, you'll wake little Freddie." Josh sat down and put his long snout up towards her as she felt around his neck. "What have you got here?" Josh whined and she knew immediately that something was very, very wrong.

Major Lytton peered out into the dark, blustery night, and bolted the door again. "The geese have quietened." He turned to Lucy. "What's the matter with this little fellow?"

Emmeline had joined Lucy, and Martha put her head around the door of the kitchen where the servants gathered in the quiet times. Lucy took the note from the leather pouch and read aloud.

"Karl, there is to be a wrecking tonight (Monday) not tomorrow. Tridd has included me. As many as a hundred expected. Attenfold rocks. Around ten o'clock. He's bringing dogs. No time to put this in code."

There was silence except for a slight swishing of Josh's tail.

Martha rushed to Lucy and grasped her arm. "Fluttenducks girl, whatever shall we do?"

"Oh Martha, does this mean Daniel is depending on Karl and Karl does not even know about it?"

George Lytton took the note from Lucy's outstretched hand and while he read it again, Martha filled the silence, shaking her head portentously as she said, "This needs a lot of thinking to be done."

"There's no need, Martha dear." Lucy looked utterly despondent. "I can see what is happening right now. Daniel is in danger from that Tridd and Karl will not be there to support him."

Martha perked up. "Our Lieutenant never, ever, not since I've known him…" She lost the thread, so began again. "No! He'll be there, he'll be there. Upon my honour, I know he and his Midnight will win the war." She clenched her fist and shook it.

Major Lytton, pursed his lips; it was evident he hadn't much faith in Martha's loyal words. He suggested they all, including Martha, move through into the warmth of the drawing room.

Lucy looked at the panting, dirty, wet friend at her feet. "Martha, fetch a towel for Josh's paws, please."

"Crumples, I'm slow tonight. I'll bring another for Josh to lie on. It be what Mrs Lytton would want, I think."

Lucy thanked her. "Yes, I'm sure Mrs Lytton would want you to look after our little hero but perhaps you should give him some water in the kitchen first, and if there's any of that mutton stew left over, give him that too."

Martha bustled away to the kitchen and Lucy followed while Major Lytton quietly apprised his wife of the situation.

Once the hero was less likely to shake rain and dirt all over the expensive furnishings of Norwell Farm, Lucy and Martha returned to the warm drawing room with the whining Josh following them.

It was only a matter of minutes before Josh was sprawled in front of the blazing fire. He'd done all he could for now and a little nap would not go amiss.

It was noticeable that Emmeline was troubled. After some discussion, it was decided that if Mr Raffles arrived tonight at all, it was likely to be within the next hour. They would wait and then in consultation with him, action would be decided upon.

No one could sit still. Lucy, having put on a brave face whilst out in the hall, now found herself feeling sick with fear. She recalled times past when her clandestine meetings with her beloved had to be far from her mother's prying eyes and those of

Karl too. The joy her memories engendered lasted mere seconds as the images were overtaken by the vision of Daniel facing Tridd and a hundred angry, grasping villagers as she imagined his true mission being discovered. None of them would see he was doing this for their own betterment. They would turn on him like a pack of – oh no, they had dogs. What sort of dogs? He was good with dogs. She could not stop a tear spilling from her watery eyes.

Josh shifted his position and nuzzled into the hem of her dress until he found her feet.

Mrs Lytton said she would make some tea and when Martha jumped up and said she would make it, Mrs Lytton firmly told her to sit back on the sofa next to Lucy, close her eyes and wait as it was likely she would be needed before the night was out.

Martha flopped down, threw her shoulders back and thrust her chest out. Needed. Chosen. What a long way she'd come since being a fisherman's wife. Flollops! She now had adventures! Daniel would be found safe at his lodgings with his cousin; Tridd might have escaped Lieutenant Thorsen's energetic attentions but the Lieutenant would catch him soon, of that she was sure. *Energetic attentions* – how she liked Lucy's words; Lucy always knew the right words. And she, a poor widow once just a step away from the Workhouse, will have played a part in the downfall of a very horrid man. She smiled at her assessment. In truth she knew her part was quite small. She put out her hand and held Lucy's gently, then closed her eyes.

Emmeline watched tenderly. She had almost forgotten that these two had been servants together in Karl's household at Watch House in Wintergate. Despite the change in Lucy's station in life, they would probably remain firm friends for the rest of their lives.

It was some while before Mrs Lytton arrived with a tray of tea but she had also made some proper cheese sandwiches, something she had always longed to do.

Under a Dark Star

Martha, comfortable in her dreams, dozed off: Lucy was wide awake, Major Lytton was busy with a pen and paper and Emmeline sat alert with her hands caressing her swollen middle. The rattle of the tea cups brought them all back to the matter in hand.

"Mr Raffles has not arrived and may not do so tonight," announced Major Lytton taking up a commanding stance as close to the hearth as the sprawling dog allowed. "I have sketched out a plan." He waved his piece of paper. "I shall first ascertain if Daniel has returned to his lodgings." He considered Lucy carefully. She was clearly very tired, a nursing mother should be with her child. "Lucy, you will stay here…"

"I cannot! I could not stay here and await news of my husband. Freddie sleeps through the night and will not need me until tomorrow morning."

Emmeline understood. "I can take care of Freddie. Are you able to give me some of your milk and I will see he is fed if you do not return in time."

"Ladies, ladies, I cannot allow…"

Mrs Lytton, having poured everyone a cup of tea, held up her hand gently. "My dear Major Lytton, Lucy is not a flower petal, she is a sturdy oak."

Lucy wasn't so sure about being an oak, but she appreciated the thought. "Indeed, Major Lytton, I think I can be useful. I know Daniel well and I think we should take Josh and he will follow me."

Major Lytton cleared his throat. "If you say so." He closed his eyes and chewed the end of the feather pen endeavouring to regain his train of thought. When he opened them though, he saw Lucy staring at Josh. Josh's nose was twitching and one ear was lifted above an open eye.

"Flumples! Someone is coming," Martha said unnecessarily.

Emmeline's face showed hope.

Major Lytton peered out of the window. "I can't see anything – good or bad. Though the geese are once again agitated." Honking confirmed his report.

Anxiety replaced Emmeline's hope. Lucy whispered to her that she was going to "see about Freddie's milk" and hurried to her sitting room.

"It's the carter!" Major Lytton rushed to the door and held up his hand to Emmeline. "Stay there until I have heard his news."

Emmeline drew in a deep breath. "Can he see Mr Raffles?"

No one responded. The parson was not easily overlooked. Josh, however, sat up and looked eagerly at the door.

Then came a shout from Major Lytton at the main door. "All's well with the parson!"

Emmeline could restrain herself no longer and struggling to her feet with one hand pushing herself away from the sofa and the other seeking to comfort her baby with a stroke or two, she bustled out into the hall and flung herself into the arms of the arriving parson.

While the devoted husband and wife reassured each other, Major Lytton took pity on the carter and the twins and suggested they shelter in the barn. "The cows are in there, mind. But there's plenty of good straw stacked at the back and room for the horse too. Up in the loft it's quite cosy."

Mrs Lytton added, "I'll send you some blankets and refreshment and you can sleep there until the morning."

Parson Raffles, relieved of his wet cloak and very wet hat, came in to a sea of welcoming faces.

Martha leapt into action. One of her favourite people in all the world had arrived and he was surely in need of a hot drink. Maybe she'd better make some more sandwiches. And the currant cakes would be welcomed too.

Under a Dark Star

"The Lord's blessing be upon you all." Parson Raffles bowed in greeting and the ladies returned it with a bob and Josh put up a paw which Raffles clasped and held. "My dear fellow, you were certainly faster on your paws than we were on our wheels!" He wiped his spectacles, put them back on and scrutinized Josh's eyes. "Something wrong?" Josh padded over to Lucy and sat down by her feet. She was grateful not only for her dog's support but also that he conveyed clearly that something was very wrong indeed.

As soon as everyone was seated, Major Lytton explained.

Once he'd finished, Raffles comforted Josh. "The bearer of alarming news? No wonder you're looking disconcerted." He raised an eyebrow. "I would be too."

Lucy slipped back in to the drawing room as inconspicuously as possible and sat down.

Major Lytton was keen to continue outlining his plan of action. "Mrs Tynton understandably feels that her husband could be in danger. She has told me before that he does not trust Tridd and he thinks he has murderous intentions."

Raffles leaned forward on his chair and examined Lucy's expression. "Murderous? Towards Daniel?"

"Daniel thinks Tridd is not sound in his mind. That he is driven by hate and too great a love of power and the things of this world. He sees Daniel as a threat to all he has built up."

"Well, that is true! Daniel is most certainly a threat."

"It was agreed," continued Lucy, "that if Daniel were to be involved in the wrecking, which of course is what they needed to convict Tridd indisputably, then Karl would be there with his men. Daniel would be protected. But the note around Josh's neck tells of as many as a hundred men, and dogs, and…" Lucy took a deep breath, "the note was never delivered to Karl so he will not know. Daniel will be on his own and if he tries to save any of the crew…"

The clock in the hall struck ten.

Major Lytton helped Lucy. "And the time mentioned in the note was ten o'clock." He handed the note to Raffles. Having regained control of the discussion, he hurried on. "Your wife has volunteered to stay here and look after Freddie, Mrs Tynton insists on coming with me, and we shall take Martha, for propriety you understand."

Martha pushed the door open with her elbow and brought in a tray. "Oh 'tis proper that *I* go, Mr Raffles, as I shall be needed."

Major Lytton stifled his rising anxiety that he was to be hampered by two women. He took a deep breath to continue only to be thwarted yet again.

"I have brought you fortifies. I knowed you just thought it would be tea but some fortifies seemed to me to be what was needed. And I am here to be needed."

Raffles came to her rescue. He was sitting next to Emmeline on the sofa and they were both stroking their ample stomachs. "We are most grateful that you have brought us refreshments *to fortify* us before our night's exertions."

Major Lytton sighed. Did the rotund parson think he was coming too? It would have to be one of the shire horses to carry him. He managed to stop himself from saying, *as I was saying*, and repeated his plan, "We shall first visit Mr Tynton's lodgings. It may be that he has not gone with the wreckers." Lucy shook her head but he continued. "Or, by the time we arrive there, it may be all over and he and his cousin will have returned."

From his conversations with Karl and Daniel, Raffles knew a thing or two about these operations. "Stripping a ship of its cargo, even with a hundred men or more, takes many hours. The only way that it can be shortened is if Lieutenant Thorsen somehow manages to interrupt their activities. And from what we know of him, Tridd is not likely to give up his booty easily."

"Nevertheless," Major Lytton pressed on, "I think we should go there first and it is not out of our way."

"That's true," said Lucy, though she wasn't keen to meet Zeb's wife.

"Perhaps, Lucy, you and Martha should not be seen at the lodgings, we don't want you to be a cause for curiosity."

Lucy readily agreed. It was quite clear that she'd agree to anything so long as they set off immediately. If Karl were here, he'd be in charge, and they'd be well on their way by now.

Meanwhile, Martha was busy proving their need of her by shovelling the ashes from the fire into the tin box which fitted snugly into the wooden carriage heater, and placed it in the hearth to keep warm. "As soon as we are ready, I'll put this in the box and it will keep us all warm." She knew it would only serve to warm Lucy's feet, but something was better than nothing.

"But now," said Major Lytton firmly, "we should all eat these grand refreshments we have been furnished with." Raffles needed no encouragement and had a plate of sandwiches and cake on his lap already thanks to the attentions of his wife. "And then we must change into warm, weatherproof clothes." He looked at Raffles and pursed his lips. Though a big man himself, George Lytton knew the parson would not fit into any of his clothes. He rushed into the hall and brought the parson's cloak and hat to dry by the fireside. As for the ladies, he'd have to take them in Karl's sturdy carriage. He hoped the wheels would cope with the rutted roads. "If we find Mr Tynton is not at his lodgings then we should make our way to the cliff tops and see what is happening. If there is activity there and no sign of the customs' men, then I will ride on to Watch House and belatedly alert them."

"And I will take care of the ladies," said Raffles.

In the end, the plan was simple.

Chapter Thirty
"Hound from Hell"

Simple? It would have been if only George Lytton had been allowed to ride out on his best horse with just a couple of his tough, trusted labourers. But here they were trundling along the muddy, rutted roads in the Lieutenant's trusty old, heavy carriage with a lady and her maid wearing two cloaks each and with their dresses tucked up above their ankles with the aid of ribbon belts. At least they were wearing boots, albeit flimsy ones. The dog, also riding in the carriage, was likely to be an asset at some point. He wasn't so sure about the enormous parson crammed inside too. He'd had to put four strong horses to the carriage to give extra speed and the possibility of pulling it out of ditches. Still, he was on a good horse himself and well wrapped up with his greatcoat and attached cloak shielding him from the worst of the weather. The Lieutenant's coachman was at last earning his keep with trying to keep the carriage moving on the road and he had to admit he was damned good at it.

He rode ahead carrying a flaming torch until he came across a disturbing sight. He flagged the carriage to a halt. Josh, having been determined to sleep until now, put his paws up to the window of the carriage and growled.

"What is it, Josh?" said Lucy breathing heavily. So long as it wasn't Daniel in trouble, she could be brave.

Major Lytton rapped on the window and Raffles pulled it down just a little so that Josh did not attempt to get out. "There's a dead dog here on the side of the road. A brown beast of a thing. His horse could not stand still and swung him around. "There's the remains of another animal further along. Half eaten by the looks of it."

Raffles put his forefinger up. "Ah, I thought Josh looked like he was being chased by a hound from hell. Probably this dog." He paused while trying to trace the reason for the dog to be dead. Surely not killed by Josh? Then truth seeped into his mind. "And it stopped to eat the weasel in the centre of the star we encountered. Poisoned." Realizing that no one would fully understand, he lowered his finger and said, "It is of little consequence. We should press on." In the greater scheme of things, he decided, the dog had died in a good cause. If he'd caught up with Josh...

And now they were stuck in the mud.

~

It was nearly two o'clock on Tuesday morning by the time they reached Tynlan House.

Lucy, Martha and Raffles stayed in the carriage. Lucy privately wondered if it would have been sufficient just for Josh to sniff around whereas poor Mrs Tynlan was now looking understandably perturbed at the sight of such a large man on her doorstep with Josh, but no Daniel and no Zeb. Nevertheless, it completely ruled out Daniel being safe at home.

Now they were drawing close to the rocks mentioned in Daniel's note. George Lytton rapped on the window again and Raffles opened it sufficiently to hear him say, "There's inadequate cover to hide this carriage. I suggest we leave it here on the road with the coachman and Mrs Tynton and Martha. Mr Raffles and I shall investigate."

"Major Lytton, I should like to come too; I shall fret if I am left here."

Under a Dark Star

"No, Mrs Tynton. It may be dangerous. We shall reconnoitre and then report back to you." He glanced at his pocket watch. "It's half past two and you'll be glad to know the rain has stopped."

George Lytton tied his horse to the back of the carriage and assisted Raffles in alighting. Josh waited for no permission and raced to the edge of the cliff. Had George Lytton been on his own, he might have stealthily collected information but, with the parson unable to conceal himself in any way whatsoever, they simply marched to the edge of the cliff. The oncoming tide covered most of the rocks which stretched out into the sea. The slim crescent moon allowed no more than a glimpse of white-topped waves crashing along the shore and on the huge boulders signifying the start of the run of rocks out to sea. Several abandoned torches did allow the two men to come to the conclusion that no one was still on the beach – neither villagers nor customs' men. Josh, however, was not convinced and stared out to sea and whined.

In the carriage, Martha was feeling rather indignant. "Weconoytrum? Whatever does that mean? It's *your* husband what's gone missing and you should be allowed to do any weconoytrumming that needs doing."

Lucy laid her hand on Martha's. Oh how she loved this good woman. "Major Lytton was an officer in the Army, he's just taking a careful look and he's going to report back."

Martha was not at all impressed. "Well, when I think back to all those adventures you had!" She looked triumphant. "You! You on the beach when the smugglers were all caught. And you being nearly killed and all." She watched Lucy carefully before adding, "If it hadn't been for our good Lieutenant, you might not have been here. Ever." And for good measure she felt compelled to add, "Not at all."

"I can no longer behave like that: I am the mother of a baby." Despite her own feelings, she smiled at Martha for Martha adored Karl and clearly always would.

Undeterred, Martha continued. "And what about you and Josh in that sinking boat? That Major Lytton doesn't know about that, does he?"

"This is not the time to remind me of times when I nearly died."

"But you didn't die! We should be allowed to look for our Mr Tynton."

This was not the time, either, to remind Martha that she had come to the island as her maid and as such, she should not be offering unwanted advice. Then Lucy relented. Martha was speaking as her friend, not as her maid. The truth was she was the greatest friend Lucy had ever known. She had made her feel welcome at a time when no one welcomed her anywhere. They had shared such joys together when they were both servants in Karl's quarters in Watch House. So Lucy voiced only the thought constantly riding high. "I think Major Lytton is recognizing that I have little Freddie to think of too."

Now Martha was quiet.

Josh was first back to the carriage and he whined at the door. Lucy opened it but Josh did not jump in; he stood back, giving her plenty of space to alight.

George Lytton put up his hand to assist Lucy and, following a second thought, he assisted Martha too. "I've left Mr Raffles walking towards the chine. I've given him my torch. Can't have him walking straight over the cliff top, can we?" He tried a smile, then looked up towards the coachman. "Move the carriage and my horse further towards the chine; stay well back. I'll take one of the lamps and you can put the other out. Light it again if you're sure we are the ones approaching." Turning to Lucy he said, "Here, take this lamp, it should last well until dawn. As the rain has stopped and the beach seems deserted, I feel confident that you will be safe to take a look."

"I intend to search thoroughly, Major Lytton."

"I will too." Martha pulled her cloaks around her and trudged behind Major Lytton and Lucy. Josh overtook them all. "As Josh is leading, I shall be the sheep dog and herd you all along." Her words were lost in the wind.

Raffles awaited them at the top of the chine. On reaching the beach, the wind howled as it soared up the cliffs and Martha and Lucy clung to their escaping cloaks. Lucy soon gave up and picked up one of the still-burning torches. Was that a boat she saw? She waved her torch but there was no response. If it *had* been a boat, it was now out of sight and into the next bay. She mentioned it to George Lytton.

His reaction was swift. "A boat? Possibly the Coast Guard cutter heading back to their station." He peered out to sea. "The wreck!" Still clutching his own flaming torch, he quickened his pace over the wet sand and the washed-up seaweed. Footprints betrayed the work of the wreckers. Here and there were signs that cargo had reached the shore and had been abandoned. He stood at the base of the huge boulders and looked out towards where he'd caught sight of the broken Brigantine. Clouds chased across the face of the moon. Lucy caught up with him and lent the light of her lamp. "I can't see anything, can you?"

"Not a thing," responded Lucy.

She and Martha started tramping along the beach, west along the shoreline which was littered with casks and broken barrels, then eastward along the cliff face where all they found was a small cave with nothing but an upturned boat at the back. Josh would not leave the rocks.

Under a Dark Star

Raffles tried to interpret the meaning of the many footprints and wheel ruts. "It seems to me," he said as he drew alongside George Lytton, "the wreckers were disturbed. Lieutenant Thorsen might have been alerted by some other means and arrived with a goodly band of men. Arrests made, perhaps, and a gaol full of prisoners!" There was no response from his brother-in-law. Josh was busy sniffing the sand near his feet, then looking at the rocks, then sniffing the sand again. Raffles looked down. "Some sort of a scuffle here."

George Lytton, never having heard of a victory over Tridd before, decided more needed to be done. "Join me in shouting?"

Raffles took a deep breath and they both bellowed out to sea. They listened, and Josh's ears were held high, nose twitching. Again they shouted and again the onshore wind whipped away their voices. They turned to face the shore and Raffles said, "Perhaps someone will hear us this way." After much roaring it was agreed that if anyone was hiding, they were not going to show themselves. Only Martha and Lucy responded by returning.

"Come ladies," said George Lytton, "let us return to the carriage. I think we should go on to Watch House."

Discouraged, Lucy followed slowly. Anxiety conquered tiredness and she looked around for Josh. He must have gone on ahead.

Chapter Thirty-One
Daniel
"As cold as the grave"

He became aware of noise. A deep grumbling maybe? Waves of noise. Singing? No, not singing. Sometimes he could hear a high pitched screeching, a hollering. He felt as cold as the grave. Too cold to move. His nose felt like a block of ice. He could see that most of him was in the sea, the rest propped up by a rock. His head was above water but blood trickled from his face. Then he remembered. He'd been swimming back towards the slaves chained inside the Brigantine. A wave had slammed him against this rock. He must move. He shifted his legs; he raised his arms. If he could move, he could swim. Damn this tide. Why did it have to be rising? This was now very deep water. The growling and hollering continued - they were calling out to him. Get moving. The noise stopped.

He must give them hope. He shouted with all his remaining strength, knowing that lives depended on it. The hollering from the hole in the hull resumed and this gave him the impetus he needed to push away from the rock. The tide was not in his favour and it seemed that for every foot of progress he made, the swell picked him up and threw him back two.

Then out of the hull a large plank floated towards him, riding the waves and making its way steadily closer. He swam awkwardly, slowly but finally he was able to make a grab for it. He heaved himself on top and found that he could only just keep his head above water, but now he could paddle the last fifteen yards and this was not such hard work as swimming. He would make it through that hole.

He surged through to a tumultuous welcome. Chained hands reached out and pulled him up. He must keep moving. He fumbled for his pockets. Please God, don't let those stones have dropped out. Finding them empty would be the last straw. With difficulty he withdrew a large stone – the hammer – and a smaller one. The eyes stared.

He made his way along to the end where the chains connecting them were fixed to a beam. He pushed the smaller one between the narrow gap in the link. It was fortunate these chains were light. If they'd been the heavier ones, used for hauling, this plan would not have worked. Only the sharp end of the stone fitted. He hammered it carefully until it forced the gap wider. Then it shattered. He reached into his pocket again – nothing. He tried the other pocket. Oh thank God! Another stone, but just the one. Shivering was so severe now that he found hammering very difficult but determination won and the gap in the link was enlarged sufficiently to ease it from the ring on the beam.

He passed the end of the chain to the first hand that reached out and heard them slip it through the rings on their metal cuffs. In less than a minute their hands were free. Now he had to hope that he could do the same for the ring which was under the water securing their feet. It took longer; he had to keep surfacing to take a breath, and each time under water was shorter. The man closest to him squatted under the water with him and held the link steady while Daniel eased the link apart. Eventually all the men in the chain were free. He counted ten.

Someone placed a blanket around his shoulders as he hauled himself up onto the bench now vacated by the slaves. A hollering came from the second chamber. Had he to go through all this again? He'd need more stones. This thought was superseded by the more immediate need to get these men to the shore as perhaps they could fetch help. Could they swim? If only they had some light. How long until dawn? He couldn't wait to find out; this cold was as ruthless a killer as Tridd. Reluctantly he tried to put the blanket back on the shelf and found it was missing. So that must have been the plank he'd been able to use. He felt along further and there was another shelf and he stored the blanket there. He slipped back into the freezing water and pulled the chain out. He would paddle back on the plank to the rock, towing the chain and the men, not able to swim it seemed, could haul themselves along it until reaching the rock. However it wasn't long enough and the water was too deep so he abandoned the idea.

Unexpectedly, he noticed an indistinct shadow in the hole of the hull. One of the men was going to chance it. Several others followed. He tried to get them to hold hands and form a human chain. This wouldn't work either. Had his brain become as numb as his hands and feet? He pushed the plank at one of the men and nudged another and set him to pulling the wooden bench away from where it was fixed to the deck. Once they realized they would have two buoyant planks, there was no holding them back and he watched until their silhouettes showed against the wash of the waves on the rocks.

Imperceptible to all except Daniel, there was a moment when the wind dropped and the sea no longer pounded the rocks. There was only a slopping sound. The tide had turned.

Chapter Thirty-Two
Lucy
"Plague of eyes"

Josh had never before seen eyes appearing and disappearing, and these ones kept sinking behind the waves, others glided above the water covering the rocks, but all advanced ever closer. He barked. Still they came. He howled and howled. They were coming even faster now. He must find Lucy.

Lucy was about to climb aboard the carriage – at last somewhere out of this abominable wind. "Martha, have you seen Josh?"

"You sure he's not got left behind? He's a one for doing last minute look arounds."

Lucy called out for him.

Everyone stood still and listened. The two men furrowed their brows. Then Lucy thought she heard Josh howling and it was agreed that Josh must either be in trouble or he'd found something significant. They all headed down the chine towards the beach. All the torches had burnt out, only George Lytton's lit their way and Lucy still clutched the carriage lamp. Josh was running towards them at such a speed that they almost fell over him. Dashing up to Lucy he sat down in front of her and howled.

"Whatever is it, Josh? What do you know that we don't?"

Josh stopped howling, barked at her then ran a few yards ahead before turning to see she was following. And this he did until he was a few yards from the rocks when he began howling again.

George Lytton led the way, holding aloft the torch though no one could see much beyond the small circle of light it created. Josh still howled. George Lytton realized that his torch was impeding their sight rather than assisting so he took it and jammed it in the sand some ten yards from the leading waves. Then they saw the eyes. Martha hid behind Lucy, and Raffles and the Major gingerly trod towards the rocks.

"*Dragons* have bright white, fiery eyes," Martha said tentatively. Gathering pace she added, "Josh sees what we can't. Oh what have we done to deserve this?"

Lucy would have liked to reply sensibly but only got as far as, "Nonsense, Martha."

"My God in Heaven," exclaimed Raffles. "Are these your poor children?" He strode towards them, his arms outstretched. "You are safe now, safe."

Raffles stood, his cloak billowing and his large hat tied on tightly, his arms held wide. To lean slaves, the well-built Raffles looked as terrifying as any slave trader they had ever seen and they huddled together. They were all bare from the waist up.

"Come, come, my poor souls. Be not afraid."

Emboldened by Raffles, George Lytton and Lucy walked towards the edge of the rocks and gradually, one by one, the black-as-night slaves staggered off the rocks and collapsed on the sand.

Martha was some way back kneeling and pleading with God to spare them from the "plague of eyes." She would not look at them. "Could they be those dragons from across the sea? Oh God, save us." Her eyes wide and pleading, she looked up. "Please."

Lucy could hear Martha and, worried that these men might be offended by her words, she turned and tramped towards her still pleading friend, her dress now dragging round her ankles, wet, heavy and sandy. "Martha, dear Martha," Lucy put her arm around her shoulder. "You must not fear. They are men and likely very cold. Why don't you collect some wood and we'll use Major Lytton's torch to light a good fire for them to warm themselves?"

Martha stayed where she was but looked up to Lucy. "Men? You say they are men? Dirtied and oily with their labours?"

Lucy blinked. Whereas she had learnt that some people were black and some white and some were in between, Martha seemed to have no idea of the good God's creative powers when it came to designing men. She must explain some day, but for now she said, "Trust me, Martha, it's a fire they need."

Martha stood up with some difficulty. "They ain't the only ones who could do with a good fire!" Relief gave her courage and energy and she set about piling wood high. She started with the abandoned torches, keeping one eye on the gathering slaves.

George Lytton and Raffles discovered the men could not understand a word being said to them, and in their turn, they could not understand the men.

"Priorities," said Lytton. His Army training took over and he designated Raffles as being in charge while he rode to Watch House. "I'll fetch Lieutenant Thorsen and his men and find a few carts to transport these poor creatures."

"Where have you in mind?" asked Raffles.

"The Ship Inn. I'll call in there on my way and have them make up a good fire and some hot broth." Without another word he just about managed a jog towards the chine but was intercepted by Martha who needed his torch to light her damp wood.

The slaves, all sitting exhausted on the edge of the rocks, awaited an invitation to come close to the fire. "My brothers, come." Raffles' words were lost on them so he went forward and held out his hand to the nearest man. The slave lifted his arm and, with his iron cuff still in place, gratefully took the hand offered.

Under a Dark Star

When they were all seated close in a circle around the steaming, spitting fire, Josh examined the slaves. If they hadn't come out of the sea, he might have been able to smell if they'd met Daniel. Then Josh heard what no one else could hear.

Chapter Thirty-Three
Daniel
"The guilt grew"

Daniel looked to the left and, from the opening in the hull, he watched the men, visible only occasionally against the wash of the waves. When he heard the strange hollering sound begin again behind him, his heart sunk. He turned and waded across to the second chamber then hauled himself up through the broken door. The hollering stopped abruptly and a rattling of chains replaced it. In this darkest of places, only sound could guide him to these unfortunate people. He felt for a hand. His numb fingers were useless so he used the palm of his hand. In doing so he touched something soft and it flinched. These hollerers were women! He was annoyed with himself for not realizing that earlier. But how could he ever have imagined stumbling across women being shipped as slaves to England? Surely this no longer happened? Stop thinking, keep moving.

He still had the stone he'd used as a hammer but he only had the larger of the smaller stones and, try as he might, it would not fit into the gap in the chain that held them to the beam. He handed the hammer stone to the woman and clenched her fist around it.

Refusing to give in to his numbing fingers and toes, he returned to the hole which led to the open sea. He could not face swimming across to the rock where there were plenty of small stones. He looked out. He'd dive to the sea bed. Before doing that, he stood chest high in the water, and saw a tiny, heartening flicker of a flame. It disappeared behind a rolling wave but when he saw it again, there was a tall, thin, bright orange column. Again it disappeared. Then nothing. Or was that movement in front of it? Perhaps it was only one of the wreckers' torches. Or had Karl arrived at last? He waited a few moments more, just time enough to see that this was a fire on the beach. Even if they were wreckers celebrating, he decided to chance shouting. It wouldn't be long before he'd succumb to the cold completely and be unable to shout. He shouted. There was no response. He tried again. The wind should be carrying his voice ashore. He put two fingers between his painful numbing lips and, waiting for a break in the sound of the waves crashing, he attempted to whistle the call to Josh that he was needed.

~

On the shore Lucy saw Josh's ears prick up. Totally focused, he dashed across the huge boulders leading out to the wreck and leapt into the breakers and was lost to her view.

"Someone is still out there!" She clutched Raffles arm and made him look.

"Ah! That is, I think, what these good people are trying to tell us." He had taken off his cloak and wrapped it around two of the slaves who seemed way past shivering and barely alive.

Lucy took off both her cloaks and draped them around the slaves, two by two, and Martha did the same. Casting all decorum aside, she drew the attention of one of them by clutching his arm and pointing out to sea. "Man?" she said.

The slave lifted his hand out of the comparative warmth of the cloak and pointed and nodded. Then he pointed at her.

What did he mean? Was there a woman out there? Some of the other slaves, shivering and teeth chattering were trying to say something too. All seemed to be fretting over more people trapped out there. Josh's behaviour told her that one of them was certainly

Daniel. She pointed to Raffles and tapped her own white cheek. "White man?"

The man nodded.

"Oh thank God!" She rushed over to Martha and hugged her and nearly lifted the little woman off the ground.

"Flollops, girl. Are you that cold? Have you got the madness?"

"Have you ever known Josh to behave like that unless it was in response to Daniel?"

~

Watching the fire won't save me or these women. I must find some smaller stones. Daniel took a deep breath but used it to whistle again – just in case. Yet he must delay no longer, he hadn't the energy to dive, so he just stepped out and dropped to the sea bed, felt around for some stones, tucked three in his pocket, then surfaced, gasping for air. He had drifted away from the hole so he fought his way back through the waves and groped his way into the second chamber.

Would these women be able to swim? Unlikely. Even if he managed to wrench some wood from the wreck would they be able to kick their way to where there was shallower water covering the rocks? The tide had now turned and would not wash them in. If only there was a hint of the sun rising.

He made a simple decision; all he was capable of. First he must free them. And with some difficulty he did. He counted six. He led them across to the larger chamber where the men had been. Despite his encouragement, not one of them would leap through into the deeper, sloshing pool. He stood, chest high in the water, and let the nearest one feel that his head was above it. But would hers be? Some of them seemed very young, not fully grown. As the benches in this chamber had been ripped out, there was nothing but the shelf overhead with the blanket on it. He handed it to the woman and she passed it back along the line; he couldn't just throw the only source of warmth into the water. He gripped the shelf and pulled – it came away so easily he nearly lost his balance. He placed the end of the plank across the opening and urged the first woman to grip it and then feel her way to the end, thus making room for each of them to do the same. The weight of the women dragged the board down. One of the women screamed, cried and would not come through but he had to ignore her protests and pulled her arm and made her clutch the wood and all the time she sobbed.

He towed the plank to the hole in the hull and forced them through. Now all he had to do was push it in the direction of the rocks where, with the tide going out, it wouldn't be quite so deep. They might even be able to walk the last fifty yards. He shoved the board towards the rocks. He knew his hopes were as wispy as the froth on the waves, but hope was all there was. Thinking of Lucy and Freddie, he decided to wrench another bench or shelf to aid his own escape.

Inside the hull, only sloshing water could be heard until a sound, a soft sob coming from the second chamber broke into his increasingly confused thoughts. It sounded like a young child. Could he have overlooked someone? He waded back and hauled himself up into the doorway again. A young girl was crouched around the corner on the near end of the bench. He lifted her tiny, naked body up onto the highest part where only her feet dangled in the icy water. The blanket! What did that woman do with it? He felt along the shelf above. Thank God it was there. He wrapped it around her. He hugged her gently; she was too frail to do much more. He lifted her feet out of the water and put them on the bench. He laid her head on his lap. To know that he hadn't the means or the strength to save her filled him with misery. And guilt. He wouldn't leave her. It was now eerily quiet, just the lapping of the water as it swelled across the broken doorway. His heart felt as if it had been crushed. Overwhelming pain and grief for this dying child seized his whole body, for dying she was, her breathing had all but ceased. She was somebody's daughter. The poor mother. Then, like a rising flood, his thoughts filled with the image of the reluctant, crying woman he had hauled through the doorway. And the guilt grew.

He thought of Freddie. How awful it would be if he were to freeze to death, alone, watching his mother pulled away from him. He would stay with this child until she died. He moved further along the bench and lifted her head on to his lap again. At least in her last moments she would have a caring hand upon her forehead. He wished he could sing. Lucy would sing. Numb lips were not conducive to any kind of talking or singing.

His heartbeat slowed, he no longer shivered, and he couldn't think of anything but the warmth of Lucy in their cosy bed with Freddie asleep in his cradle beside them. But he hummed. This little scrap of humanity would know she was not alone.

A panting sound. How strange. His befuddled brain fought to know what this panting could be. With a huge effort, he remembered his whistle to Josh and here was Josh surging through the broken doorway and paddling onto the bench and attempting to get on his lap. He shifted a little to make room for his faithful dog who, overjoyed, licked his face and tried to put his front paws around his neck. With his free arm, he pushed Josh down. How could he do that? How could he push this loyal friend away? Josh was not at all deterred and continued licking and nudging him until, climbing onto his lap, there came the recognition that someone else was there. He backed off onto the bench and investigated. Putting his long snout up to Daniel, he whined. The body next to his master's was beyond all hope and all help.

"She's gone, Josh. You know that, don't you?" mumbled Daniel.

Josh sat on the bench, leaning against his master. His master was too quiet. And very cold.

All thoughts of the fire on the beach left Daniel; he knew he no longer had enough strength to get there. The death of this child crushed his last hope to fight.

Josh nudged up closer. His master was not going to die, not while Josh lived. Josh leapt off the bench and back into the water and paddled out of the hull.

Chapter Thirty-Four
Lucy
"Through the deep waters"

"Martha, the boat!"

"What boat?" asked Raffles.

Lucy dashed to the parson. "There's a small one in that cave." She waved her arm in the general direction of the cliffs. "Josh knows Daniel's out there," she said pointing to the rocks. "Will you help me drag it out?"

"A boat? What a gift! Of course, my dear, of course." He turned to Martha. "Keep this burning brightly; we're depending on it not only to create a little warmth but to be a beacon of hope to anyone still on the wreck."

Martha had been drying some wood close to the fire and smaller bits were now dry enough to feed it. She threw on all the driest and this time there was a lot less spitting, but after a quick burst of flame there was still mostly only smoke. "I'll get me some more." She glanced across to the slaves and her look told Lucy that she hadn't quite worked out where on God's earth they could have come from.

Lucy ran towards the cliff face and soon found the upturned boat again.

"Leave this to me, Lucy," said Raffles panting from his exertions to catch up with her. He thought this little lady – for that is what she was nowadays, indeed always had been – would not be much help in dragging a heavy sailing craft across the sands.

Within moments he realized how wrong he was. He pulled, she pushed and oh how she pushed. They dragged the boat to the shoreline much quicker than he'd imagined possible. "It's amazing what love can do," he murmured.

"We have no oars," Lucy called out to Martha.

Martha immediately collected several pieces of wood. "These long bits will do as paddles."

"They'll have to," said Raffles as he helped Lucy with her lamp into the boat then took the wood from Martha. "Now don't you worry about those men; just keep them warm and keep the fire blazing to guide us back." Blazing? Well he could hope. He looked up at the sky. Dawn was breaking somewhere in the world but not over the Isle of Wight, not yet anyway.

Raffles climbed in and Martha gave it a last push into the waves before rushing back to the fire to dry her feet on her frock. The receding tide was also a gift, or so the Godly parson declared in between puffing and paddling. Although the boat had oar locks, without proper oars it was easier to paddle than to try to row. Lucy was hoping the vessel was seaworthy and was very grateful that the wind seemed to have dropped and the clouds had mostly cleared. Stars shone brightly in the sky and the crescent moon, though now far in the west, gave enough light to keep them off the rocks.

Only a few minutes passed before a most terrible howling began. It was as if it were from the depths of hell. Lucy could only discern a moving white patch on the rocks but that frightening yowl was undoubtedly Josh and a very distressed Josh too. Paralyzed by fear she could paddle no longer. "Mr Raffles," she hesitated, "That's Josh. I think we might be too late."

"Faith, my child. Let us assume it is a desperate cry to summon us. Call to him and we'll take him too." Josh needed no invitation. He had already plunged in the sea and was paddling towards them. While Raffles balanced the boat on one side, Lucy hauled Josh in on the other. He could only spare a quick greeting to his master's beloved before rushing to the bow, barking.

Lucy's face brightened. "He's letting Daniel know we're coming."

"You see, he is alive! We must keep paddling."

Lucy's hands hurt but she ignored the possibility of blisters and resumed frantically trying to propel the heavy boat until she heard hollering. "Mr Raffles, whatever is it?"

The panting parson also stopped paddling and squinted towards the rocks. Not believing in hounds from hell or any such nonsense, he deduced they must be more slaves. Suddenly he exclaimed, "More slaves!" Raffles was aghast. "Women!"

Knowing that the parson's sight was not his best sense, Lucy peered as well: definitely women and they appeared to be naked. She tried to fathom who these strange, shrieking women could be, though she had to give them credit for making themselves heard in such challenging conditions. From what she could discern, there were six of them, all holding hands and up to their waists in the sea.

A very distressed Josh rushed back to Lucy, then across to Raffles, then to the bow where he resumed barking.

"Daniel's not with them or Josh would let us know."

"I think your good dog has his priorities right. We must leave them to continue to the shore where they will find a fire and help. Our mission is to find Daniel who is undoubtedly on the wreck." Raffles gripped his paddle at the same time as Lucy plunged hers back into the water and not another word was said until they reached their goal.

Josh leapt over the bow and swam through the hole. Raffles and Lucy struggled to find a way to anchor the boat close as Lucy was adamant they should not ram it over the entrance. If they holed it… She couldn't bear thinking of the consequences.

Raffles turned the boat sideways on and through sheer strength in his arms he held the heaving vessel alongside.

Lucy lowered herself into the first chamber. The sea came up to her shoulders. She reached for her lamp and stood, eyes wide as she stared at the bare inside of the hull. She hoped the deck below her feet was intact. To fall through a gaping hole was unthinkable. She pushed her way through the freezing water towards the sound of Josh's barking. Lifting her dress above her knees, she climbed through the doorway and was relieved to find she was in shallower water. She held the lamp high. In the corner of this small ante-room she saw Daniel, still as a tombstone, eyes closed and head lolling back. But he was softly humming and cradling a bundle on his lap.

Lucy waded towards him and hung the lamp on a hook above his head and leaned close; his breathing was slow and shallow. She whispered in his ear, "Daniel, it's Lucy." He didn't move and continued humming. "It's Lucy." He stopped humming. Was there a slight movement of his eyelids? Josh was alongside him and appeared to be sitting on some feet as he licked Daniel's face. Shocked, Lucy took a step back before pulling open the damp blanket. A child. A dead child!

Josh's ears pricked up and he made a low grumbling noise. There was a crack and the whole of the broken stern slipped further into the sea and the deck below her feet sloped even more. She was now waist-high in water which also covered the child. And Daniel still did not move. Josh and Lucy exchanged looks and with one accord they knew they must act immediately.

She lifted the wet bundle and waded across to the boat. The water was deeper now and she only managed to keep her head above it if she pushed hard against the deck and bobbed up for air and then dropped back under again. She fought her way through to Raffles who was crouching as the boat was now at least a foot higher in relation to the hole. It was clear he daren't let go of his hold on the opening. With great difficulty Lucy balanced on the rim of the hole and held the little body over her head and tipped it into the boat. She tugged the parson's coat, hung on to the edge of the boat and shouted, "Daniel is alive, but only just, Mr Raffles. I'll bring him out."

"Glory be to God," called back Raffles. "I can hold on."

Lucy returned to the ante room and the light of the lamp revealed a second hook on a nearby beam and around it was a rope with a handle. Oh dear God! It was a whip. She lifted it off and slung it around the back of her neck, then taking hold of Daniel under his shoulders she hauled him up and pulled his right arm around her own shoulders and hung on to his hand. With her right hand she seized the lamp. His weight was more than she'd be able to manage. Should she have changed places with the parson? Should she take out the rope and fasten the boat and then both of them carry him out? Josh's ears pricked up again. Please God don't let this ship sink further. She must hurry. Why hadn't she thought to assist Daniel first and then go back for the dead child? How senseless. Her lack of reasoning might cost Daniel his life. Freezing cold and now very angry with herself, she took a step forward but he remained still. She used her foot to push his right leg ahead and slowly he began to walk of his own accord.

"Lucy," he slurred.

"Yes, I'm here, my love." She must give him hope. "And we have a boat."

Daniel pushed onward until they reached the doorway. Lucy stood him up against the opening and encouraged him to lift his legs over the high base of the door. The drop on the other side meant that he hardly had his neck and head above water and, like her, he was bobbing along the bottom.

Damn, damn, damn that shift in the hull! Where was God? How could she help Daniel across to the boat when she could not swim or even keep her head above water? She'd have to abandon the lamp. She must hurry, she couldn't leave him to struggle alone. She held it up to have a last look inside the hull – the terrible prison from where the slaves had escaped. Just to the left of the doorway she saw a hook. She leant across and hung the lamp. That might help him. She took a deep breath and dropped down completely underwater into the lower chamber and pushed him towards the boat. She surfaced and gasped for air. Her mind had been totally focused until she'd seen the dead child, and now it swam with a torrent of guilty thoughts obliterating good sense. Focus returned: she took another breath and, submerged, she pushed Daniel forward, and tried supporting him under his arms. Then she felt Josh swim past. She surfaced. He'd been a good sheep dog and made sure everyone was out. She sank to the bottom again and felt ahead for Daniel. He wasn't there. She bobbed to the surface. Josh was swimming behind him and nudging him upwards and towards the boat. Her thoughts sloshed around her head in confusion. She should not have doubted God. God had made this intelligent dog and he'd made water buoyant. She went ahead of Daniel, took his hands and pulled him.

Managing to get to the parson, she took off the whip around her neck and handed it up to him. He immediately tied it to the boat but she could see nothing to fasten it to in the hull.

Standing on the rim of the hole, Lucy took hold of the whip handle. Please God, please let there be something. Her eyes stung; everything was a blur. Into her mind popped the old image of Josh towing her to safety when she'd been in the holed boat. The rope barely reached a post but she managed to wrap it around once. She called Josh. He took the handle in his teeth, like a stick, and paddled, keeping the handle from drifting away.

"Josh is holding the rope, Mr Raffles; I doubt he can do so for long."

"He's doing well. The boat is in position."

But Lucy could not hear, she'd slipped beneath the water to push Daniel up onto the rim. Now that the parson had two hands free, he hauled Daniel in. Lucy felt the rush of water as he left and she surfaced and climbed onto the rim. She could see Raffles in great difficulty because Daniel's weight nearly tipped the boat over.

Though exhausted, she must do one last thing: she called, "Keep going, Josh! Pull back the boat!" She lost her grip and slipped to the bottom of the hull, unable to breathe again and with little strength to bob up. A strong arm reached down and grasped her under her shoulder, pulling her up on to the base of the hole, then it disappeared. She heard the parson yelling something about moving Daniel to help balance the boat. She leaned forward and clutched the side of the little boat and held on until Raffles returned to lift her to safety.

As he tried, the vessel began to drift away and wobbled dangerously. With one arm, Raffles pulled it back. Josh frantically tried to keep the rope taut and, with the boat once more alongside the hull, Raffles lifted her in and laid her next to Daniel. Josh did not need calling; he swam back and was hauled in by Raffles. He shook off as much water as he could and rested between the prostrate Daniel and Lucy and put out a paw in reassurance to Lucy. The little bundle was tucked into the bow. Raffles sat at the stern and paddled first one side and then the other. Progress against the tide was slow but Martha must have found some dry wood and the blazing fire drew him on. As he got into rhythm, he sang one of his favourite hymns:

Under a Dark Star

"When through the deep waters I call thee to go,
The rivers of grief shall not thee overflow,
For I will be with thee thy trials to bless,
And sanctify to thee thy deepest distress."

Chapter Thirty-Five
Karl
"Weasely servant of hell"

So Tridd had escaped. He'd used that old trick: the rope secured on the cliff top and left to dangle unobtrusively providing a swift escape. All they'd caught was one of his dogs and the growling, slobbering beast was now nailed in a barrel. If they'd taken a vote, it would have been pushed over the cliff but he'd had visions of the creature, madder than ever, returning to take revenge on its tormentors.

Buckby gleefully volunteered to roll the barrel to the inn despite the furious objections of the dog. "That's the last time he'll threaten me with this damned dog. And I'll roll him in a barrel too if it's the last thing I do. Tridd had better not cross my path again."

Tolly's wife agreed to tend the wounded but she didn't like the sight of blood so the best she could do was to lay them on the floor and keep a good fire burning in the hearth and await the doctor from Brigton. Zeb's body was taken upstairs; other bodies lay outside at the back of the inn. The shipwrecked sailors would be buried in the graveyard too.

Now here they were again: hiding, watching, waiting. This time they were behind the church wall and out of sight of anyone using the track which led up from the inn. The land was considerably overgrown providing good cover in which to hide. If any gravestones moved, they'd be able to see the reason why. How he'd chuckled when the two little urchins had told him about the antics in the graveyard. He looked at his pocket watch. Did that say two o'clock? He fervently wished he knew where Daniel was. Comrades didn't desert each other. Besides, Lucy would never forgive him if Tridd mercilessly killed him. Perhaps he was safe somewhere. He took a deep breath and ensured that rope was still tied to his belt. He hoped to need it.

They were observing only half a dozen stragglers in the graveyard, left behind to tidy up. His men were keen to arrest them but Karl had a better idea. He'd come to the obvious conclusion that the villagers had dumped their booty and fled. There was only one place big enough and close enough to store the likely amount of goods they had plundered and that was inside the church which was now securely locked. His only interest was to find Daniel and Tridd. It would serve his purpose better to have the villagers on his side.

"Tutte, you take two men round to the other wall and make sure no one escapes. Flowers, you do the same on the north side and we four will cover the rest. We'll encircle them, close in and take them to the porch where at least we'll be out of this wind." Karl looked at his two best men – still eager in stark contrast to some of the others. "Any questions?" Not waiting for an answer he whispered, "Go!"

In less than three minutes, he faced the six men who were almost pinned to the huge church doors. Two of them were married to those silly girls who adored Daniel. He was cross with himself for feeling resentful; the girls had been helpful, but why was it always Daniel who attracted the women? Damned floppy blond hair!

It was dark in the porch so he despatched one of his men to bring lamps or torches from the inn and Tutte and Flowers to watch the far side of the church. Meanwhile he began his interrogation.

"I am not going to ask your names." The captured men did not move. "You'll naturally be suspicious as to the reason." He knew Tomkins and Buckby should know them anyway. He would have felt more in control if he had room to pace the ground but he contented himself with running his eyes along their faces – or what he could see of them. "I want to know two things. If you know the answers it will be in your best interests to tell me." Two torches were brought and held at a safe distance. There was not a sound from the men who all had their eyes to the ground. "I am not going to arrest you." He paused to evaluate the effect but there was none. "Except Tridd. And one other person." This time the captives' eyes flickered upwards but only for a second. In days gone by, he would not have tolerated what could be insolence but he knew these men were afraid and fear was a powerful, constraining emotion. "I want to know where Tridd is. If you tell me, it will save me time, that's all, because I shall capture him whether or not you assist." He looked into the eyes of the three men who had raised their heads out of curiosity. "If any one of you tells me, and it proves to be correct, you will each receive a half sovereign." Now he had the attention of them all. No one would know who'd done the telling. "If none of you does, you *will* regret it, so do not rely on someone else to do the telling."

Facing the captives again, he said, "The second question I want you to answer is: where is Daniel Tynton?" Answering this question should not endanger their lives unless… He dare not think along those lines. He took a sovereign from his inside pocket and held it up then put it back and patted the pocket. He did not expect an answer to either question but this was the easier one surely? And the greater reward. "I am going to ask you individually." He paused, "One by one, that is, and it will never be revealed which one of you has given me the answer. If more than one gives me the verifiably correct answer, I have more than one sovereign." He smiled. He liked stepping outside of the rules and he could afford to do so.

He arranged his men so that eight were guarding the villagers in the porch and he and Tutte would interrogate each man away from the others. One by one they were questioned but the only answers given were that they'd tell him if they knew but they didn't. The nearest he got to an answer was from one of the girl's husbands, Fawcett.

"Don't know about Tynton but Tridd might be in his fort. Normal times, that's where he'd be after a good wrecking. Goes north sometimes, if there's trouble. Don't know why or where. And this ain't no normal times."

"If this proves true…" he hesitated, "we will capture him and you shall each receive a half sovereign."

Fawcett looked up, his eyes hungry for money but Karl could not blame him for that. He sent him back to the others. Turning to face the bedraggled villagers he sent them away and told them to tell no one. Then he despatched Flowers to Ryde. "Contact the Coast Guard and have them monitor the ferries and any small boats crossing. Hurry, Tridd may already be on his way."

Buckby cut in. "He doesn't usually go to the mainland, sir. He likes the night life and spending his money."

Karl was angry with himself. How stupid– he must be tiring, he'd forgotten that Tridd thought of himself as untouchable and was more likely to be revelling than fleeing. "Flowers, have the Revenue men comb the town – and Cowes too; in fact, all along the northern coastline."

Flowers rushed off to the inn and soon the drumming of hooves could be heard. Karl smiled in satisfaction. Men like him were hard to find: men like him won wars.

Buckby and Tomkins looked tired and as old as some of the tombstones, and the Coast Guard support were keen to leave but he had more for them to do. "It will not be easy but we must break down these doors to the House of God."

One word was written on all their faces – *how*?

At the back of the General Store was storage for logs and he commandeered a tree trunk awaiting chopping. Regaling the men with tales of knights of old storming forts of the thieving rich, he led the way back to the porch whereupon they began pounding the solid oak doors. Shouts came from behind the church and he told his men to abandon the tree trunk. Success! He marched to the other side of the church.

"Caught him, Lieutenant!" Tutte was holding the leg of Parson Rafe Driver as he attempted to climb out of one of the few windows that opened. But Parson Driver was not going to be taken easily. He slashed a knife at Tutte's hand, narrowly missing it as Tutte quickly pulled away. Karl grabbed the parson's flailing arm, bent it back almost to the point of cracking and the knife dropped.

He wrenched the scrawny parson through the window and forced him to sit under it. Tutte stood on the yowling parson's shoulders and Karl pushed Tutte up through the open window, thus preventing any more destruction of the doors by opening them from the inside.

He tied the parson's hands behind his back and marched him around to the porch.

As Tutte pulled open the damaged doors, Karl thrust the parson through. Little could be seen until half a dozen candles had been lit but then Karl thundered, "Look you weasely servant of hell, look!"

His own men remained silent but the men of the Coast Guard gasped. "It's like a pirate's treasure trove."

Rafe Driver spat back, "Those London vicars are walking knee high in gold. Why am I stuck in this unbearable abyss? Why me? Why me?"

Karl tapped his painful arm and he yelped. "You are unworthy to serve the King of Kings at all – anywhere!" He hesitated, it was as if Raffles was doing the talking! "May God forgive you because I know I cannot." He tapped his arm again. "The lives of many sailors, the impoverishment of this parish, indeed this whole part of the island and much more is because of your greed for gold and power. And yet you have so little of either." He took a deep, satisfying breath. "You are under arrest."

His work was not over, but he allowed himself a moment of triumph. "Take this wretch and imprison him in Watch House." Tapping the parson on his arm again, he handed him over to Tutte. "You ride, he runs. And when you get there, release those poor unfortunates we've been feeding. They'll be strong enough to walk back to Brigton now." Turning around he glanced at his pocket watch, gone three o'clock, still a while until dawn. He addressed those still standing aghast. "Men of the Coast Guard – well done! Now secure this church and graveyard, and two of you keep watch, the others get what sleep you can. At dawn, those on guard can return to your homes and those who've slept are to stand guard until you are relieved. Any man found asleep will be regarded as guilty of dereliction of duty. Buckby and Tomkins, come with me to the inn. What might we find there?"

Chapter Thirty-Six
"Where, be damned, were you?"

The wind was dropping, the sky clearing, but the relentless sound of crashing breakers focused Karl's attention on his unfinished work. Perhaps tomorrow the sun would shine and the waves would merely lap. Tonight there was still much to do and his two best men were fully occupied, one with imprisoning the despicable, weasely parson and the other with tracking the violent, power obsessed Tridd. Tridd's dog, in a barrel at the back of The Ship Inn, heard them coming and barked furiously. Buckby and Tomkins could not resist hammering on the nailed-shut lid as they passed. Karl initially ignored their childish delight until the dog became so enraged that the barrel tipped over and rolled around the rough, stony yard. He must prevent this operation from turning into a farce, besides, the dog was not to blame. "Enough! Have a care – dead men are laid out here." He looked around. A faint light from a lamp in a back window illuminated the bodies of those who would never walk the sands again. And sailors who'd never sail again. There'd be more corpses on board their smashed ship, no doubt about that. He loaded his pistol, squatted by the barrel, hammered on the side and when the dog responded by barking, he cocked the gun, took aim and fired. Silence. It would suffer no more.

Karl strode around the corner and came to an abrupt halt. What might they find at the inn? He hadn't reckoned on nearly a dozen black men in iron cuffs sitting cross legged around a brazier.

Under a Dark Star

The sound of squeaking wheels coming out of the darkness caught his attention, as did the bare-chested women, being wheeled in the cart. They were followed by others trailing behind whose bare feet bled, and all being shepherded by Major George Lytton.

"By Jupiter! If I live a hundred years I'll never see the likes of this again." He turned to catch Buckby and Tomkins staring, their jaws dropping visibly. "Major Lytton, are these what I think they are?"

Lytton ushered the sodden, frightened women to sit by the fire. "Indeed, they are." The slaves, though exhausted, were overjoyed to be reunited and initially whispered, all the time wary of being punished for speaking. Lytton raised his voice above the increasing volume. "And all but drowned; left for dead in the sinking wreck. How they got out is something they hold as their secret."

"Secret?"

"None of them speaks English. I found Martha sitting alone with them on the beach trying to keep a fire going with wet flotsam."

"I'm surprised to see you here, but Martha? Why on earth is *she* here?"

"It's a long story which I'll tell you one day. It starts with that incredible dog of Daniel's."

"You're not going to tell me that Lucy and Martha are looking for Daniel?"

"You've jumped to the heart of the matter. Lucy, the parson…"

Karl exclaimed, "Parson Raffles! That man gets everywhere. In your head, in your life…"

"Mr Raffles is with Lucy."

Karl ignored his men, the slaves and the Major, and dashed to the door of the inn. Inside he saw only injured villagers who'd

Under a Dark Star

been wheeled there by his men. From the open doorway he turned around to interrogate the Major. "She's not here, is she? Where, then, is she?"

"Shut the damned door!" squawked Tolly's parrot which it followed up with irritable screeches.

"Keep what little warmth there is inside and I'll tell you," said Major Lytton. Karl slammed the door. The slaves ceased their whispering and leaned closer to the poor excuse for a fire and further away from anger. "Martha tells me that she and the parson have paddled out to the wreck."

"What!" spluttered Karl. "Did you know about this?"

"Of course not! Perhaps I'd better explain a little more," he huffed. "Daniel intended you to receive a message, tied around his dog, but the dog did not get through to you it seems. Remarkably, it found Lucy and delivered it to her.

"He would," stated Karl. "What was the message?"

"It told of the wrecking planned for tonight at Attenfold rocks and warned of many involved." He didn't allow Karl time to interrupt again and hurried on. "Lucy knew Daniel would be in trouble if you were not in support; as did we all. The parson had arrived to visit his wife who, as you know, is with child. He, Lucy, Martha, and the dog and I set off for the rocks. I'd tried to convince them that I, and a couple of strong farm hands on sturdy, fast horses would be quicker and safer, but Lucy would not be persuaded."

He took a deep breath. "She's not easily persuaded." That was a certainty: if she were, she'd be his.

"By the time we arrived on the cliff top, the action was over. There was no sign of you, yet we had heard a ship's guns on our way here. I set off to find you. When I returned, according to Martha, the dog became convinced that his master was out on the rocks or maybe even on the wreck, though how he got there is still a mystery."

The bodies of the sailors by the rocks flashed through Karl's mind. Had Tridd slaughtered them all? Could Daniel have tried to stop him? Daniel could take care of himself; he remembered the fight he'd once had with him over Lucy; but Tridd used knives. Would Daniel? He became aware that Lytton was watching him and so were Buckby and Tomkins. Yet the slaves were all looking in the direction of the beach and daring to whisper and point. Perhaps they knew there was more than Martha to be found there. He must find Lucy. And Daniel.

"So Lucy and the parson are paddling towards the wreck. What in? A leaky boat?"

The Major ignored his sarcasm. "Martha is staying to keep the fire burning brightly to guide them and the dog back."

"Josh is with them?"

"Barking all the way."

"So are you saying that Martha saw them reach the wreck?"

"She can't be sure, but she saw the light from the lamp they took with them disappear and then it reappeared."

Karl's patience was running out. "And is it now getting closer?"

"When I was on the beach, I could see nothing and do nothing. Never has dawn seemed so long in coming. My priority was to escort these slaves away from the sands and to hand them over to you. Which I now do!" Major Lytton was not accustomed to dealing with bad-tempered officials even if they were on the same side. "Earlier, I'd ridden out to alert you at Watch House and what did I find?" He too could be belligerent when the occasion called for a bit of grit. "Two children, no higher than my hand," he held his hand out level with his waist, "playing with a fire on the roof. And…" his voice grew louder, "…a *woman* would not even

Under a Dark Star

answer the door to me. I'd dealt with the geese, and then had them nipping my backside. Where, be damned, were you?"

Karl could not stop the thought *well done Flo* from bringing a curl to his lips. He took a deep breath. "I thank you for the safe delivery of at least some of the cargo." He indicated the slaves. "There are several matters to attend to." This was said as if he were compiling a list of provisions. "First, may I make the assumption that you will not be returning to Norwell Farm before Lucy is found?"

"Of course!" the Major barked.

"Has a doctor been called?"

"Of course!" Lytton was becoming more annoyed with Karl's every utterance so he took command. "I shall attend to the injured and the dying. You are then free to concentrate on any…"

"An excellent offer!" Karl had played this game of "kingpin" before and enjoyed every minute. "You have my authority to use Watch House should you and the doctor require temporary extra capacity for nursing these miserable wretches." He waved his arm at the slaves and the inn. This man was annoying him and had induced him into a poor choice of words which he regretted. "Flowers is there now and he will allow you access. It might prove useful if you could ask him to sort out some spare, warm clothes and send them to the inn." Flo would attend to any who arrived at Watch House, he was sure of that. What a nurse she'd make! He could probably do with some nursing himself when he finally made it back. "Tomkins, Buckby, you are to watch over these…" he waved his hand at the slaves and as he did so he thought of Lucy again. She wouldn't be so dismissive of these unfortunate foreigners. He had so much to do, but he must do it well. "… watch over these ill-fated men and women. Commandeer some wood from the General Store if Tolly is running low. Keep them warm." He turned to Lytton again. "Tomkins and Buckby know that none of these villagers is to be arrested."

"Not arrested! I thought I was assisting in an operation to rid this island of wreckers and layabouts."

"You are," responded Karl. "If you can find it in yourself to trust me, you will find the island a better place to live."

"And you?" said the Major. "You shall be doing what?"

How dare he! If he weren't useful at this moment, he'd be told to go back where he came from in no uncertain terms. Foolhardy man, bringing Lucy into a situation like this. It was at this point he realized that the carriage with coachman standing nearby were his own. "My coachman will assist you in your transportation needs – to Watch House or perhaps there is a hospital reasonably close." He was angry with himself now. He must stop this parrying back and forth. "I shall go to the beach and find Lucy and Daniel. Tomorrow I shall find Tridd."

Chapter Thirty-Seven
"A wail of sheer misery"

Karl found Martha shivering in front of the fire on the beach. She had always been a capable servant but now she excelled herself with this fire, albeit small with just a couple of high, flickering flames. It was more than most could have created from mainly wet flotsam. He was alarmed when he saw her staring as if she were dead, oblivious of all but the sound of Raffles' fragmented singing.

"Have you no cloak? Surely you…" he stopped, chastising himself for not remembering the sight of the slaves sharing cloaks. One of them would undoubtedly have been hers. Surely not Lucy's too?

"Oh Lieutenant! They're coming, they're coming! Oh please God let them be alive."

Karl, not known for being tactile or dealing inappropriately with a servant, put his arm around her and drew her to the side of the fire. "Listen, can you hear the words?" This dear little woman was loyal to the end, standing alone, her skirts half tucked up and half trailing in the wet sand, and her heart full of longing for the safety of those who stood in the stead of a family; what a treasure. "Raffles will bring them home. Listen to those words."

A glimmer of hope glowed in Martha's eyes as, floating through the darkness and accompanied only by the sound of the receding tide, the words could be clearly heard:

"That soul, though all hell should endeavour to shake,

I'll never, no never, no never forsake."

Karl said, "He wouldn't be singing that if either of them were dead."

Martha clutched her hands together and held them to her breast. "Suppose he means their souls are all that's left of them?"

Karl, his arm still around her shoulder, drew her closer. "Have faith, Martha; the hymn is about not fearing when the odds are against you."

She summoned all her hope and gradually faith took its place. "They're alive?"

"Yes. They're alive but they will need to be taken to the inn immediately. Have you any more hand carts?"

"No! Oh no!"

"I passed one on the way down here. Fetch that and then run up to the inn, tell Buckby, Tomkins, or Tutte if he's back, to bring another. Quickly, they will be here any minute."

A task. Needed. Useful. Martha liked nothing more and he knew the running and bustling would warm her more than this fire.

Karl called out to the approaching Raffles. "Ahoy there!"

The singing stopped and the strained voice of Raffles answered, "Hoy!"

Then, as if in response to his faith, he saw the little boat with Raffles at the back, paddling one side, calling out, then paddling the other side. Despite the encouragement he'd given to Martha, his faith wavered; it was not his strongest resource. Just the indestructible parson? No sign of Lucy? Or Daniel? Could they be lying down? But Josh? Wouldn't he respond? He took off his uniform coat, his boots, stockings and shirt, flung them into the cart and plunged into the freezing sea. He swam to the bow, pulled himself up and peered inside the boat.

"They're alive, but only just," gasped Raffles.

Karl pulled himself along to the stern and kicking his powerful legs he propelled the little boat the last thirty yards until it beached. Then he leapt aboard and with great difficulty lifted Josh off Lucy and Daniel and heaved him onto the sand. Within seconds, Josh returned and stood with his paws against the side, attempting to clamber in. But Karl was already lifting Lucy and taking her to the hand cart that Martha had left. He grabbed his coat, threw it in and gently placed her on it and covered her as best as he could. She shivered; any movement was a good sign but he must make haste. He called out to Raffles, "Help is on its way; I'll go and hurry it along."

Raffles was slumped over and panting. They'd need a cart for him too. Karl picked up Lucy, still wrapped in his coat, stumbled across the sand, then ran with her up the chine, stopping only to direct Tomkins and his rumbling hand cart and offering encouragement to Martha.

When he arrived at the inn, he ignored Buckby and the slaves and crashed through the door shouting to the innkeeper. The ever surly innkeeper was behind the bar, pouring tots of brandy into small glasses. "Tollervey! That room of yours upstairs – make it ready to receive three urgent patients for the doctor. Is he here yet?"

Tolly was not known for his speed and had not got around to answering when a voice behind Karl said, "I'm Doctor Joliffe. Let me see this woman you're carrying. Put her on this table."

"This *lady*," began Karl, "is not going to be examined in front of these wretched felons. I'm carrying her upstairs, and you can attend her there." The dozen or so injured villagers wasted no emotions on taking offence: they were of the opinion that they'd be hanged or, at the very least, transported.

Doctor Joliffe was not used to being given orders. "There is a body in that room, certified by me as dead. Zeb Tynlan lies there until…"

"Tollervey! Move him."

Such was Karl's shout that Tolly jumped, slammed down his bottle of brandy and clomped upstairs. Karl followed him up and into the room where Daniel had first slept. Tolly lifted the dead weight of Zeb, slung him over his shoulder and took him down the stairs meeting the doctor coming up.

"Lucy," Karl whispered her name as he laid her gently on the bed. He stroked her forehead and gave not a thought for his own discomfort in his wet breeches. "Lucy, I will always be here for you." His heart was breaking. What had he done? Why had he ridden to Bethlehem Farm and told Daniel of his plans to come to this wretched island? He'd never forgive himself if she didn't survive.

Doctor Joliffe knocked and entered the room with his medical bag. "Now let me see this young lady. Lieutenant, I suggest you change into dry clothes before you catch a fit of the sneezing."

Karl ignored him. "How is she, doctor?"

The doctor lifted her out of Karl's coat and placed her on a blanket. "She'll be all the better for being in dry clothes and a warm bed!"

"Will she live?"

"Yes," said the doctor listening to her breathing. "Yes, she looks strong and the quicker you leave, the quicker I can attend her."

He was not at all sure about leaving Lucy in the care of this unknown quack but the doctor stood in front of the bed, holding his medical bag and did not move until Karl backed out of the door. "She is a lady and I hold you responsible for treating her as such," Karl said with menace.

"And I shall hold you responsible for paying my fee, Lieutenant."

Karl bolted down the stairs, clutching his coat. Outside, he picked up his stockings and slung them on the hitching rail and put his damp shirt and uniform coat on. Then he seized one of Lucy's cloaks from a slave and dashed back upstairs with it. The doctor was removing her petticoats. "This is L…" Damn! He nearly revealed her identity; until Tridd was locked away, it would not be wise. "This is her cloak." He covered her with it while the doctor continued to remove her wet clothes. Again Karl dashed down the stairs and found Mrs Tollervey. He took the time to explain to her that he'd like her to chaperone the young lady and light a fire in the small hearth. She was an amiable woman and readily agreed. He slapped a few coins on the counter in front of Tolly, and demanded hot tea for the slaves.

"And one for Polly," screeched the parrot.

As he passed the slaves who were still sitting cross-legged around the brazier, he took two more of the cloaks, leaving only Lucy's second cloak. In return he attempted to explain that warm drinks would soon be theirs.

"Buckby, come with me."

"But, sir, suppose they escape?"

"This is an island. Where do you think half-clothed, black, iron-cuffed slaves can hide? We have vital matters to attend to." He picked up a couple of logs and threw them into the brazier. "Follow me. Now!"

On the beach Tomkins had lifted Daniel into one of the hand carts and Josh was once again lying on top of him, refusing to move. Martha stroked Josh while Tomkins tried to help the parson out of the boat. He was having some difficulty trying to hold the boat steady and encourage the exhausted man to haul himself out.

When Raffles finally stood on the wet sand, he turned and lifted a bundle from the bow.

Once both Daniel and Raffles were in the hand carts it was simply a matter of wheeling them up to the inn, though pushing the cart with Raffles and his bundle across the beach was anything but simple. Karl wheeled Daniel and Josh, with a cloak on top of them, and Tomkins and Buckby struggled with the parson. Raffles refused the cloak saying that he was the only person who hadn't been in the water. "Wet feet, that's all I have to worry about. Put it over our good friend. His very life is in danger."

On their arrival at the inn, Tutte greeted them with a sack full of dry clothes. But the wildest greeting came as Karl wheeled Daniel and Josh past them. The slaves all stood and began hollering and hooting, banging their iron cuffs together and stamping their feet. Josh leapt out to defend his master from these noisy strangers. Karl tried to calm Josh but he would not stop barking and circling around these people who sounded and smelt like no others he'd ever known. Then Daniel lifted his head and attempted a whistle. Only Josh heard. He immediately quietened, rushed to the cart and put his paws up on the side. Daniel raised an arm to comfort his faithful dog.

Raffles clambered out of his cart with a nod of thanks to Buckby and Tomkins, and painfully hobbled to Daniel's side. "The Lord be praised!" The slaves began their hollering again until he lifted his arms and put his right forefinger to his lips and lowered his left hand and they sat down. Only the crackling fire and Josh panting could be heard. Raffles went back to the cart and lifted out the bundle. The body of the girl was still wrapped in the scrap of blanket, but her legs and feet hung down into the cold night air. One of the women let out a wail of sheer misery and the parson handed her the bundle. She cradled her child and wept noisily as he prayed for the soul of the child and the life of the mother.

Lying back in his cart, Daniel managed little more than to close his eyes once again. Raffles leant over to whisper, "It seems you are a hero, my son. One day soon you must tell us all about it."

Chapter Thirty-Eight
"A graceful form, perfectly balanced"

Daniel lay on a make-shift bed alongside the sleeping Lucy. Mrs Tollervey had nowhere else to put him and reasoned with Karl and the doctor that so long as nobody else knew, it was best to disregard respectability and she could nurse them more easily. Karl suppressed a smile and kept quiet about their relationship. The doctor had carefully removed Daniel's wet clothes and he now lay wrapped in Tollervey's own blankets next to a small but effective fire. As she wrapped his head in her own woollen shawl, she declared she had nursed many a cold fisherman, and knew how to bring the heat back to their bodies. "Leave him alone, don't touch him," she said sternly. "I'll give him a warm drink soon. And the lady too."

The doctor whispered to Karl that she was highly regarded in this ministry and backed away. "One less for me to worry about."

She retorted, "Huh! When have you ever worried? And don't send me any bills."

"Send your bill for these two people to me," Karl said decisively, then added, "I'll pay within good reason. And there'll be payment for good nursing too, Mrs Tollervey."

Once the injured villagers had been attended to by the doctor and sent on their way home, Karl moved the slaves inside. The doctor refused to examine the slaves and marched out declaring he'd be sending the bill for the villagers to the Lieutenant as it was the Coast Guard who had caused the injuries. Karl declared he was in no way responsible for payment and the doctor should present his bill to each patient. He did not regard this as heartless because he viewed it as an incentive for them to find honest, paid employment which would enable them to pay the bill. Creating employment was another matter. Daniel and Raffles could take care of that. Perhaps.

In the comparative warmth of the inn, Karl sorted through the sack until he found his own clean white breeches and an extra shirt and put them on. He went outside, flung his wet breeches across the hitching rail and, despite the cold, he brought a stool and sat close to the still burning brazier. A golden globe rose in the east and its sparkling rays shimmered across the sea. At last the dawn, and it would be a fine day. He had delivered one of his promises. He had found Daniel. Tomorrow he must find Tridd.

Tutte, Buckby and Tomkins were asleep on a couple of straw mattresses in the store room at the back of the bar. Understandably, the innkeeper complained non-stop to his wife as they trudged upstairs to a cold bed. Karl, however, knew he needed to stay awake for a few hours more, then he would sleep. Looking across to the rising sun he saw two little figures skipping and jumping down the slopes towards him. The urchins. Really must find names for them soon.

His mind skipped to Flo. Would she realize she could now make her escape from both Tridd and himself? He must get back soon and reassure her she was not a prisoner and give her the consideration she deserved. He thought of Lucy who would likely make a full recovery, but she was the wife of a fine friend. He must turn his attention to… to whom? Not one of these prissy ladies his mother kept pushing his way, of that much he was certain.

The boys bounced up to him. "Mornin' sir," they chorused.

"Good morning to you both." He was extremely pleased to see them: to say this crusade was undermanned was an understatement and these lads were an unexpected but welcome addition.

"That Major man sent us to see what you be a doin'. He says to say he's got four men with sore heads. Bleedin' they were. Flo bandaged them and the man says they're to stay there 'til you get back."

He took a long, deep breath. Of course, Lytton was there, Flo was not alone with that evil man who calls himself a parson, and desperate villagers. He'd overlook their calling her "Flo" for now, there'd be time enough to teach them manners. "Well, I think you can help me with what I be a doin'."

They grinned. "That Tutte fellow, he let those two men out of gaol. Was he meant to?" When Karl nodded they grinned even more. "And he's put that ol' parson in and locked him up! Shoutin', he was. Shoutin'."

Curly decided it was his turn to say something. "More splutterin' and coughin' than shoutin', I'd say. And that Major man keeps tellin' him he'll shut him up good and proper."

He laughed, rubbed his hands together to warm them, then said, "Run around to the church and ask the Coast Guard if they've had any trouble. Then report back to me here."

Curly gave what he thought was a salute and his pal did likewise and they ran off towards the church.

He stood up and stretched. Oh what a blessing daylight is. He pushed open the door of the inn. A warm, smoky atmosphere greeted him. The chimney needs sweeping; why don't they look after this inn. The slaves were all asleep on the floor, not one dared sit on a stool. Time to take a look at the metal tags they were wearing around their necks. He knelt and examined one. Made of copper, it had a number and the word "PAID" engraved on it. They were delivery tags. He'd like to trace whoever was expecting to receive this unfortunate man. He examined another: same number. But other tags revealed different numbers. So more than one man was involved in this illicit trade. He'd trace them. They'd not escape the law.

~

"Flo*rence*," said the woman who had sat up all night awaiting his return. "Flo*rence*. Only that Tridd man called me *Flo*. I hate it and I do not like him. He hurt me."

Karl, seated near the stove, looked concerned: no one should hurt such a charming lady. And he too would hate it if someone insisted on calling him something other than his name; he'd soon put a stop to that. He beckoned her to sit opposite him. His concerned expression was superseded by a suppressed smile. Her ruby red dress, black velvet spencer, and her glorious dark hair had dried out and seemed incongruous in the stark surroundings of Watch House. She was delightful. Sensual. The way she missed out the letter 'h' sent a frisson of excitement through his tired body. She had not taken flight; she had attended to the stove, brought in wood, kept a pot of broth hot, tucked the urchins into the beds left vacant by Buckby and Tomkins, and much more besides. Yet she looked wonderful, warm and welcoming. To have someone like her in his life was becoming a possibility. "No one will call you Flo ever again: I shall see to that." He'd not trouble her to tell him more about being hurt. He knew. He knew all too well what a blackguard Tridd was. He looked at his pocket watch. Nearly nine o'clock. "How shall we address you? What is your surname?"

"Sir, it is Fivaz."

He smiled and repeated, "Florence Fivaz, what a beautiful name." Florence returned his smile. "And should we address you as…" he hesitated, she was obviously French "…as Madame or Mademoiselle?"

"Sir, I am not married, I have no family and I shall be most honoured if *you* will call me Florence. You are my hero."

She pronounced this last word without the 'h' and Karl felt his whole body react. He could not stop a broad smile; tired as he was, this woman infused him with energy, the kind that could carry her off to bed, yet clearly she was a lady and that is how he would treat her.

"I am the one who is honoured." He could not stop another smile and he was aware they were becoming bigger. He must be careful. What was a French woman doing on an English island? There'd be time to find out. For now, he would give her the benefit of the doubt. "My men, indeed everyone, will address you as Miss Fivaz." He'd accord her the honour of the *English* title. She might need some guidance so he added, "You should address me as Lieutenant and my men as Mister." Buckby and Tomkins hardly merited the title of Mister but maybe, given time, they could be regarded as men of worth, property owners one day perhaps. To be called 'Mister', if only by a delightful French woman, might help them aspire to that station in life. His mind wandered to Martha. She was the one servant whom everyone called by her Christian name. Her surname, *Fagg*, though a good Kent county name, was just too blunt. Sleep – time they both went to bed. "Let me escort you to the top floor again and you shall sleep there, in privacy, at least for the next few hours." He stood up and she followed him.

~

It was mid-afternoon when Karl, sleeping in Flowers' lumpy bed, woke up. Above him, in *his* bed, slept Flo. He corrected himself – Flo*rence*. A satisfied expression crossed his face. He noticed a bowl and jug of water nearby; he'd wash, dress then wake her himself. On the floor below was Tridd's foot-licker; how good it had been to pass him by earlier, all trussed up and gagged. Muted

Under a Dark Star

sounds from the ground floor reminded him that the men would need directing, they'd evidently woken up already. As soon as Karl had arrived at Watch House, Lytton readily agreed to take the four badly injured men to their families, then to take Raffles to Norwell Farm in Karl's carriage and send his more comfortable one to collect Lucy and Daniel; so that was taken care of; they'd be well cared for there. The slaves! They were also here somewhere. So much to do still. He rubbed his cold hands together, then washed, dressed in another clean shirt, and his uniform breeches – women loved men in uniform – combed his hair, dashed up the stairs and called out to her. Florence wasn't there He looked around and saw the pathetic bunch of primroses he'd placed in her bed at the fort. She'd brought them here and placed them in a little jug of water. That's just what Lucy would do. He took a deep breath and skipped down the stone steps, past the pathetic parson again, and on down to the ground. Before his eyes could seek her out, he was confronted by the slaves. He glanced across to Tutte. "Did the Coast Guard escort them here?"

"Yes sir. I was surprised you didn't hear the racket the geese made; they woke me up, and then they thumped on the door." Momentarily, he imagined the geese thumping on the door. Thoughts of Florence had created a merry mood.

"So the Coast Guard delivered the slaves and then went on their way home?"

"Yes sir. And just after we'd woken up, we took the bodies to the graveyard. There was an empty grave that the Guard had discovered and we piled the dead in there. Except Mr Tynlan, of course. He's lying in the church itself, near the barrels of olive oil."

"How many dead?"

"We've located eight sailors so far and only three villagers. And Mr Tynlan." Tutte could see Karl's disapproval and tried to lift it by saying, "Of course, some of the bodies didn't fit inside, and we just laid them on top, so we've covered over the whole grave with a tarpaulin. Looks better."

"We must contact Parson Raffles and ask him to arrange burials, if he feels so inclined. What about the little black girl?" Karl was visibly anguished.

"We didn't know whether to put her in the church or the grave but the grave was full, so we put her in the church. We did wonder if that was allowed, her being of unknown origin."

"You did well. A blameless child." He sighed. "And who is guarding the church now?"

"Three of the Coast Guard stayed there, as you instructed, until they were relieved by the Guard from Bruton. Major Lytton called them out, as agreed, and six armed men are now guarding what's in the church."

"Tutte, organize a rota to cover the next week so it is secured until we arrange the sale of the goods or otherwise dispose of the cargo." Karl turned to Tomkins. "Have these people been fed?"

"The slaves, sir? Yes sir."

"With what?"

Tomkins looked at Buckby for inspiration.

"Well sir, I gave them all some water and they had Flo's broth."

He glanced around the room. Where was she? Florence stood up from where she had been sitting on the floor by the side of a cupboard and came forward to Karl. He gave her an admiring smile before he turned back to Buckby and said sharply, "You will address this lady as Miss Fivaz."

Buckby and Tomkins looked at each other and Karl interpreted their look correctly. He didn't mind. Why should he mind that it was obvious he appreciated her attributes?

Under a Dark Star

"I shall be happy to make porridge but there are very little oats."

Oh, her English! He could listen to her all day. "Just make up what you have," and here he could not stop himself from imitating the way she spoke. "Make a leettle porridge for the slaves." Something had to be better than nothing. "Buckby you are to go to the store and commandeer a sack of oats and some sugar." He'd seen the storekeeper staggering up the chine with a cart full of loot – now he could help keep the slaves alive. Then he remembered that Tridd ordered everything to go to the church before distribution, mostly to himself. "Or get something from the church."

"Milk too please, Lieutenant." Florence was already emptying all the oats into a clean pan and adding water. "Bread! We have no bread. And perhaps les confitures?"

Karl translated for Buckby. "Bring back some jam, a dozen pots if you can. And if they've got any meat and potatoes, bring those back too. Tomkins, you'd better go with him. Tell them I'll pay later. Where are the boys?"

"We're 'ere, sir." The two boys leapt up. "We'll help."

"I want you to stay here and help Tutte get the slaves up to the next floor and make them as comfortable as possible. Provide water to wash with and some to drink." Karl turned to the slaves and spoke very loudly in an attempt to explain that they were to go up the stone steps, wash and soon there would be some porridge for them to eat. "Tutte, you get this operation going and then we'll have our room back down here. And give the weasely parson a bowl of water to wash himself in – he stinks. You can release him from his ropes and the gag. And don't go near him, especially when he's coughing. Make him wash his breeches."

"Should I give him another pair?"

234

"No. Make him wait." His shirt would probably cover the necessary.

Tutte was a natural leader and beckoned the slaves to follow and they did. He clapped his hands at the boys who, unusually, had been more inclined to stare at the strangers than help.

"Buckby, do you know if anyone has told Mrs Tynlan that her husband is dead?"

Buckby shook his head. "Perhaps Tolly's sent a message, or perhaps Mrs Tynlan is out searching or gone to the inn."

"When you are at the store, make enquiries, and at the inn too. If no one has seen Mrs Tynlan, I want you to visit her as soon as possible and explain to her the happenings of last night. Take your time and ensure she is comforted. Perhaps take her to one of her friends."

Now it was Karl's turn to notice Buckby's facial expression which betrayed a feeling not noticed before. This could solve a few problems.

At last he was alone with Florence. He wandered over to her by the sink. "My apologies for bringing you to a place so bleak and cold. It is only for a short while."

"I am safe. That is good." She looked him straight in the eyes. "I thank you. I am pleased to be helping the poor strangers."

They'd make a good team. He had plans, much to accomplish, and she would bring a softer touch, distributing largesse elegantly. He smiled; he was even thinking in French now. His dreams were interrupted by his stomach rumbling. "Forgive me, I haven't eaten for a long time." Then he remembered her bowl of broth she'd saved for him. "Apart from your broth."

Immediately Florence opened a small cupboard above her head and pulled out a covered dish. "I have here a little cheese." Wrapped in a clean white handkerchief was a hunk of bread. "This is stale, but better than nothing, no?"

How remarkable. Not only had she saved him something special but she was voicing his thoughts too. "It most certainly is."

"You shall sit by the stove and I shall warm the bread."

He did exactly as she said. How annoying that he must make plans to track down Tridd. He'd said he'd find him tomorrow and now tomorrow had arrived. He knew his foe could be in Ryde thanks to the informant at Kaddakay church. For the moment, however, he would watch Florence move. Such a graceful form, perfectly balanced, with ruby red lips matching her dress and her bountiful black hair tumbling over her shoulders. He leant back in his chair, put his hands behind his head, stretched out his feet and allowed his thoughts to wander.

Under a Dark Star

Chapter Thirty-Nine
"Not quite the naval way"

Once darkness fell over the diamond isle, Karl knew he must say farewell to Florence. He had waited until there was little chance of being seen and now it was undoubtedly time to bring Tridd to justice.

"I must go. I can sit here and enjoy your delightful company no longer."

"You will not go alone?"

A hint of a smile crossed his face. "Yes, alone."

"No! You must have men with you. Lots of men."

He could not have been more pleased with her response. Nevertheless, he turned away and climbed the stairs to his room at the top. He changed into his uniform, gathered up his dark woollen cloak in preference to his cumbersome leather one, and picked up his pistol, sword and belt. He walked slowly down, passing his sleeping men, and taking time on the last step to watch Florence as, once more, she bustled around the cupboards. He took a deep breath: she was the one woman who could help him forget Lucy.

"It may be a short while before I return, but return I shall, and you will then know that you'll be safe from that man. Until I do, do not open the door to anyone and under no circumstances should you leave Watch House. You will not be alone here, and I hope to be back within a few days. The men have their orders but at the moment they need their sleep. Tell them I'll find Tridd. Take care of the boys." He knew he was making this farewell last longer than necessary so now he simply stood and treasured her.

Florence took a deep breath and clutched her hands together under her breast. "May the good Lord go with you."

He strapped on his sheathed sword and withdrew it. "I have this trusty blade, you need have no fear." She put her hand to her mouth. He sheathed his sword immediately. Walking towards her, he held out his hand and took hers from her lips and kissed it gently, fleetingly, and let it drop.

"Please, I ask you to be very careful."

He bowed, turned and strode away. He must not think of her again until Tridd was secure in gaol.

~

Around ten in the evening, he arrived in Ryde. Why had this town been mentioned specifically? What brought Tridd here? Bawdy houses? Gambling? His mind went back to the day on the island when he'd walked into the first inn he'd encountered. The one where Tridd, yes that much he knew, was playing cards. Was it for...? Anger rose in him. Time to verify that later. He must start his search now.

He carefully tied Midnight to the hitching rail outside the rowdy tavern, noting that an ill-dressed man was loitering near the door and clutching a tankard. Revenue man, perhaps? He sauntered over and was accosted by the loiterer.

"I wouldn't go in there in that uniform, sir."

"Revenue Officer?"

"Yes sir."

Karl needed to be convinced and asked for the name of his senior officer. He did not recognize the name but said nothing.

He had no intention of going inside; he'd planned to offer a half-crown to a needy-looking customer but this man was a better solution. "I'd like you to verify that Tridd is not in the bar nor in any of the upstairs rooms and I'll cover your post here."

The Revenue Officer looked startled. "Upstairs rooms? I'd be a dead man the first time I opened a door."

"So how do you know he's not in hiding here?"

"This is his favoured inn so we've been on watch at the front and the back since we received word from you, sir."

Karl had grave doubts. Yet from the noise and the language coming from inside, he was sympathetic to any representative of the law who'd try to search a bawdy house alone.

"Was it searched before you took up your post here?

"Oh yes sir. There were eight officers from Cowes, with pistols too." The man paused to establish if this particular senior officer was impressed. He wasn't, so he continued, "And we, that's those of us from Ryde, we then took our places. We take turns. We cover all the inns in this part of town. Tridd's not one to favour high class hotels."

"I am relying on you to ensure he does not slip away from the island nor find somewhere to hide until you can no longer spare the men to look for him."

"We do our best, sir." Karl was about to ask a question but discerned that the man had something more to say. The man licked his lips and began. "He's known to take a woman down to the beach." The officer, now having shed his loitering stance, pointed along the coast. "There's a sheltered cove, about half a mile, I'd say. He wasn't there when we last looked."

"When was that?"

"Only yesterday, sir. In the evening too."

He weighed up this information. He needed to be wary of a trap. Had this man been paid to say this? Reassurance came when the man suggested he take six men with him.

"My thanks to you for your assistance."

Under a Dark Star

~

Karl easily found the cove. Six men! No. He would bring Tridd in himself. Unaided. Except by his sword. No one, least of all Florence, should be won as a prize; this man must come face to face with justice. He tied Midnight to a tree and stroked his velvety muzzle and patted his shiny black coat. Midnight's ears pricked. "Quiet now. I'll be back soon."

He pulled his telescope from his inside pocket and took a look at the beach. A thin wisp of smoke curled its way up and drifted inland before dispersing. If this is Tridd, he is remarkably careless. Or, more likely, too confident. He took off his cloak and uniform and stowed them in his saddle bag. Now he was dressed all in black. He placed his cap securely on the saddle and pulled on a black knitted hat. Next he threaded his belt through the loops on his close fitting cotton breeches.

Collapsing his telescope and tucking it into a pouch on his belt, he deduced that the smoke was about one hundred yards away. If Tridd had one of his dogs with him, it would alert him to his presence. He patted his pistol on the left side of his belt, and the rope tied at the back, and crept towards the tell-tale smoke. It came not from an open fire but from a chimney.

Using his telescope, he could see that a cabin had been built against the low clay cliffs. When he came closer, he noticed that it was quite sturdy with only a stable door, both the top and the bottom being firmly shut. No chance of peeking through a window: there were none. No dog either, for it would surely have smelt and heard him. He listened at the door. A female voice. And a man's. Disappointed, he knew there was insufficient space to wield his sword. He stepped away and glanced up; the roof sloped towards the cliff. There'd been a recent fall – a few scattered rocks lay close.

He moved back to the door. Maybe the top wasn't bolted. As he reached out to see if he could wrench it open, he heard panting coming from further along the beach. He turned and to his horror he saw a shape, the same mid brown colour as the cliffs, and it was hurtling towards him. He drew his flintlock pistol, cocked it, took aim and fired. He'd been only twenty feet away from a vicious mauling. Instantly the whole door flew open and slammed against him. He clung on to the pistol but had no time to reload before an arm around his neck wrenched him out from behind the door into the light from the cabin. He received a swift knee jerk to the back of his knee. There was no doubt it was Tridd. And he stank of brandy. Tridd now pulled his neck further back but was frustrated in this by backing into the door. Karl took his chance. He slammed his elbow into Tridd and with his right hand he smashed his pistol butt against Tridd's head and wrested the arm from around his neck. He spun round and faced the glowering murderer.

It was years since his last fist fight. Now he was fighting for his life and his sheathed sword hampered him rather than defended him. Why did his foe only stand and stare? To give the woman time to get away? Unlikely. But useful perhaps? He called out, "Woman! Come out and run!" She did.

At the same time, Tridd rushed at him as if to smash his fist into his face but Karl ducked, butted him in the chest, picked up his legs and flung him over his shoulders. That trick wouldn't work twice but with his enemy prostrate on his back, it allowed him time to back away and draw his sword just as Tridd scrambled up. It was odd, this killer just stood staring at him. Those eyes probably terrified the locals: for Karl they provided the opportunity to advance with his blade. With a flick he slit Tridd's sleeve at the shoulder and then he slit the other side. "Turn around."

"You're that Thorsen. All done up in black don't fool me. There ain't no way you're taking me in. You're a dead man."

Tridd's arms hung by his side but his eyes showed no sign of defeat. Karl noticed why. Sand trickled from his clenched fist. His sword flashed to Tridd's hand and nicked the skin. "Sling that and I'll take your hand off."

Tridd neither let go of the sand nor turned around.

"Unless you want this sword in your belly, turn around, drop the sand and put your hands behind you."

Tridd slowly turned around facing the open door, then shot inside, slammed the door and bolted it.

A satisfied smile crept over Karl's face. He reloaded his pistol and sheathed his sword. He silently piled the rocks against the side of the cabin and put dead grass from the cliff fall on the low part of the roof. He picked up some nearby driftwood and broke it into strips and placed them on top of the grass. Then, using the rocks, he climbed up. He tore a few lumps of the crumbling clay from the cliff and stealthily walked across to the chimney. He used the clay to block the escaping smoke. He crept across to above the door. He laid down his gun and sword, then took the rope from his belt and tied a lasso. He'd not lassoed anything since he was in the navy when he'd captured a rampaging pig on board ship, yet he was confident this would work.

All he had to do was wait and while he did, he fashioned the dried grass and sticks into something resembling a large bird's nest. Tridd coughed. Good. He silently turned to the chimney and lifted the clay. He lodged some stouter sticks a little way down then placed the nest on top. As soon as he saw it smoulder from rising sparks, he replaced the clay keeping all the smoke inside. No doubt Tridd would put out the fire in the hearth, but smoke drifting down the chimney would not be so easy to stop.

When Tridd began coughing violently, Karl picked up his rope ready to drop it over his body. But Tridd did not oblige by coming out. He opened the top half of the stable door and leaned out to take a few deep breaths. Karl slipped the lasso around the only available part of Tridd – his head – and pulled. Tridd, still coughing, grabbed it and tried to wrest it away. Karl tugged on the rope, tightening it considerably. Leaning over the edge of the roof, he shot Tridd in his left arm. Tridd immediately ceased struggling, yowled, and swore profusely. The lasso was evidently not tight enough, so Karl tugged until Tridd no longer protested. Karl reloaded his pistol then jumped down, making sure the rope stayed taut.

"Open the door and walk out slowly."

Tridd had no intention of obeying someone else's orders. "Never," he croaked, and desperately pulled at the rope with his right hand.

Karl reached for the bolt on the inside of the door and kicked it open, smashing it against Tridd causing him to lurch backwards, thereby tightening the rope again. Karl jerked him out of the doorway, spun him around and, ignoring the croaking, he tied the other end of the rope to his two hands pulled behind his back. "Get moving!"

While Karl retrieved his sword from the roof, the subdued killer staggered towards the cliff path. Karl only used his sword once and that was to encourage his drunken prisoner to avoid the dead dog.

Not quite the naval way of doing things. But the job was done.

Chapter Forty
Lucy
"Escaped the sawbones"

Friday 21st March
Joeline Lytton knocked on the door of Lucy's little sitting room at Norwell Farm. She hardly waited for an answer before rushing in. "Karl's caught Tridd!"

Daniel leapt up. "Well that didn't take him long!"

Mrs Lytton looked radiant. "He is a remarkable man. If only he'd come here years ago, the poor would not have had to endure such terrible troubles."

Lucy, still holding Freddie in her arms, studied Mrs Lytton. Yes, there was no doubting her admiration. "Where is he?"

Mrs Lytton could not hold back a broad smile as she said, "The Lieutenant, so I hear, is on his way to visit us."

"No, I mean Tridd. Where is he?"

"In gaol." Mrs Lytton's thoughts returned to Karl. "We shall be able to ask the Lieutenant more when he arrives."

Daniel invited her to sit but she declined. "If he's on Midnight, he won't be long."

She had the look of a younger woman as she said, "I must hurry. He might need to stay here for a day or two." She dashed out and firmly closed the door behind her.

Lucy smiled at Daniel. "I'm glad he has his devotees."

"And I hope one day he'll have one in particular – but not you!" Daniel pushed his pale blond hair out of his eyes. "Will you trim my hair for me?"

Lucy patted the sofa next to her. "Of course I will, and this time I shall keep a lock of it to give to you when you are old and grey." She watched him laugh and knew she could guess his thoughts. "Oh please come back and sit next to me, it's just so very, very good to be near you and to know you are almost fully recovered."

Daniel readily sat close. "Oh it's just a numb toe; that will soon fade. I'm so relieved to see that you have no lasting repercussions from your ordeal."

"I've been fortunate."

"Fortunate?" He turned his head so he could look straight into her warm, brown eyes.

Lucy, feeling the full force of those wonderful blue eyes, could feel herself melting. "Yes," was all she could say.

"I'm the one who is fortunate to be married to you. I can't remember too much about being trapped in the hull, perhaps later my mind will allow me to recall more, but I do know that without you, I wouldn't be alive now. How can any man be so blessed as to have a wife as brave as you? You would be a credit to the King's army."

She laughed as she imagined herself in long black shiny boots and a heavy red tunic. "I'd have to take Josh with me."

Josh, hearing his name, raised an ear and opened an eye but promptly went back to sleep by the fire. They were talking about him, not to him, nothing was required.

Daniel looked lovingly at his faithful dog. "He's been dining on the very best of everything. Martha is spoiling him, as usual."

"He deserves the best; we could not have managed without him. And you are the one who has trained him."

Daniel smiled. He moved closer and wrapped his arm around her shoulder. With his other hand he tickled Freddie under his chin. "My son, our beautiful son. I hope he will grow up to find a love such as we have." He took Freddie from her arms and gently placed him on the floor and gave him a ball to play with. Freddie clumsily bashed the ball and then crawled after it. "Eight months old and see how fast he is."

Lucy's face shone. "I was so relieved when you began to recover and you escaped the sawbones. I couldn't bear for him to touch you in case he sawed something off."

Daniel drew Lucy into his arms. "Sawbones? Where did you learn that dreadful word?"

"That's what everyone calls him, apparently, as it is his remedy for most things. And, can you believe that the people defend him just because he is the only doctor who will visit this part of the island?"

He reflected for a moment. Yes, he'd seen quite a few people with fingers missing, or struggling on crutches. He hadn't thought much about it – it seemed to fit in with many a smuggling community. "I've had such a lucky escape." Then he added quickly, "Not luck, I owe my life to you. How could you have risked everything to find me?"

"Waiting for you here gave me time to think and I reflected on my life with my mother. You were the only happiness I knew. Dear Parson Raffles kept me sane but I always lived for the moment I'd see you again. I often relive the time I first saw you on your farm."

"Ah... the porridge?"

"Yes. If I had not been so hungry I don't think I could have come so close to you."

"By then I'd decided I would marry you." His blue eyes sparkled.

"Oh you were so cruel!" Lucy laughed. "I had no idea you even had a fancy for me."

"I never forgot that first kiss I stole from you some years earlier. Now that the word 'kiss' has been mentioned..." he leant forward until his lips touched hers and this time her kiss was readily offered. It was interrupted by Freddie banging his little fist on her foot. She leant down and picked him up and Daniel wrapped his arms around them both. "I would gladly give my life if it saved yours." He looked down into her brown, eager eyes and saw the love waiting there for him. "Let's put Freddie in his cradle and sneak upstairs and lock the door."

"I don't think he'll sleep yet. I'll ask Martha to look after him and settle him when he's ready." The little sitting room was some distance from the kitchen, so Lucy stood outside in the hall and rang the hand bell until Martha peered around the kitchen door.

"I thought you was all asleep in there. You should be. You ain't supposed to go a running around." Martha's almost toothless grin was as engaging as ever and grew bigger as she walked towards Lucy.

"Take care of Freddie for us and we shall do as you think best and go upstairs for a short rest."

Martha's eyes lit up. "I thought I was never going to be asked; you've not left his side since you came back and I be aching to give the little one a cuddle. Aching, I am, aching."

Lucy loved it when Martha returned to her old, natural way of speech. Despite all her efforts to *better herself*, as she called it, and one day serve in a grand house, Martha slipped back whenever she was excited. "Freddie will be ready for his afternoon nap in half an hour or so."

"Did you like the little cradle I made for him?" Martha laughed as Lucy nodded. The 'cradle' was nothing more than a drawer from one of Mrs Lytton's cabinets. "I'll watch him

Under a Dark Star

carefully, you know I will. I'll defend him from dragons and monsters." She put up her fists and waggled them around.

Lucy laughed, but all she could think was how close she had come to losing everyone she loved. "You may wake us up when the Lieutenant arrives."

"The carter told us he'd caught that wormy rat yesterday and he was in the town gaol. Easy for our Lieutenant, eh? He'd escorted him to the gaol in some place beginning with N."

"Newport. Daniel says they'll probably hold the trial there in a few days." As much as she loved her devoted friend and servant, Lucy had other things on her mind so she hurried on. "Freddie is playing with his ball."

"Time to play with my little flumple wumple!" Martha wiped her hands energetically on her apron. "Now you go and rest and leave me and young Freddie to our games."

Lucy put her head around the sitting room door and gave Daniel the smile he'd clung to in his darkest hours.

~

Karl had endured a cold journey crossing the central chalk ridge which spanned the island. Consequently he leapt off Midnight, patted him, and flung the reins around the hitching post leaving Miller to attend to him. The door to the farmhouse was opened at the very moment he arrived and he bounced in with a satisfied smile before sitting on the bench while one of the servants pulled his boots off and replaced them with leather slippers.

Mrs Lytton swept towards him, her cheeks aglow and, as Karl bowed, she dropped a low curtsey, delivered with an unstoppable beam. "Welcome. You are more welcome than ever. To have rid us all of that…" she hunted for a word to describe Tridd's activities but had no chance before her husband rushed up the hallway, bowed, and ushered Karl into the drawing room.

"You deserve a hero's reception but I trust you will settle for our high regard and heartiest congratulations." Major Lytton poured him a glass of his best brandy. "That'll warm you through. You'll stay the night?"

Karl took the glass. "I'm most grateful for this," he held it high, "and I'm pleased to accept your offer of hospitality." He took a sip. "It's not over yet. The trial is set for the Wednesday after Easter and by then I hope that Daniel will be able to travel and bear witness to the murders committed by Tridd. I shall be able to support his account as I found the bodies."

Major Lytton stood, legs astride in front of the hearth, and invited Karl to sit close by. Rocking on his heels, he confirmed that Daniel had recovered almost fully and that Lucy was also in good health. "Despite the cold and the wet, we have all returned to full vigour with the exception of your poor coachman who is sniffing and sneezing. He's been on light duties until today." Peering out of the window, he added, "He's taking care of that fine horse of yours."

"First-rate fellow. Usually has the assistance of a groom when we're at Whitchester Manor but he's not too high and mighty to help when necessary."

Each brought the other up-to-date on the happenings on the south of the island until Karl glanced around. "I thought Daniel was here? I need to speak to him."

Right on cue, Daniel and Lucy came through the door together, with a maid following behind with a tray of tea.

Karl leapt up and bowed. "Your rosy cheeks tell me you have recovered well, Lucy."

Lucy added a blush to her rosy cheeks. Why could nothing be hidden from his searching eyes?

Daniel, the author of her flushed appearance, bowed. "My congratulations. To capture that tricky Tridd is worthy of a medal."

"Sit down, sit down," said Mrs Lytton as she motioned to the maid to pour out the tea. "Your Martha has insisted on baking these biscuits and I feel sure she'd like us to eat them all."

Karl tilted his head in acknowledgement then responded to Daniel. "I could not have achieved his capture without your guidance and participation. And those slaves would have drowned, or died of the cold had you not rescued them. I want to know every detail when there is time. First I want to ensure Tridd's punishment."

Lucy saw that Daniel approved. Now they were both on the same side of the law, he appreciated Karl's persistence and endurance. "Our agreement was that we would not be pressing for the wreckers to be hanged but that transportation would be their sentence."

Karl interrupted, "You're about to say, I hope, that Tridd should not be sent to Van Diemen's land but should bear the full penalty for murder. Remember, he is likely to have been responsible for the loss of many, many lives, including the Americans who first came to our attention only a few months ago. How many lives has he ruined or terminated in his time here?" Karl turned to George Lytton.

"I cannot give you a specific answer but it undoubtedly runs into hundreds," said the Major. "He has only got away with his activities because local people who objected seemed to disappear. Magistrates and Riding Officers were bribed, and constables and watchmen never came near the back of the Wight. There is such a sparse population on this part of the island and communication, as you know, is difficult. Few have been aware of all that has happened. I am ashamed to say that I should have done more."

Mrs Lytton waved her arms to stop him saying more. "You cannot blame yourself, my dear. You had no support whatsoever from anyone!"

Daniel continued with what he had intended to say. "I believe Tridd must pay the law's price for murder. It would be quite wrong to send him away and hope that he will reform and make a good life for himself. A crocodile will always seize, sink, swallow and smile."

Mrs Lytton, puzzled, looked to her husband for clarification.

"I'll explain later," he whispered.

"However," said Daniel, "I now do not believe the villagers should even be transported. I have come to know them and while many of them are rough and inclined to commit misdemeanours, with Tridd removed and improvements in their conditions, there is every chance they will repent and reform." He turned to Karl, raised his eyebrows and grinned, "Remember that? One of Raffles' favourite topics."

Karl laughed. "Yes, but it was Repentance, Reformation and Restitution! These villagers haven't a hope of making restitution."

Lucy could not hold back. "Perhaps they could make this a better place to live in the future and that would be a kind of restitution to the living if not the dead."

There was a moment's silence before Daniel squeezed her hand and said, "How true."

Karl regarded her for a moment, admiration showing in his eyes, then turned to Daniel. "There is one," he said, "who should pay for violation of his Holy Orders. He pursed his lips. "I feel it is not right to deport such a..." Karl remembered there were ladies present, "such an *evil man* to Van Diemen's Land. Petty thieves yes, but not Rafe Driver. There is much I haven't told you yet."

"Then what are we to do with him?" asked the Major.

"For the moment he can remain where he is, incarcerated in Watch House," Karl said with a satisfied smile. "I don't think he is receiving favourable treatment." Lucy watched as Karl's anguished thoughts played across his face. He became aware that everyone was waiting for his decision on Driver's future but he changed course. "Now about the slaves. I have contacted Wilberforce." Major Lytton showed no indication of knowing who 'Wilberforce' was. "Wilberforce leads the fight against slavery and I have sent him the information on the slaves' copper tags around their necks to see if their so-called owners can be located. And prosecuted."

"Excellent work!" Major Lytton had also been converted from critic to admirer.

Karl continued. "The Coast Guard are arranging transportation of the slaves to Ryde and from there they will be taken to London and either repatriated or found employment in service."

Mrs Lytton handed round the plate of biscuits. "Do have another."

Major Lytton indulged his wife, and himself, and took two. "Is there any other news we should be imparting?"

Lucy announced, "Yes, today Raffles is burying the slave child. He and Mrs Raffles left here early this morning; he too has recovered well, and they will both now stay at the parsonage until the birth of their child in the autumn."

"Very wise," responded Karl. "The long and arduous journey is not recommended in her condition."

Daniel added, "I think Raffles is itching to take these sinners under his wing and turn them into saints."

"And I tell you, he's just the man to do it," said Martha pushing her way through the door and clutching a plate of cake.

"Carrot cake," she stated, then muttered, "and it weren't me what put carrots in it. Silly idea."

Karl greeted her like a long lost friend. "We'd eat anything, Martha, just so long as you serve it to us. You are a heroine." Martha stood like a statue. "Accompanying your Mistress on that adventure will save many lives in the future, and it's something of which you can be most proud."

"We are so grateful to you," said Lucy.

"And forever in your debt," declared Daniel.

Martha burst into tears.

Chapter Forty-One
Karl
"A sense of foreboding"

Friday 28th March
The morning mist lay over the horizon like a grey chiffon scarf, curling its way across the sea. Karl brought Midnight to a halt just to stare and appreciate the sight of the sun tracing it with silver. He had stayed much longer at Norwell Farm than anticipated. There had been more furniture to convey to the parsonage and then Lucy, Daniel, little Freddie and Martha were taken by carriage to be with Raffles and his wife. Now, a whole week later, he was returning to Watch House, leaving Raffles to conduct the Good Friday service in his new parish.

His horse stamped his hooves impatiently and he knew he should continue the journey to see how his men were faring; it had been a few days since he last rode to Watch House. But first he would visit Mrs Tynlan. Buckby had apprised her of her husband's fate, so it was mostly a matter of courtesy. Courtesy? No gentleman would visit a lone woman and definitely not at this time in the morning but, he reasoned, if he didn't visit her now he probably never would.

Becky opened the door a little and was surprised to see the uniformed officer of what she still called 'the Revenue'. Embarrassed, she closed it to within an inch or two.

"Mrs Tynlan, I have come with a message from Mr Tynton."

"One moment please, sir, I am not yet respectable."

"Take all the time you need and I offer my apologies for calling so early."

Five or more minutes passed before Becky opened the door with a nervous smile. Now dressed and with her hair combed and piled on her head she asked Karl to come in and sit down. He continued to stand, feeling uncomfortable as she dithered by the scullery doorway, clearly wondering if she should offer some refreshment. Apparently she decided against this and sat down, thus allowing Karl to sit too.

"Mrs Tynlan, may I offer my condolences for the loss of your husband."

She stared at the floor.

"Mr Tynton is recovering from a brutal ordeal, otherwise he would have returned to visit you. You will probably have heard by now that he is married." He reminded himself that he must put a stop to Lucy's marriage rising to the surface at every opportunity. "And he is with her now. They both suffered badly from the cold but it is hoped they will fully recover soon."

Becky looked up, her eyes full of fear. "I ain't got no one, sir, no one to help me."

Karl raised his hand. He could read this little woman as easy as headlines in a newspaper. "That situation will change and your good name is not compromised. *Everyone* was ruled by the power of this Dark Star. That's what you all called him?" She nodded. "You need have no fear regarding your husband's involvement with Tridd and wrecking…"

"Sir, my husband was a good man but Tridd had a hold over him."

Karl could forgive her interruption if she had information to give. "Tell me; I have time to listen."

Brushing away a tear, she began. "They were both dumped in the House of Resolution when Zeb was just this high." She indicated about two feet tall. "He was an orphan but Tridd was older and a bastard child, and when his mother got the pox, she put him in there. He never knew his father and he never saw his mother again."

Undoubtedly tragic, but, regrettably, many a child started life like that. "So what was this hold Tridd had over him?" Karl tried not to sound too impatient.

"As Zeb got older, one of the guardians who visited regularly," she lifted her eyes to meet Karl's and immediately looked down again.

"The guardians being those responsible for the care of the poor, sick and elderly in the House?"

"Yes sir. One of them, well he said he was a guardian, took a liking to my Zeb." Karl gave a hint of a smile, but Becky saw and frowned. "He, he…"

Karl realized his error and helped her. "He abused him?"

"Yes sir."

"He beat him?"

"Not that, sir. He being only about nine years old at the time was not able to defend himself from the man's *appetites*."

Karl's stomach churned. The brute must be brought to justice. "Do you know the guardian's name?"

"I ain't finished yet, sir." She took a peek at Karl to see if she would be allowed to continue. "Tridd, now he was older, fifteen or more, was big because he used to steal the others' suppers. It weren't easy for the breakfasts and dinners 'cos there was always someone watching, but he got away with pinching stuff off the supper dishes."

"So Zeb knew he was a thief?"

"No, what I mean is, Tridd was big, bigger than all the others and strong too. He used to do outside work, breaking up stones in the quarry, for the roads. Some of the others were picking on Zeb 'cos this guardian brought him presents sometimes, to keep him quiet, and the others would take them off him."

"What sort of presents?"

"I don't know too much but Zeb said he'd been given a pair of leather boots, not new, but good ones and someone took them off him but Tridd got them back for him. Weren't no good to Tridd 'cos they was too small. Zeb used to run errands for him and they looked after each other. Tridd knew about the guardian but couldn't do nothing about it. Not then anyway."

"But later?"

"Yes sir. Later. The guardian was found dead in a pool of vomit with something cut off him." Becky shifted in her seat, she was clearly embarrassed and very upset.

"Was no one arrested for the murder?"

"No sir. It was some of the boys who found him, including Zeb." She hung her head and mumbled, "Tridd said to feed him to the pigs."

There was silence until Karl asked, "And this was never discovered?"

"Zeb said they didn't hear anything more about it. He told me he wasn't the only one it had happened to, so I suppose they all got together and it's been kept quiet all these years. At the time it was a big mystery, he'd just disappeared."

Karl stared hard at her. Poor woman. He'd help her by concluding the story. "So Zeb knew that Tridd had murdered one of the guardians?"

"Yes sir. Though the other guardians said he weren't one of them. But don't you see? Tridd is not all bad. He looked after him. When Zeb was older and came to work for my father, he was a decent young man. Of course, my father didn't think he was good enough for me, but Tridd told my father that Zeb would make me a fine husband." Karl could imagine the conversation. Becky

Under a Dark Star

continued, "I had a small dowry and we bought this land. We *bought* it. We ain't tenants." Her eyes flickered up to Karl's. "Tridd never got Zeb to take part in the wrecking. We used to store some of the stuff but Tridd kept him out of the actual wrecking until last week." Becky stared at the floor again yet Karl sensed she hadn't finished. "Zeb says it also happened to Tridd when he was too little to defend himself."

So Tridd had waited until he could defend himself and others too. Perhaps there was a shred of decency in the man. Or was he just using Zeb for a while. "Can you think why Tridd killed your husband?" Karl knew why but verification would be welcome.

Becky's face creased and tears rolled down her cheeks. She wiped them away, sighed and said, "I think it was because he was too friendly with Daniel, them being cousins. Tridd was jealous and I expect he thought Zeb had told him all his secrets so Daniel had to die."

She was undoubtedly right but it was not the main reason he was killed. Karl drew in a deep breath. "Tridd told Zeb to go to the wrecking so that Daniel would also be there. It was Daniel he wanted to kill. When Zeb saw the fight with Daniel, Tridd killed Zeb to stop him being able to testify against him."

Becky sniffed. "He wouldn't have told on him." Her tears began to flow freely.

Karl stood up and wandered around the cold and dark little parlour. "Tridd thought Zeb's allegiance had shifted." There was nothing more to be said on this.

"How is Daniel? Will he come to see me?"

"I'm sure he will. He wants to talk to you about looking after this place." He thought this was a good time to introduce his plan. "I'll send Buckby with a few provisions and he'll give you a hand with chopping some wood."

"Thank you, sir. He has been." She hesitated. "He said he'd come and see me on his day off."

Karl nearly exploded. "Day off! He won't be having one of those until after I've gone – we've far too much work to do and so few to do it."

Becky clenched her fists to her chest. "I'm sorry, sir. I didn't mean to get him into trouble."

Karl was angry. Angry with himself. Again. "I'll make sure he comes to you before that. I'll send him here tomorrow. Can you find something for our two little urchins to do? You have a spare room so perhaps they could stay here with you? They're in need of a little kindness and mothering and will readily give you a hand to help with the land. What do you think?"

"Oh sir, I'd be very pleased. Mr Buckby told me about them. But there ain't enough food for us all."

"I'll make sure you have enough to feed them for a week or two and then you let me know if you and Buckby between you could care for them." There – he'd said it! He might not be around to say it later, so it just had to be said now. "You'll need to give them names." He stood and walked towards the door.

As Becky stood up, Karl noticed light in her eyes at last. Daniel had said she was a good little homemaker, maybe she could begin again and Buckby, though also recently widowed could look forward to a new life – as a landowner perhaps? Buckby, having no relatives on the island, had been loudly complaining of his impending homelessness. It was good that he'd a glow in his eye for Becky. And with Daniel's donkey, they'd be off to a good start. It was still early days; he should not enthuse too much, yet he knew that in impoverished areas practicality overrode propriety.

His talk with Becky would become an enduring memory, of that he was sure, yet the overriding memory would be how Tridd killed and did not attempt to conceal it, even leaving the body of his comrade on the beach. Who usually did the clearing up?

~

The geese noisily made way for Karl; they'd done a grand job. Lytton had helped this operation in several ways and the geese were an excellent idea. He knocked loudly and Florence opened the door. He'd love to take her into his arms – soon, soon. One of the boys rushed past him to take Midnight to the stable. He was impressed and took a moment to watch the lad pat the horse and lead him away, chattering, mostly nonsense, all the time.

Buckby, Tomkins, and Tutte stood up and all grinned widely. He'd see they all benefited from having worked so hard for him but for now he just acknowledged their silent respect. Silence except for a hacking cough from the gaol upstairs. "Has he been coughing all this time?"

"Miss Fivaz says we're not to go too close in case it's catching," said Tomkins.

"Not that we needed telling," added Buckby.

"We must get him over to Newport gaol and before a magistrate," said Karl. "The quicker the better. Tomorrow without fail." He looked around. Ah… the other boy was holding a dish of large eggs and handing them to Florence. Good. "Flowers not back yet?"

"Should he be, sir?"

Karl took a deep breath. Flowers had met him in Newport and stayed to deal with the paperwork for the handover of Tridd and other matters. Flowers, normally being stationed at Newport could handle everything and it gave Karl extra time to reassure himself about Lucy and Daniel. Furthermore, he'd given Flowers some time off to attend to his mother's funeral so long as he returned midday today. He glanced at his pocket watch. "He should be here shortly after noon at the latest." He shifted his shoulders as a quiver ran down his back. His mind flicked back to the days in Kent when all had seemed well for the first time in years and then Lucy went missing; pushed out to sea by her mother in a leaking boat. His apprehension increased to a sense of foreboding as he remembered when, in January, he'd visited Daniel's farm to discuss this mission and the deep shiver of his soul when Raffles had said *it's as though they are in league with the devil*. He must deal with everything without delay, nothing must be overlooked, and then get off this island. With Florence.

Curly, who'd looked after Midnight, slipped in quietly and stood next to his friend. They both liked to listen to Karl's briefings.

There was no sign of the slaves. "Coast Guard taken the slaves?"

Buckby was quick to answer. "Yes, sir. I've given the women my wife's clothes." Written all over his face was the pain of her no longer needing them. "And Mrs Tynlan gave them her late husband's clothes, so some of them are decent and warm now."

"Some of them?"

"Well, we didn't have enough for them all but Mrs Tynlan got her friends to part with a few old rags. Better than nothing."

So Daniel's smuggled cargo had come in use even for the slaves. Becky and her friends now had new clothes and didn't mind parting with some of the old. "Fine woman that Becky Tynlan. I'm making it your duty to take care of her. Tomorrow, take the boys up there. They're going to stay with her for a while – see how they get on. You'll need to call in at the store on the way." He dug down into his pocket. "This guinea should cover all she needs for a few weeks. And if you're planning to have a meal with her, make sure you take her plenty of wood and meat. And," Karl gave great emphasis to his next words, "the boys are to be taken to Brigton church every Sunday, without fail."

Buckby turned to look at the boys, or was it to hide his rare optimism? His mood was catching and the boys smiled, though a little uncertainly. "Well, you'll love it up there, proper home it is. Curtains and cushions and…"

"That's settled then. And, Buckby, you are to look in on her every couple of days. Understood?"

"Happy to do my duty, sir."

Undoubtedly. Perhaps she could cure him of saying *well* nearly every time he spoke. Good luck to her – he hadn't managed it. Now, what could he give these three men to do so that he and Florence could have time together alone? A thought occurred to him. "Tridd's dogs are probably still locked in the fort and there's the dead mangler in the barrel. Off you go. Deal with them all." He waved his hand towards the door. At least the one in the barrel would not present a problem. He really should have shot it earlier.

"All three of us, sir?" said Tutte.

"It'll take all three of you to handle them. They'll all be hungry, so get some meat and use that as bait."

"What with, sir?" asked Tutte.

Karl patted his nearly empty pocket. "Here's a couple of shillings for meat. And don't come back until all the dogs are…do you have a dog pound here?"

"No sir."

"Well either start one or shoot them. I can't imagine those dogs becoming anyone's pets, can you?" An answer wasn't necessary. "I want the fort cleared out too; make arrangements for that. I shall be liaising with the island's Member of Parliament as to its future."

"Should we wait for Flowers, sir?" Tutte was puzzled.

"No. I want you all out of here and doing something useful right now"

The men looked a little mystified for all of a second or two until they noticed Karl watching Flo doing some baking.

"We'll get the boys to muck out the stable, shall we, sir?"

Karl didn't answer. They already knew what Karl was thinking and he didn't care. It was time to think of his own future.

Chapter Forty-Two
"He'd enjoy every minute"

At last they were alone, only harrowing coughing disturbed his thoughts. "Has he had anything to eat today?" Karl indicated the parson above them.

"Yes, I have given him a little broth. Perhaps he could have one of these eggs I am boiling? You think yes?"

"How many eggs do we have?"

"We have fifteen, Lieutenant."

"*Two* for each of us," he pointed to the empty chairs, *one* each for the boys and one left over. "Yes, Florence, that is a kind thought, give him an egg for his supper." He hoped she noticed his correct pronunciation of her name.

"And a little of the bread I have baked?"

Karl nodded in agreement and quietly said, "Who knows what has driven him to violate his vows?" He reflected on Becky Tynlan's tale of Tridd's and Zeb's early lives and pushed the thoughts away. Time enough to ponder later.

"The parson told me Tridd was very nice to him at first and promised him money for his church. But he is not a stupid man."

"Who? Tridd?"

"Yes. He heard the coughing, like we do. He knew he had not long to live."

Karl put his hand to his mouth. If he'd given it any thought, he would have realized the parson had consumption.

"He is soon to meet his maker, do you think? And he is frightened," said Florence.

One of Raffles' phrases came to mind: *God is not mocked.* Somewhere in the Bible were words about whatever you sow, that is what you will reap. The parson had cause to be troubled. He stood and looked at Florence, his head on one side. "Perhaps we should take him to a hospital rather than the gaol. Is there one in Newport?"

"I do not know. I have not heard of a hospital on the island." She shook her head. "Ah, but I think the House of Resolution has doctors." She stared at Karl. "You think we should take him there and God will be his judge?"

She said everything so delightfully simply. Why bother with man's law? He smiled at her; it was so good to feel a smile on his face. She was kind and compassionate, even to this weasel of a man. There was one advantage in being here in this forsaken place – he could do what he liked. He'd have the parson sent to the House of Resolution, it would be marginally better than gaol and perhaps they could ease his distress in his last days. He would suggest this to the parson: the magistrate and gaol, or go direct to the House of Resolution? The parson would choose the latter and he'd be declared a pauper. This would soon be true as he'd relieve him of any furniture and furnishings found in the Kaddakay parsonage and impound them ready for a new incumbent. Any personal valuables would be donated to… he'd find a good cause. Raffles would advise the church authorities and the stipend would be ended. He'd advise the M.P. of course, eventually. Probably better to keep this solution between themselves.

He picked up one of the chairs and set it down by the stove. He pointed to the other by the hearth. "Come and sit here with me, I have something I wish to discuss with you."

Florence complied with a slightly worried smile.

Under a Dark Star

"I shall be leaving for my house in Kent soon. Watch House will be manned by members of the Coast Guard – Buckby, Tomkins and new recruits from the village possibly, and there will be no place here for you." Again he was angry with himself. Why did he always address gentlewomen as if they were sailors or Revenue men? He watched her shift uncomfortably. He must *listen*. "Tell me, how did you come to be living on the island?"

Florence lowered her eyes. "I was captured."

He felt a little better; she too came straight to the point.

"By whom?"

"I was to be betrothed to a Count. He was much older than I and my father had little money and I suffered from only a little dowry. The Count, he said he loved me. He had been married two times before and there was talk; talk about how they had both died young. I was warned by my maid, she knew a servant of his. She said I should not marry him but my father was angry with me." She closed her eyes and shook her head slowly and a tear fell from the corner of her eye. "My father said if I married him there was a chance he would help my family."

Karl looked dubious, found a handkerchief and handed it to her. "Please forgive me for causing you such pain."

She took the hanky, wiped her tears and thanked him, then continued. "I must tell. I ran away to an aunt who lived by the sea near Boulogne. But the Count, he found me. And he sold me!" She shuddered. "He sold me to a visiting English sea captain."

Karl drew back in shock. "An English ship's captain! When was this?"

"In the summer of 1819." She glanced at him and saw that she should continue. "He was an old man, many lines on his face. He brought me to this island and he was kind to me. When he found he was dying, he bought me a little café so that I could have money."

"To support yourself after he'd died?"

"Yes, Lieutenant. But he had a son and the son was not happy about this. Then suddenly he took his last breath and the son claimed the café as his own. I had no papers to prove it was mine. I went to a magistrate and he laughed at me, calling me a frog, and he said I had no place on this English island."

Karl bit his lip. He could imagine this all too well. "So what happened?"

"One night, the son came and took me to an inn near my shop and locked me in a bedroom. He said that by midnight I would belong to a friend of his. I asked him who and he said he didn't know which one yet. Then he laughed and said 'it depends who wins the game'." Tears flowed freely now; she mopped them up.

He recalled the four men playing cards in the inn at Ryde and fury flooded through him. He clenched his fists. "By thunder! They *were* playing cards for you!" His suspicions were confirmed. And Tridd had been the winner. He could have stopped it. He stood up and paced the floor. "Don't distress yourself further. I know the rest of your story!"

To hide his anger, Karl put a couple of logs on the fire and filled a kettle with water. Some tea would be needed soon. "It is clear you cannot stay on this island, so I propose that you come back to Kent with me and remain as my guest." He was totally unprepared for Florence's reaction. The French were certainly different.

"Oh Lieutenant, Lieutenant! You are my hero." She rushed towards him and flung her arms around his neck. "Thank you, I have been too worried. Far too worried and now I can smile. I will work for you. I can cook. I can…"

She had no time to finish. Karl's arms were around her, his lips on hers, kissing her in a way she had probably never experienced from any of the men in her life. This brusque naval officer finally had a chance to show that he could be a most gentle lover. "You shall be my guest, not my servant, Florence."

She pulled away from him just slightly, enough to see him clearly. "I thank you for the kiss. I shall be pleased to be your guest."

Karl thought he understood her meaning. She would like to be courted. He could do that. In fact he would do that very well and he'd enjoy every minute. She was adorable.

The sudden squawking of the geese punctured this precious moment. Thumping on the door followed. He took a second to smile at her. His mission here was almost finished, and a new life was opening up, so for once he sauntered to the door. The buried germ of fear grew as he opened the door and Thomas Flowers burst through.

"He's escaped!"

"What!"

"Tridd's escaped."

Chapter Forty-Three
"Overwhelming agony"

Saturday 29th March
"One more task, Daniel. One more, then we can go home." Karl had left orders for his men to continue searching for Tridd and then ridden over to the parsonage at Brigton late on the Friday afternoon and stayed overnight. Lucy was not pleased to see him particularly when he'd asked Daniel to 'come riding' with him today."

Daniel sighed. "I am relieved that at least this operation hasn't taken as long as we envisaged."

Raffles sat at his desk in the drawing room window trying to write his sermon. "I think I'll give up on this," he tapped a pile of papers with his pen, "I can't seem to find what I am supposed to say. You'd think I could manage an Easter Sunday message without too much trouble, but the words just aren't coming."

Daniel looked across at his good friend and said, "We're leaving now. Once it's quiet, without our chatter, inspiration may come."

"No, it's not you. I would know if it were."

Karl jumped up from his comfortable seat. "Daniel's right. The sooner we find Tridd, the sooner we can go home."

Mrs Raffles put her head around the door. "It's so good for us all to be together again. I shan't want you to go."

Daniel gave her a huge smile. "You are wonderful to take my wife and me into your home, not forgetting little Freddie, of course."

"It is my pleasure," she said gliding towards him and absent-mindedly stroking what Martha called her *pudding*. "We have Martha to help us as well as our two daily servants and my cousin is so generous." She waved her arm around the well-furnished room. "She said it gave her a chance to modernize her farmhouse." She appeared to think hard before saying, "I know it's selfish of us to have you here, but at least she has her home to herself again."

"It's as though we have established an outpost of our county here on the island," said Daniel as he welcomed Lucy clutching Freddie. He gave them both a parting kiss. "One day soon, when we are in our own home again, Josh will wake you with a rose every morning." He winked at her.

"I shall never forget that time. The roses were such a mystery. I should have known they were from you." It had been one of the most special times of her life, a treasured memory. She held out her hand to touch him again before he left.

Martha stood in the hall, determined not to miss her two heroes leaving. She had made each a currant pie and a small loaf of bread, cut and lavishly buttered. She'd added slices of mutton and there was a meaty bone for Josh and bottles of ale. As soon as they put on their coats, she handed the precious parcels to them and watched as Daniel limped his way towards Fiddle. Josh was at his heels, inspecting them and deliberating.

Raffles also watched, and a seed of a sermon was sown. Daniel paid a heavy price to save people from tyranny: his frost-bitten toe might cause him to limp for evermore; he might even have lost the toe. Emmeline had applied every herbal remedy she knew and he had prayed for full healing but still he limped, just a very little.

Under a Dark Star

It was a bright, sunny morning, a good day for searching. Karl surreptitiously showed Daniel the pistol under his coat. "You ought to have one too. I have a couple at Watch House."

They turned their horses, raised their hands in acknowledgment of their good friends and family and set off once again to comb the island for signs of Leon Tridd. They cantered as far as the next village when they slowed to a trot.

"Could someone local be hiding him?" Daniel remembered his father when he was being sought by Karl a couple of years ago; he was hiding in his own farmhouse. "Some of these cottages could have hidden cellars."

"There are over one hundred men searching systematically all over the north of the island. If we don't find him by this evening, we'll call up reinforcements and search the south – every cottage and outhouse." Discouragement was an unfamiliar feeling for Karl, but he had to admit to it this morning.

For once he found it hard to give all his concentration to his mission. "Daniel, I have such plans for Florence. She really is exquisite. I am nearly thirty – time I married, don't you think?"

"Indeed." Daniel would like nothing better than to see the man who worshipped Lucy happily married with a woman of his own. "From what you say, she would make a fine Mistress of Whitchester Manor."

"I shall give her time. She will be my guest initially and then, maybe in a month or two…"

"A month or two! Karl, you jest surely! A lady, for that is what you say she is, will expect a little more time than that. She has been through a terrible experience. You must give her the opportunity…"

Karl interrupted firmly. "Opportunity! Opportunity to say 'no'?"

Daniel laughed. "Take your time. It is important you get to know her well. She is, after all, French, and they have recently been our enemy."

"It is true my mother will not approve both because she is French and because she won't be able to solve the puzzle of her former place in society. I shan't be telling her. Florence came from a good family." Karl remained silent on the matter of a scheming father. "She is undoubtedly a fine…"

Karl hadn't time to search for le mot juste because a cart clattered around the corner and came to a halt in front of them.

"Well, get out and go and tell him," said the carter to his two nieces sitting either side of him. "Go on, I haven't got all day."

Karl held back. Daniel was the man to deal with scatter-brained girls.

Daniel dismounted and led Fiddle towards them. He inclined his head. "Hello my jolly Joliffes. What is it you want to tell me?" They bobbed slightly; they seemed to be in a hurry. He had no idea who was Jilly and who was Jessie so he felt relieved that at least he'd made them smile. Josh took the opportunity to lie down at their feet.

"We think we know where Tridd might be," said the girl on the left.

Daniel's eyes lit up. "I knew you were special." It wasn't said lightly; he'd known these cheerful girls would prove to be on his side.

"I'm Jilly," said one of them helpfully. "We've learnt this from the baker who provides bread for the gaol in Newport. He said that Tridd bribed two of the gaolers."

"Bribed? What with? He was searched and had nothing to bribe anybody with."

"Well he did," said Jessie. "He bribed them with keys. He said he kept a key to the fort and another to his money box hidden in the hills somewhere."

Daniel was not surprised. "So he told them where to find the keys in return for his freedom?"

Jessie nodded. "The gaolers were not easily fooled. They made sure they had the keys first but when they went to the fort, they could not find the box."

"So they went back to Tridd?"

"Yes," said Jilly. "And he said he would show them if they let him out."

"But they were not foolish," said Jessie. "They said they wouldn't let him out until they had the money."

"And he said he wouldn't tell them where it was because they might not come back and let him out." Jilly said. "And this went on all week."

Daniel sighed. He could see where this story would end up. "So they let him out, thinking they were the ones with the keys, and they had even come to an agreement to share the money?"

"Yes, that's right!" Both girls were astonished.

"And now there's no sign of Tridd and no sign of the two gaolers either?" said Daniel.

The twins looked at each other and then both spoke saying that two bodies had been found in the river.

The carter leaned forward and said, "They thought you'd like to know."

"When was this?"

"The baker told us early this morning as soon as he discovered them," said Jilly.

Daniel groaned. "We received the message that he'd escaped yesterday afternoon, but we didn't know about the gaolers."

"We'd not have known either," said the carter, "but the gaolers told the baker 'cos they said they couldn't trust Tridd and if anything happened to them…"

"Surely the whole island must hate this man!" But Daniel knew the power of fear was stronger even than hatred.

The carter took a moment to think and realized he was not the first to report the escape, so he emphasized the extra information they'd brought. "He's ruthless. Dangerous. To kill two men with his bare fists, well, he ain't normal. Those gaolers have truncheons, you know." He sniffed and wiped his nose with the back of his hand. "Murder, it is, murder." He looked Daniel straight in the eye to stress the significance of this. "Course, it takes courage to tell tales and I'll be starting work late today." He decided a moment's silence would stress his message. "But we thought you should know."

Daniel understood and reached into his pocket. This information was definitely worth gold and these folks had a tough life. He handed a half sovereign to the carter and two crowns to the twins then bowed. This was what they liked – being treated as young ladies.

"Tis a pity you're married," said Jilly and they both blushed and curtseyed unsteadily.

Daniel mounted his horse and galloped off with Karl a yard or two behind.

"I could hear most of that," called Karl. "The fort has already been searched but we should go there immediately. If I'd had more men I would have left a small army on guard."

"He won't be there. He will have gone by now. Taken the money and bribed a ferryman." Daniel slowed Fiddle so that he and Karl could make plans. "He might even have a boat moored somewhere and be sailing off to the mainland clutching his loot."

Karl could feel the Viking steel in his bones setting hard. "He won't be able to leave from Ryde or Cowes. They'll be on watch, that's for sure. Let's start at the fort and see if there is anything there to give us a clue as to where he could hide or run to."

"Are your men at Watch House?"

"Not until late tonight. I've told them to return to the fort by dusk and show their presence for an hour or two to keep Tridd or the villagers out. There's others searching at night."

"So is Florence alone?"

"At the moment she is. The boys are with your cousin's wife, Becky, and that rat of a parson has been taken to Newport's House of Resolution coughing and spluttering all the way, well away from Florence. She knows not to answer the door unless our special knock is given." Had he done enough to protect her? She had the geese and she knew to light the fire on the roof if she felt she was in danger. Yes, she would be safe. But against Tridd? Doubts turned his stomach over.

They rode in silence, cantering most of the way. Daniel stopped once they were in sight of the fort to give Josh some water. He was five years old now and not quite as frisky as he used to be. "Let Josh go ahead and sniff around a bit."

Karl felt in his pocket for the keys Florence had secretly acquired and when Josh, his inspection completed, sat down by the gate, Karl opened it and they rode inside. "The dogs have all been moved. Probably soon be dead as I can't imagine anyone wanting to resettle them."

Daniel chuckled but didn't mention that they'd almost certainly be in meat pies before too long. They dismounted, tied their horses to the hitching rail inside the walls, then closed and locked the huge wooden gates. Not having a key for the main door to the house, and the option of climbing a rope no longer existing, they tested the windows. There was one around the back just low

Under a Dark Star

enough to be smashed close to the handle and within a few minutes, Karl standing on Midnight, had climbed inside and opened the door at the front. Josh was very reluctant to enter and despite a firm, reassuring talk from Daniel he only managed one paw over the threshold. Daniel relented, left him outside and didn't close the door.

Ever since he'd first climbed into Florence's room, Karl had wanted to see more of this fort, and to analyse Tridd from what he surrounded himself with. He scouted around all the rooms to ensure the escaped prisoner was not in hiding. He inspected the cellar too; terrible smell. A large, empty wooden casket lay on the kitchen table: Tridd had taken his money. He looked around and noted that silver candlesticks and other valuables were still in their places. So the man was travelling light.

Daniel laughed at this observation. "What you mean is that the gold is too heavy for him to carry anything else!" Then he noticed Karl had several dresses over his arm.

Karl initially ignored Daniel's inquisitive look but, shifting from foot to foot, he said, "It will be good to see her wearing something other than her red gown."

They closed the main door behind them and searched for Josh. Daniel whistled and Josh came running, barking all the way. "It's best to pay heed; he's not often wrong."

The ominous look Daniel gave Karl jarred his nerve again.

Josh wasn't wrong. There was a small, fenced-off garden on one side of the fort, with a vegetable patch and a square of grass and some small bushes against the wall. Josh jumped the fence and resumed frantically digging at the base of one. Daniel and Karl promptly pulled the bush up; it came up too easily. They stood in shock at what lay beneath.

Karl drew back. "It's clearly a woman not long buried. She's still got skin and hair."

Daniel was holding on to the scruff of Josh's neck and stroking him, and remembering a conversation with Becky.

"Becky told me there'd been a woman here at the fort who'd not been seen for a few months. I think Florence was her replacement, perhaps in the hope that no one would notice the disappearance of the other."

Shaken, they led their horses out, locked the gate and sat on the grass on the surrounding hills. Their bottles of ale and the comfort of Martha's provisions might steady their nerves. Neither of them spoke until Josh lifted his nose from the bone Martha had packed, sniffed the air, then whined.

A thin plume of smoke rose from the direction of Watch House. Every nerve in Karl's body was taut as he yelled, "Quick!" Florence has lit the warning signal.

They rode as if on the wings of the wind. The thin plume became billowing black smoke and, as they came closer, flames – twenty feet high – flared from the roof. The clipped wings of the geese prevented them from flying so they pushed over the smoking fence and were scattering, honking loudly. The glass windows exploded. The huge oak door was on fire. The whole of Watch House was ablaze and never before had Karl come so close to overwhelming agony.

Chapter Forty-Four
"Tomorrow, sometime, somehow"

Daniel slipped his arms over Karl's head and pinned his arms to his side. Karl kicked and used all his strength to break his hold. They fell, and still Daniel held on. Not until they heard the crashing of the wooden floors to the ground did Daniel let go. Karl clenched his fist and hit him on the chin before rushing over to the crackling inferno.

He circled the tower to see if he could get closer. Fire raged through every shattered window and burning timbers dropped from the roof. Could there be a chance she'd found somewhere safe?

"Florence! Florence!" Damn Daniel! He was right, of course: there was no prospect of saving her. None whatsoever. He tore his eyes from the fire to glare at Daniel but Daniel had mounted his horse and was gesticulating frantically towards the cliff.

Karl's eyes stung. A tear dropped down his smoke-blackened face and he rubbed it away with his sleeve. Daniel was racing after someone or something. Another crash behind him drew his attention and the physical pain of this heart-breaking scene immobilized him until a thought burst through. She has escaped!

He raced to Midnight and leapt on, galloping furiously to follow Daniel. Deep in his heart he knew it wasn't Florence; she wouldn't run away. Or maybe someone was chasing her on foot? He dug his spurs deep into Midnight's flanks. Hope flooded his body with energy. He lost sight of Daniel who'd disappeared behind the last rocky outcrop of Rose's Ridge.

The voices he heard filled him with dismay. Both were male. He slowed to walking pace and saw ahead of him the figure of a dark-haired man crouching behind a rock some fifty feet up the ridge. Daniel was still on his horse. Of course, with his limp, he'd find it difficult to pursue on foot.

"Is he armed?" called Karl.

"Not as far as I can see."

"Who is it?" He was beginning to grasp that this must be the man Tridd left to finish the job for him.

"Jim Brantiani."

"Of course."

"Remember, we don't know if this is the man who set the fire and we don't know if Florence was inside."

But Karl knew. From the depths of his soul he knew Florence was dead. Tridd would have made sure. He should have heeded that foreboding. He shouted up to the man who was now scrambling further up the steep ridge. "Come down or we'll drag you down."

The man turned and roared, "You'll never catch me!"

They watched as he lit a torch and held it high. Was he going to set light to anyone who chased him or set light to himself?

Karl drew his pistol and shot him.

~

It was mid-afternoon when Karl thought he saw Tridd. He'd ridden to the Coast Guard at Laurie's Point without Daniel. Daniel took Brantiani's bleeding body to Newport. He might even be dead by now; it was a difficult, bumpy journey. The ache in Karl's heart blocked any feeling of guilt or compassion. It only allowed a driving sense of justice which urged him to seek the real butcher.

"You say you saw him?" One of the men who'd stood guard at Kaddakay church ushered Karl through the door of the Coast Guard headquarters.

Despite the urgency, Karl's eyes noticed the man's smart uniform and his ready-for-action demeanour. At last, some respect for the status of their office was filtering in. "Yes. I can't be sure it was him, of course, but I noticed a small sail-boat, with a dark sail, making its way around the coast towards here."

"Launch the cutter," cried the Guard and immediately a series of sharp whistles rallied the crew who scrambled from all directions down the cliff banks to the moored cutter. "You coming Lieutenant?"

Karl didn't need an invitation, he was already running.

~

Karl sat hunched on the sofa in the parsonage. He should have known. Tridd was not an ordinary murdering criminal – if there was such a thing – he was clever, possibly the most cunning he'd ever dealt with. The boat was a decoy. Valuable time had been wasted and though he'd ridden all the way along the south coast of the island towards the east, he saw no other boats capable of anything other than hugging the shore. Nevertheless, the Coast Guard would be ordered to search every one. But the damned man had probably sailed west under cover of darkness leaving Jim Brantiani a few coins and many threats to light the fire that almost certainly killed Florence.

His thoughts were interrupted by Martha bringing him and Daniel what she called 'some well-earned thick nourishment'.

Lucy gave her good friend and servant a radiant smile; it reflected the relief she felt now that Daniel and Karl had returned to the parsonage. Raffles squeezed Emmeline's hand and said, "I know it's nearly midnight, but do you think, my dear, I might be allowed just a little more of cook's delicious rabbit stew?"

Emmeline smiled indulgently. "Martha, is there a little more?"

Martha had been given the honour of becoming 'housekeeper' and with that high station came the responsibility of making decisions. She consulted her feelings rather than her mind for most of these. "Of course! You must keep up your strength for the morrow – the most important day in the world." She threw her arms wide.

"Thank you, Martha. Easter Sunday is indeed the most important day in the *year* when our Lord Jesus triumphed over death." He reflected for a moment. "And it is my fervent hope that the whole world agrees."

All except Martha were seated around a dying fire in the warm drawing room and all confessed to being very tired. Karl and Daniel exchanged glances that spoke of gratitude for the kind of hospitality that doesn't demand etiquette. Bowls of rabbit stew and tankards of mead tasted all the better for being presented on a tray. Karl allowed himself a moment of consolation – the Coast Guard at Laurie's Point seemed transformed. They'd even said they'd find a role for Tomkins. Buckby should be comfortable enough with Mrs Tynlan. He'd be a landowner – probably more than he'd ever aspired to. He took a deep breath. Maybe one day he'd be able to look back and say he'd left the island a better place. He must remember to suggest more pay for Tutte and Flowers; they were good men. Tomorrow, sometime, somehow, he must face returning to the ruins of Watch House to find Florence. The remains of Florence. Could she be buried in Brigton? Would Raffles conduct the funeral?

Lucy watched Karl. Never before had she noticed how his face, though almost imperceptibly, betrayed his feelings.

Under a Dark Star

Raffles also perceived Karl lost in thought and so asked Daniel, "Brantiani is alive, in gaol and faces hanging?"

"Karl's bullet is in his shoulder. It was a good shot and served to make him drop the torch before he caused any more damage. When we find the bones of Florence in the ruins, yes, he'll hang. We cannot save him from that."

"Did he confess?" enquired Raffles.

"No. But he kept muttering about a screaming woman. There's no doubt Florence was inside. It seemed to be troubling him. I don't think he'd been told about Florence."

"By thunder! If I'd heard, he'd never have muttered again." Karl's eyes flashed with anger. "And!" he announced, "He, Tridd or both, slaughtered the few survivors who made it ashore from the smashed boats on the rocks. Twenty-seven bodies found so far, all scattered around the coast, and at least a dozen with knife wounds. And the woman at the..."

Emmeline put her hand to her mouth to stifle a gasp. "I think I shall retire, Mr Raffles."

Emmanuel Raffles looked mortified. "My dear Emmeline, I am forgetting your condition and I beg your forgiveness too, Lucy. Please withdraw and no doubt we shall shortly follow."

The ladies stood, curtsied, and withdrew.

As soon as the door was closed, Daniel clenched his fists. "Yet more families without breadwinners! I thought I'd done enough! I thought there'd be no more hangings but he and Tridd are unlikely to repent and reform." He took a deep breath and stared at Raffles.

"Ah, you do listen to my sermons. You even remember them!"

"You know, Raffles," said Karl, "I shall miss you but I think you are the man for the task."

"You mean the duty of resolving many problems after you've all gone?" Raffles teased them both with a cheeky grin. "I have listened to my unquiet soul. I am formulating plans already. I shall start a school."

Daniel chuckled. "And I can personally testify that many will profit from that."

Raffles bobbed his head in acknowledgment. "And perhaps a home for homeless children." He shook his head and pursed his lips. "Those poor urchins." He took a deep breath and sighed. "Unlike the boy King, I doubt I shall be able to establish a hospital. I must leave that to someone else." Then he cheered up. "And with Emmeline at my side and soon a new soul to care for, I shall enjoy every minute"

Karl almost choked. *Enjoy every minute*. Those were the very words he had thought about Florence. Was he fated never to meet the right woman? Guilt flooded him: all he had ever given her was a bunch of primroses which she had treasured. If only there had been time to give her more, to give her happiness.

"Would you like me to conduct her funeral?"

Karl looked at Raffles. What a man. He could even read thoughts. "Would you bury her in Brigton?"

"Most certainly, if that is your wish. I shall attend to her grave regularly."

"And if there's any justice in this world, Tridd, having taken too much gold will have sunk in the choppy seas last night." Daniel could offer nothing more in the way of distraction than the thought of justice.

"Sunk? Yes, almost certainly. Possibly by the island's Coast Guard patrols."

Raffles added, "Indeed, it is most likely for the wind was gusting fiercely at times. I shall be here to ensure that should he ever be seen again, you will be informed immediately."

Karl's eyes grew hard. "And if that happens..."

Chapter Forty-Five
Raffles
"Let not your past echo into your future."

Easter Sunday Morning at Brigton
From the front of his church, Raffles peered over the top of his spectacles and his heart was touched by what he saw. It was full to overflowing, and just as they had done in Wintergate, rows of villagers stood at the back. The sun shone through the stained glass windows and onto the faces of the congregation. Some faces looked yellow, others blue with green hair. There would come a time when this would bring a smile to his face, but that time had not yet arrived. The anguish of Karl hung over him, and his words the night before rang in his ears: *And if that happens, I shall disembowel him with my sword.* And aching with all his heart, he thought of Saint Peter who had cut off the ear of an approaching soldier when they took Jesus to be crucified. Jesus had drawn Peter back to the path of virtue and Raffles had no doubt Karl would be restored too. As for the villagers? They'd come from far afield. Well, miracles do happen. The work of the Holy Spirit! Attending the service on Easter Sunday was a fine start. Or were they here only for the promised Easter eggs, colourfully decorated by his wonderful wife? Or cook's little cakes? Would there be enough? Still, that was a good problem to have, except he might have to go without.

As everyone knows, news travels fast in small communities and each member of the congregation had heard of the previous day's happenings long before they'd entered the grounds of the church. It had stolen their joy at being rid of Tridd, the man who'd thought of himself as Lord of the Manor. Yet they had still brought the daffodils which nodded gaily in overcrowded vases on every available ledge within the church. And although he'd not got beyond the seed of a sermon, he now knew what he would preach.

Emmeline, Lucy and Daniel sat in the front pew, next to the Lyttons. Karl had declined to come. Martha sat at the very back near the door with little Freddie sleeping in a basket. Raffles, knowing Karl needed a quiet time alone, had encouraged her to come and bring the baby. He noticed a woman with two small, well dressed boys with very short hair sitting half way to the front. Could she be Becky, Daniel's relative? Yes, and as instructed by Karl, she'd brought little Arthur and Tomas. God was indeed good.

He mounted the pulpit. He was sometimes unable to be bound by tradition, besides, who was to know if he departed from the order of service? He lifted his eyes to heaven and then faced his packed congregation. This was a rare day. Today he would stay in the pulpit and not wander around. Today he would expound on rising from the dead, the power of the risen Lord, communities rising again and people set free from slavery in all its forms. In a measured, quiet voice he began.

"There was a monk called Telemachus. He hid from the world so that he might live a quiet life of prayer and meditation. One day Telemachus realized he had chosen a life given more to his own selfish needs rather than a life given in the service of God and man. He should be in a city of sin and need. Rome! So to Rome he went. Walking. And Rome was now supposed to be a Christian city."

He suddenly remembered he'd not told the congregation how long ago this was. "Fourth century. They no longer threw Christians to the lions, but there were still gladiatorial games, much loved by the populace long fed on bloody fights. Captives were made to march into the arena and cry out, 'Hail Caesar! We who are about to die salute you'."

He looked around. These good people knew little of the outside world. He must make his message clear. "Men fought each other to the death. Telemachus went to see the games and was appalled to see hordes of people watching men kill one another."

He paused for a moment in the hope that the villagers would make the connection between the Romans and their own neighbourhood. "Telemachus leapt the barrier and ran into the ring and separated two fighters. The crowd roared. The gladiators pushed away the old hermit, still in his holy robes, but he came between them again. The spectators hurled stones at him and urged the gladiators to kill him. By order of the commander of the games, a gladiator raised his sword and plunged it into Telemachus. Unexpectedly the crowd was silent: shocked that a holy man should give up his life and be killed in such a way. The games ended abruptly and *never again resumed*."

He peered over his spectacles. His congregation was also silent. Did they even know or care who the Romans were? In a loud voice he thundered, "By standing up to violence, Telemachus did more for the cause of a loving, peaceful Christianity than he ever could have done hiding away." He gave them time to think. "A 'Telemachus' came here," he coughed, "well, two came. They came to stop the violence. And now you are like the crowd at the games. I see you are silent just as they were. Appalled at the senseless loss of life, all to satisfy base appetites."

It was no good, he couldn't stay in the pulpit. Perhaps he should have made the message simpler. If he'd written it out it would have been better. Marching up and down the aisles, he spoke louder and louder until he was sure they had made the connection to their own situation. The congregation was enthralled. They had never seen such charisma, such authority, such power, and they loved it.

With no organist, the only accompaniment to the hymns was Major Lytton scraping away on his violin, yet he played it with such vigour that it was becoming a valuable feature of the services. Only those in the front pews could read the words in the hymn book, so Parson Raffles once more mounted the pulpit so that he could read each verse loudly before singing.

"Christ the Lord is risen today, Hallelujah!" He thumped the pulpit and read the first verse before saying, "He is risen, and all those who die loving Jesus Christ will rise again. Today we mourn the loss of many of our community in Brigton, Kaddakay and other villages. We also mourn the loss of a lovely French girl, burned alive because of one man's hatred and revenge. Yet we here today know that the love of Jesus showed us that after death, *there is life!*"

Most sang falteringly, and not always the right words but, with each verse, the mood of the congregation improved. By the time they reached the last verse, their voices soared in triumph and there were ripples of enthusiastic comments as they sat down.

"Corruption brings poverty!" Raffles thumped the pulpit. "Let not your past echo into your future." Once more he thumped the pulpit. A terrible cracking sound heralded the splitting of the front panel. Undeterred, he continued. "If ever again there is something rotten in your villages – *root it out*. Stand together and remove all that is evil."

Into his mind came the phrase that had begun this mission and he boomed, "All that it takes for evil to triumph is for good men to do nothing."

And at the back of the church, standing next to Martha, Karl, having arrived late, whispered, "Amen to that."

The End

Under a Dark Star

If you enjoyed Under a Dark Star, I should be so pleased if you would leave a review on Amazon.

If you 'Follow' Anna Faversham on Amazon you will be kept up-to-date with new releases. The Follow button is near the author biography/author picture.

If you would like to contact me, please visit my website www.annafaversham.com. I'd love to hear from you and I'll be happy to help with any questions you might have.

Other books by Anna Faversham:

Hide in Time *A time travel romance*

Book One of The Dark Moon Series: **One Dark Night** *The choices we make determine our futures*

Book Three of The Dark Moon Series: **One Dark Soul** Journey into a dark heart. *Lucy has survived hard times but by 1825 she finally has it all. Why does she throw it all away?*

Under a Dark Star

Twenty Questions for Book Clubs

1. What did you like best about this book?
2. What did you like least about this book?
3. Which characters did you like best?
4. Which characters did you like least?
5. If you were making a movie of this book who would you cast?
6. Share a favourite quote from this book and why did it stand out?
7. What other books have you read by this author? How did they compare to this book?
8. Would you read more of the author's books?
9. What feelings did this book evoke for you?
10. Which songs does this book make you think of?
11. Which character in the book would you most like to meet?
12. Which places in the book would you most like to visit?
13. What do you think of the title? How does it relate to the book's contents? What other title might you choose?
14. What do you think of the book's cover? Does it convey what the book is about?
15. How original was this book?
16. Bearing in mind this was set in 1823, were you able to relate to this book?
17. Did any of the characters remind you of anyone?
18. Was the pace too fast/too slow/just right?
19. Is there a message you will take away with you from this book?
20. If you had the chance to ask the author one question, what would it be?

Under a Dark Star

My thanks to my writing friends
for their patience and advice

Lexi Revellian
lexirevellian.com

Alan Hutcheson
Author of Boomerang and The Baer Boys

Printed in Great Britain
by Amazon